Rising From the Ashes

Allie Grecco Series - Book 1

Katy Pierce

D1562687

Copyright © 2021 by Katy Pierce

All rights reserved.

No portion of this book may be reproduced in any form without written permission from the publisher or author, except as permitted by U.S. copyright law.

Contents

Description

They tried to cover up the wrong case. Allie Grecco will make them pay.

Allie Grecco is living a double life. Thoughtful friend, office drone, and girly college student by day, she becomes a deadly hunter by night, lurking New York City's seediest alleys to eliminate scumbag predators the cops can't—or won't—catch.

Since her discharge from the military, it's the only thing that keeps the nightmares at bay. But everything changes when Allie realizes she's not the only hunter out there.

When one of her sting operations is interrupted by another ex-military operator, Allie learns a secret about her day job at Soldiers for Hire, and is soon put to the ultimate test... a case that could alter the course of her life forever.

A civil rights lawyer is missing, and the cops have declared her dead. It smells like a cover-up. Allie Grecco won't have it. Not on her watch.

Rising From the Ashes is book one of Katy Pierce's Allie Grecco series, perfect for fans of L.T. Ryan. A thrilling roller-coaster ride of one soldier's journey to face her demons—vigilante-style.

I'd like to dedicate this book to anyone who's afraid to walk away.

If you're in a bad place, just get up and walk away. There's no need for you to explain yourself. It's your life and it's the only one you'll ever get. Do what makes you happy.

Chapter 1

W herever Mila was, she couldn't remember how in the Sam Hill she'd gotten there.

The low ceiling was crumbling and festooned with hairline cracks—or was it? Even though Mila was lying still, the fissures seemed to wave slightly, like kelp in the sea. She felt like she was underwater too.

The kelpy ceiling swam as she turned her heavy head against the mattress, squinting into the dark room. There was a water bottle nearby, sitting on the edge of a beat-up nightstand. Her throat was so dry.

Mila lifted herself on unsteady elbows to grab for the bottle, struggled to uncap it, and downed half in a few enormous gulps. She set the crinkly plastic back on the nightstand to catch her breath and tried to focus her stinging eyes.

It must've been some kind of bedroom, but not like any bedroom Mila had ever seen before. There was a bed—the one she was lying on—with mussed sheets and no pillows, the nightstand, and what looked like a dresser up against the far wall. Something soft and lumpy lined the walls, almost like the inside of an egg carton.

She wasn't in an egg carton, was she?

Mila's temples throbbed as she forced herself to look closer. There were strange silhouettes hanging over some of the wall lumps. Weapons, she thought at first—like prized heirloom rifles above a fireplace—before her foggy brain recognized them for what they were.

Sex toys. The whole room looked like an embarrassing banner ad, one that she'd normally scurry to close before her roommate saw.

Mila swam back through distorted memories to her apartment, and to the last things she could remember. To when she was getting ready to leave. To when ending up in an egg carton didn't even cross her mind.

• • • ● • ● • • • ·

Mila craned closer to the mirror, checking her eyeliner for probably the fourth time. It was okay if the wingtips were a little off, right? Guys didn't usually notice stuff like that. Her ex sure hadn't. Maybe city guys were pickier.

Pulling her palms off the sink, Mila gave herself one last critical look-over before letting out a nervous sigh. She'd managed to smooth most of her flyaways into a seamless golden-blond sheet of hair, but it suddenly seemed flat. Her foundation was blended evenly if you didn't look too closely. The fuchsia lipstick was maybe a

little much—Mama would have said it was, anyway—
but this was going to have to do. If she futzed with her
face any longer, she'd be late.

Flicking off the bathroom light, Mila walked out into
the tiny living room, where she was greeted by a sharp
wolf whistle.

"Look at you!" Alisa exclaimed from the couch. "You
don't look half so country now, do you?"

Mila blushed. "Does the makeup look decent?"

"It looks great." Alisa held up her fingers in a lazy
okay sign. "I told you that lipstick goes with that dress."

"Thanks." Mila tugged the snug hem down just a little
more. It was shorter than she was used to, but she'd
better at least try to look the part of a Park Avenue girl
tonight. She didn't want her first big-city date to smell
the small-town Alabama on her.

"So, you planning to find out what this guy's
apartment looks like, or...?"

"I already told you I don't do that on the first date,"
Mila insisted, but couldn't stop a second blush from
rising in her cheeks.

"You said 'that's not how it's done at home,' but this
isn't Podunk Hollow. This is New York, baby!"

"New York or not, I'm still gonna be me."

Alisa rolled her eyes. "Whatever you say, Alabama.
Knock 'em dead." She winked. "And I promise not to say
anything if you don't come home tonight."

Alisa's words followed Mila all the way outside. They
had seemed a lot more embarrassing than foreboding at
the time.

• • • • • • • • • •

Jolting out of her memory and back to the strange room, Mila was struck by the desperate need to examine herself. Her chin tipped down.

She was inexplicably dressed in a navy-blue and white school uniform. That wasn't how she left her apartment. That wasn't how she'd ever dress, for anything. It was the sailor suit kind, the Catholic schoolgirl kind, the kind that seemed more like a costume than something a student would wear. The skirt was a mile too short, the V-neck too deep, and the top exposed too much midriff. Then a second realization hit her—and with it, a cold claw of fear. She also wasn't wearing any underwear.

Her mind was spinning. She couldn't remember putting anything on, much less taking off her underthings, and her heavy fingers barely seemed capable of doing up the fiddly buttons on this blouse. She was strung out, she realized. She must've been drugged—it was the only explanation.

Drawing her knees together, she noticed the ache between her thighs for the first time. Mila knew she'd been raped.

She squeezed her eyes shut, hoping maybe she was dreaming. Maybe it was a nightmare and she'd wake up if she concentrated hard enough. But no matter how hard she tried to straighten the spiral of her thoughts, the cottony feeling in her head didn't go anywhere, nor did the cool sheets beneath her, nor the scratchy schoolgirl fabric.

How had she gotten there?

Mila tried to think back, tried to remember who had done this to her. She remembered a bar, so she took a deep breath before revisiting it in her mind.

· · · ●·●·● · ·

The noise in the bar was overwhelming. Mila squinted at the clock, willing down the prickle of building tears.

He was over half an hour late, and he hadn't read any of her messages. It was obvious he wasn't coming.

Lifting a hand to wipe away makeup-stained tears, Mila abandoned her club soda at the bar and rushed for the restroom. An older woman with a smoky voice knocked on the stall door and kindly asked if she was all right, but she'd been otherwise left in peace to cry out her disappointment. She missed home; she missed her friends and family; she missed her high school boyfriend, as imperfect as he'd been. At least he was familiar. At least he'd never stood her up.

She couldn't have been gone for more than five minutes.

Once she'd sobbed herself dry and cleaned up her eyeliner as best she could in the grungy mirror, Mila returned to her seat and her soda, right where she'd left it. She was going to pay her pathetic one-drink tab and go home, and probably delete all her dating apps. But first, she was going to finish this glass.

She flopped onto the barstool, drawing a sympathetic look from the bartender.

"Can I pay my tab, please?" Mila sniffed.

The bartender looked her over for a long moment. "Just a second, honey," she said, and disappeared into the back only to return with a dark bottle of beer. With an odd sense of ceremony, she popped its top and clunked it down in front of Mila. The glass was already beginning to sweat in the warmth of the bar. "On the house," she added with an understanding look.

Mila didn't want to stay for one more second. But even in Podunk Hollow, Alabama, it was rude to refuse a gift.

· · · · ● · ● · · ·

When she opened her eyes again, the horrible room was still waiting for her.

What the hell happened? Did she top off her soda? Did she drink all of it? She couldn't remember. It was all either blurry or blank. It felt like that night at the bar couldn't have been more than a half hour ago.

Mila pushed herself up, sliding off the mattress to stand on shaky legs. Everything was sore, everything hurt. Steadying herself against the battered nightstand, she looked down at her body. Ugly purple stains glared up at her, and—clear as day—three fingers of a handprint, each thin bruise stark against the pale skin of her thigh.

Mila began to scream—involuntarily, uncontrollably.

A sharp bang on the door snapped her to attention, her hands flying to her chest. Mila froze.

"Put on the blindfold!" a man demanded from behind the door. Mila soundlessly searched the gloom, confused.

"Let me go! Please!" She heard her voice but couldn't feel her lips moving.

"On the nightstand," he clarified impatiently. He sounded young—no older than his thirties—and his voice might've been honey-like if it wasn't barking at her through the door of a prison she still didn't know how she'd ended up in.

Still dizzy, Mila had only just located the strip of cloth spooled on the nightstand when the voice commanded, "Put it on right now or I'll make sure you never see anything but the inside of this room ever again."

The tone—cruel and icy—was so different than it had been just a few seconds ago, and it sent a shiver racing down Mila's spine. She hurried to obey.

"Now, sit on the bed," he directed next.

"Please." Mila sank to the edge of the mattress, lost in the darkness behind her blindfold. The fabric soaked up her tears. "Please don't hurt me."

"Put your knees together," he said, and Mila had no choice but to comply.

Seconds passed, each warped and bloated with tension. She expected to hear the door open—she expected to hear footsteps—she expected to hear something—but she didn't. She didn't hear anything.

"Now," the voice said after the long pause, its dulcet nature tinged with a sadistic sort of glee, "wait for me."

"Who are you?" Her own voice quivered.

"Wait for me quietly, or the answer to that question will be the last thing you ever hear."

Mila's lip wobbled. She waited quietly, holding perfectly still, but no one came in.

With every instant she waited, her fear thickened. It swelled and churned until Mila felt the hot wash of bile rising in her throat, and she choked and hiccupped hysterically on the edge of the mattress, too afraid to wipe her tears away.

Still, no one came in.

She didn't know how long she sat there crying, but it was almost a relief when her head drifted back up into the clouds, and everything went black again.

• • • • • • • • • •

The next time Mila woke up, she was facedown in the middle of the mattress. She was alone, and the blindfold was back on the nightstand, folded neatly. Everything was just as dark, just as nonsensical, just as stretched out.

She was just as lost as she'd been before.

But then a thought, bright and solid, emerged from the mist swirling between her temples. It cut through her confusion like the beam of a lighthouse across a black sea. She had to turn her cheek on this mattress and look around again. She had to memorize every single detail of this room, about the voice, about what was happening to her. She had to.

She wanted to tell the police everything. If she ever got the chance.

The idea of dying in this awful room probably should have scared her. It probably should have made her feel *something*, at least. She should've been losing her mind, but Mila felt numb, as if she were a piece of driftwood bobbing atop the waves.

She had to remember. She didn't want to become an unsolvable court case wedged in the corner of a newspaper. She didn't want to become one of those girls nobody believed.

She didn't want everyone to think it was her fault. Her fault for going on a blind date in the big city. Her fault for getting roofied. Her fault for wearing too-loud lipstick and a too-short dress.

There were two empty bottles on the nightstand now. Mila only realized she must've drunk a second one when she began to slip away again. The world spun, and at the center of her consciousness, the bright light of purpose burned out.

She closed her eyes.

She opened them.

Things had changed again. Now she was wearing the blindfold. Now her face was smashed into the mattress, sweaty hands gripped her body, and someone was between her legs.

"Shit. Not yet," the voice grunted, though its honey-steeped edges were ragged now. It was so much closer, yet through the sludge of Mila's mind, it sounded like he was calling to her from some distant shore. "Go back to sleep. Be a good girl."

Thick fingers squeezed the back of her thigh.

Mila thought about screaming. But you can't scream underwater. She didn't want to drown.

She kept quiet, not moving a muscle, pretending to pass out. It wasn't hard with the drugs flooding her head and weighing down her body. Maybe he'd let her go if he thought she was too stupid to remember the room, the empty bottle, the sailor-schoolgirl outfit. Maybe—if she went limp and acted like a dead girl—everyone would feel sorry for her, and it would all go away.

Mila shut her eyes tight under the blindfold. When he was done, he left her lying on the bed, skirt hiked up over her back.

She heard the jangle of a belt, the zip of a zipper, and footsteps moving away. The doorknob turned. In the next instant, as hinges swung wide, Mila swore she heard someone else scream. Then the deadbolt thunked back into place, and she was plunged into silence again, wondering if the scream had been her own.

She held her breath, listening for a sign that someone was still there with her, that she wasn't fully alone. That there was still life out there, beyond this room. That whatever this was—whoever he was—it would soon be over.

She heard nothing. Only her shallow breathing, loud in her ears.

Tears slid down her cheeks, overflowing the blindfold, seeping into the bed. This time, she didn't bother wiping them away.

A new thought, dark and dense, rose from the fog: It might never be over. What if this was it? What if this was her life now?

Chapter 2

Allie slapped the alarm off before its third note. The red *4:00 a.m.* burned brightly in her dark bedroom, but Allie Grecco never hit snooze.

Not unless she wanted to have the nightmare. Not since her first and last mission with the 75th Ranger Regiment. Not since they'd torn off her tan beret.

On mornings the nightmare managed to get ahead of her alarm, Allie woke up choking on the phantom stench of blood, her body dripping sweat, her mind engulfed by the grisly red lake that lapped at her bare dream feet. Even on quiet mornings, she could almost taste its coppery pang in the air.

It was dark outside when she climbed out of bed. Anyone not fundamentally ruined—like she was—would still be sound asleep. That's how she liked it.

Allie clicked on the bedside lamp, tucking in and smoothing out her sheets with military precision.

These days, her training uniform amounted to little more than a pair of athletic pants and a university sweatshirt tugged over a plain white tee. She threw her hair into a ponytail the same way she did every morning and brushed her teeth, keeping her gaze trained on the faucet below the mirror so she wouldn't have to look into her own eyes.

It scared her. Not the way she looked, but the reflection itself, peering back from the other side.

Mirrors had long made Allie feel like a ghost, even when she was a teenager. It was as if she'd been split in two, and maybe Other Side Allie was the realer one. It freaked her out.

Spitting out the minty foam and wiping her lips with one wrist, she checked the other for her watch. 4:20 a.m. Still plenty of time before she left at half past four. Allie didn't have superior officers to hold her to a strict schedule anymore, so she held herself to it.

She tiptoed into the kitchen, filling the coffee pot by the glow of the nightlight. She put in a new filter and scooped in the grounds, careful not to rustle too much. Rejoining civilian life had Allie longing for those old army mornings, where everyone on base was up before sunrise, and she could make as much noise as she wanted.

Now she had Libby to worry about. And Libby loved to sleep.

And Allie didn't particularly want to explain her Ranger-certified exercise routine to her soft-eyed, well-meaning, dangerously nosy roommate.

Coffee maker prepped, Allie slipped out of the apartment at four thirty sharp. She jogged down the stairs, past the sleepy front desk guard, and out into the crisp November air. The eastern sky was just beginning to turn gray over the ocean, and the sun hadn't yet breached, but New York made enough of its own light to illuminate her way. She pulled up her hood and took off through the streets of Rego Park.

Relief flooded her with the very first step of her daily three-mile run. Allie could finally lose herself in the mind-numbing comfort of exercise. Nothing else chased off the nightmare or its lingering horrors. Nothing else granted her a few precious hours of sleep at the end of another day.

A few hours later, after the run and a grueling bout of strength training in the park, Allie returned to her still-dark apartment. Before stepping inside, she leaned her ear against the door. Silence. Libby was still asleep. As with most days, she would never even know her roommate had been up before the sun. Exhaling in relief, Allie pushed inside for a quick shower before changing back into her pajamas.

It was just another morning. Another successful stealth mission. Freshly showered, Allie tossed her sweaty athletic wear in the general direction of her laundry hamper, and snuck back out to start the coffee maker, leaving the pot to heat up.

She was padding across the wood floor and back toward her room when the sound of a rattling doorknob stopped her in her tracks. Libby's door swung open.

"You're up early," Libby observed, kneading a squinty eye with the heel of her hand.

"So are you," Allie returned, frozen in the middle of the floor.

"Ugh." Libby yawned widely, scrunching her freckled nose and cheeks, and trudged out of her bedroom to swing an immediate right, into the bathroom. She shut the door softly, but kept talking from inside. "I'm not sure it's safe to say I'm up yet. I may be standing, but I think I'm still half-asleep."

"Then go back to bed." Allie felt stupid talking to a door.

"I can't. That freaking guy with the leaf blower is out again," she answered. "I'm too angry. I won't be able to go back to sleep."

Allie didn't remember seeing anyone blowing leaves; he must've started while she was in the shower. At least Libby didn't seem to know Allie had left. "Yeah. He woke me up too," she lied.

"Say, babe... I wanted to know if you—"

Before Libby could strike up a conversation about anything off-limits, Allie retreated to her bedroom. She changed out of her pajamas for the second time that morning, putting on a neat pair of opaque tights, a skirt, and a floral blouse. The shirt was patterned with little white daisies, and as she did up the last few buttons, Allie mused that her mother would have thought it was cute.

Fluffing her drying hair with her fingers, Allie headed for the kitchen. Her gentle knock on the closed bathroom door let Libby know she'd already started making coffee.

Libby's morning routine was much more involved than Allie's. While she was primping and braiding, Allie pulled two mugs from the cabinet— a pink one for Libby, and the one with Murder Prevention Juice printed on the side for her. When the pot was done, she made up Libby's coffee first, spooning in sugar and adding creamer until it looked like a latte. She left hers plain.

It wasn't much longer until Libby joined Allie at the kitchen island. Setting her phone on the counter, she scrubbed a hand through her ginger curls, leaving them prettily tousled. She looked a little more awake with her eyeliner done, but only just.

"I was going to complain about how rude it was of you to walk away and leave me talking to myself —again—but I'm so glad you made coffee, I don't even care anymore. I don't think I'd make it through lecture without the caffeine."

"I feel the same way." Allie passed the pink mug over. "I'm gonna need it for work today."

Libby took an appreciative sniff. "You're a lifesaver," she groaned, and brought the mug to her lips for an experimental sip.

"Did I put in enough sugar?"

Libby swallowed through a noise of approval. "Just the right amount of sweet! Just like you," she added with a saccharine little smile and a poke to Allie's shoulder.

The giggle Allie let out was fake, but her smile wasn't. The friendship wasn't fake, either, even if she hid herself beneath a mask of femininity and overly sweet pleasantness. Libby was the only one who ever smiled at Allie so genuinely. Nobody else in her life, and definitely nobody at work, would ever call her sweet. This was why the mask was so important. She couldn't risk letting Libby see through to her real self, or Allie would lose her, just like she'd lost everyone else.

Better to pretend she was loveable and keep the one person she had.

"Busy day ahead of you?" Libby asked, wrapping both hands around her mug and leaning her elbows against the island.

"Yeah," Allie sighed. She needed to do something with her hands too—something girlish enough not to be suspicious—so she gingerly tucked a strand of her wheat-blond hair behind an ear. "There was a mix-up last week, and I'm going to have to clean up all the assignment schedules. Probably gonna be late again."

Libby frowned, giving a sympathetic cluck of her tongue. "Sorry, babe. I don't know how you manage to work so much during the semester. I'd be so tired all the time!" She illustrated the point by yawning again behind her hand. "But it's cool that you have, like, a real job already."

Allie grunted in agreement, taking a long sip of coffee to avoid a more substantial answer. Libby didn't know how badly Allie craved structure. Neither the criminology classes nor the security company shifts were about paying rent or jumpstarting her résumé. They were about clinging to any semblance of military rigidity she could get.

Libby only knew that Allie had been in the army. She didn't know Allie had been discharged under other than honorable means, and she sure as hell didn't know why. She probably didn't even know what an OTH discharge was. And if Allie had her way, she never would.

Allie took another delicate sip, the black coffee sharp on her tongue. A comfortable silence filled the kitchen before the rumble of Libby's phone against the counter spoiled it.

"Not another university alert." Libby read the message hurriedly, a frown creasing the corners of her mouth. "God. It's about those girls who were abducted."

"Was there another one?" Allie asked innocently, drawing her eyebrows together.

"As if they'd tell us. Just another generic warning and equally generic assurance that we're safe on campus."

"How could we possibly feel safe if they're not able to catch the guy?"

"Listen to this." Libby read directly from her screen. "'We assure students that local police are doing everything they can to keep you safe.' Are you feeling safe yet?"

Allie snorted. "Hardly. Anything else?"

"Just tips. Check in with your friends, don't walk alone at night. No-brainer stuff."

"Well, don't you just love the irony of it?" Allie narrowed her eyes. "We wouldn't have to do any of that if they'd work harder to get this pervert."

"Exactly!" Libby closed her phone with a sharp snap. "There's a serial rapist wandering around kidnapping students, and nobody has done anything about it! Should I just be on the lookout? How does this email make any sense to anyone?"

"Mhm," Allie agreed into her coffee.

"And thank goodness those girls returned alive. I just can't help worrying that it might escalate to... you know..."

Allie was almost positive it wouldn't—not with this particular perp, anyway. Maybe if his identity was threatened, but not in the compulsive way some serial rapists graduated into serial killers. She wasn't about to share her insider knowledge of the investigation with Libby, though. Allie just nodded sadly and fiddled with the handle of her mug.

"And you know what really drives me up a wall? This whole story is based on just two accounts," Libby added, still riled up. "Yet I know for a fact that it's happened more than twice."

"Do you, now?" Allie lowered her mug and narrowed her gaze.

She knew, of course, there were more victims than the university had reported. Allie had been following this case very closely on her own, but it was a little surprising Libby knew about it too.

"Yeah. I've heard people in class talking about girls who didn't go to the police. I guess they figured the cops were a lost cause."

"Because nothing came out of whatever they did about the first two."

"Right. And I don't blame them for not wanting to be grilled. You know how it is. Unless there's a corpse, everyone makes it out to be the girl's fault. I heard as much from a girl who knows a girl who was attacked last weekend. Can you believe that?"

Allie stared into her coffee. She knew the feeling all too well.

She also knew those girls—all of whom had been heavily drugged and shuttled off to a second location—probably didn't have anything to report. This was a practiced pervert. He had never let his victims see him or been caught on camera. Some had remembered a male voice and vaguely described a disturbing padded room, but none of it was concrete enough to seal the fucker's fate.

"Anyone I know?" Allie asked, careful to sound like a morbidly curious criminology student instead of an interrogator. It was the best kind of lie—one that was sort of true.

"Do you know Alisa? From toxicology?" A photo-perfect image of wide cheekbones, a button nose, and straight-cut bangs flashed in Allie's head, though she'd probably only spoken to the young woman once or twice. "It's her roommate. Mila."

"She sounds sort of familiar. What's her last name?"

"Turner, I think."

Mila Turner. Allie made a show of dwelling on the name, cocking her head and tapping her chin. "Yeah, that sounds familiar. I think I've met her in passing around campus."

She hadn't, but she made a mental note to talk to Mila, to see if she could share anything that might turn into a lead. If Allie could just get started on this shitbag's trail, she might even be able to take out the trash before he managed to hurt anyone else.

And when she got her hands on him... well, she'd teach him a lesson about pain and suffering that was so harsh, so blood-soaked, he'd never sleep again.

"Penny for your thoughts?" Libby's question snapped Allie out of her violent fantasy.

"Just wondering how the police managed to drop the ball so badly," she fibbed.

"Yeah." Libby gazed into the creamy surface of her coffee, looking introspective herself. "I just... I wish someone could really do something, you know? Before the next girl gets hurt."

Allie downed the rest of her coffee, then set the mug on the counter with a definitive clink. "Someone *should* do something, shouldn't they?"

Checking the time, Allie rinsed her mug, grabbed her backpack, said her goodbye to Libby, then headed out for work.

She made a stop in the building's service room, like she did every morning, where she changed into her unofficial work uniform: baggy jeans and a black t-shirt. Because the full truth was that Allie was almost never herself—not at home, not at work, not at school. The truth was that the only time she could really let loose was when she was bloodying some creep in an alleyway.

If Mila Turner could tell her anything useful about the Weekend Rapist, Allie swore she would finally track him down, and once she did, she'd put an end to his reign of terror and introduce him to the real her.

Chapter 3

The front office of Soldiers for Hire was perhaps a tad less sleepy than most offices were at nine in the morning.

Allie wouldn't know. She'd never worked in a regular office.

And she wasn't about to start now, apparently, because according to Allie, the best thing about this job was its staff. Soldiers for Hire exclusively employed ex-military personnel, and in turn, it put them to work connecting veterans with whatever services they needed to transition back into civilian life. That was the whole point of the organization. It was a bridge between retired soldiers and the rest of the world.

Shouldering through the front doors, she gave the secretary a curt nod, then stalked to her back wall cubicle as quickly as possible. That was the most acknowledgment Allie ever offered her coworkers. When they gave her a choice, that is.

She did not get a choice today.

Allie must have dropped her backpack to the floor a little too loudly, because no sooner than she'd managed to land butt-in-seat, a voice called out.

"Mornin', Sunshine!" shot at her across the flimsy cubicle barrier.

"Phoenix." She sighed, not bothering to disguise her distaste.

Somehow—via means beyond Allie's powers of comprehension— Frustrating Phoenix in the next-door cubicle was their boss's best friend and right-hand man. The insufferable man was a permanent fixture in her workspace. He was also either too dull to understand Allie was uninterested in pointless office pleasantries, or he was very dedicated to converting her into his office wife. All he succeeded in doing was pissing her off.

She stiffened in her chair and plastered on her unfriendliest scowl, just in case he decided to stand up and peer at her. He didn't, thank god. Phoenix left his desk to putter off somewhere else, hopefully far away, and so Allie booted up her computer and pulled out the lowest drawer of her filing cabinet. She had just fished out a handful of olive-green folders when approaching footsteps and a familiar voice snapped her to attention.

"—not going to send operatives out for something like that," her boss was saying into his cell phone. Allie's back straightened unconsciously, and her face tightened in a manner beyond normal deference for a boss. He hated to be called by his name, and especially hated to be called Mr. Bennett. Yet he was one of the two co-owners of Soldiers for Hire, and as such, commanded the respect of his employees without needing to demand it. Most of the time, Allie just referred to him as "sir."

"What? What is it? What are you talking about?" Phoenix's wheedling barged into a conversation no one was having with him. "Is it a funny mission? 'Cause if it is, I'd volunteer in a heartbeat. And for real, it might actually be good for publicity, so... what is it?"

"It's nothing and it's not up for debate. No operators working security at the putt-putt," Mr. Bennett said, shooting Phoenix a hard look, and his tone conveyed that there would be no arguments.

"Oh, you're no fun," Phoenix pouted.

"Grecco." Mr. Bennett glanced in as he passed the opening of Allie's cubicle, giving her a short and courteous nod. She was greeted with a half-second glimpse of sandy-blond hair and a scruffy beard above his customary black t-shirt and jeans. Mr. Bennett didn't have the rigid appearance or sharp dress of the other COs Allie had served under, but he carried himself like he knew what he was about, a trait she found comforting.

"Sir," she responded, quashing the urge to salute.

He continued on to the next cubicle, where he paused to ask about an equipment order. Released from the scrutiny of an authority figure, Allie turned back to the thick folders spread across her desk.

"Say, Grecco... How long have you been here now, anyway? Has it been a year already?"

The hand that had been reaching for files thumped into her lap as a fist. Phoenix was leaning on the frame of her cubicle.

She shot him a stern glance that sailed right over his head. Just as tall as Mr. Bennett and as lanky as army guys could get, Phoenix had short red-brown hair growing out of a military cut, and always smiled like he had something up his sleeve.

"I don't get it." Phoenix took an exaggerated look around, as if he'd never seen the four bare walls of Allie's cubicle. "You ever gonna actually move in here? If you quit, I probably wouldn't notice for a week."

"I don't need decorations to do my work," she countered evenly, turning back to her computer, hoping he'd take the hint.

"It has nothing to do with decor, Grecco. You don't even have a calendar. I gave Shauna a calendar with puppies on it. Do you want me to get you one?"

"No need. I use an app."

"So you're not a puppy girl." Was he still talking? "What about kittens?"

Allie didn't like to be called a girl at the age of twenty-eight, especially by a man, and especially by a man from work. She didn't even want to be thought of as female there—she just wanted to do her work and go home, ideally unharried by office funny guys who might take any show of kindness or humor the wrong way.

"Would you at least change your desktop background? What if I sent you a *picture* of kittens? If I emailed you a picture of kittens—an adorable picture of adorable kittens—would you take five seconds to open it, right click, and *set as—*"

"Back off, Phoenix. I'm kind of busy. Can you just let me get back to work?"

Phoenix lifted his hands, backing away from the cubicle like he was being held at gunpoint. "Yes, ma'am," he obliged, and turned away to bother Mr. Bennett, leaving Allie to her work.

Mr. Bennett often roved the office on his own agenda, but Phoenix was almost never seen without him. They'd been inseparable since their own active-duty days, and they carried a distinct army-buddy energy into the office.

If Allie had known she'd be working beside two ex-Rangers when she filled out her application, maybe she would have looked elsewhere. And if she had known they would remind her so much of Matthew and Judd—the two men who had destroyed her, each in their own way, and gotten her kicked out of the 75th—Allie would have thrown the job offer in the trash.

Sitting in that uncomfortable chair, listening to them banter, her face reddened from the neck up. Bonds of brotherhood—or whatever flame-eyed, melodramatic metaphor men in military friendships liked to use—couldn't be trusted. They'd choose each other over everything else. Over every*one* else, even when their loyalties were misplaced.

They'd break your heart and ruin your life without a second thought.

A dull pain pulled Allie out of reminiscing. Snapping her hand open, she examined the red crescents her nails had left in the flesh of her palm. They were almost deep enough to draw blood.

Allie shook out the pain from her hand and her heart. No one could hurt her like that again if she stayed closed off. No one could hurt her at all if she never gave them an opening.

She'd barely gotten started on the scheduling problem before someone else was knocking on the plastic frame of her cubicle. It was Mr. Bennett holding a stack of documents.

"New assignment for you, Grecco. These are the evaluations and treatment recommendations for our new batch of soldiers. Get them entered into the system ASAP and pass off copies to the right departments."

"What about the mix-up from last week, sir?"

"Don't worry about that," he said, tapping the thick handful of papers with a forefinger. "This is your top priority now. Everything else can wait until this is done."

"Yes, sir." Allie accepted the printer-warm stack into her hands. If it had been anyone else, she would've just motioned to her *incoming* mailbox.

"I'll have some scheduling adjustments later today for Thanksgiving week. Keep an eye out."

"Yes, sir."

Allie was all business at work, and so was Mr. Bennett. All either of them cared about was results and maybe, in Allie's case, being appreciated for those results. She respected that about him, and he certainly didn't seem to mind it about her.

Before he could depart, another pair of footsteps threatened the already crowded space between the cubicles.

"It's cold out there!" said a jolly, masculine voice. Stan—the other company co-owner—joined Mr. Bennett in the doorway of Allie's humble gray cube.

With his salt-and-pepper hair (the salt seemed to be winning), deep-set laugh lines, and expensive suit, Stan looked a little out of place beside Mr. Bennett. Yet even as he greeted each and every person in the office with an easy smile, he comported himself like someone accustomed to being obeyed, no questions asked. Being an insanely rich criminal lawyer apparently bought you a nice air of authority to match your suit.

"Have a great day, Allie," he said, crow's feet crinkling around his eyes.

She kept her chin straight and soldierly. "You too, sir."

"I see your game now," Phoenix said. He'd crept back up to her cubicle, a tilted grin on his face.

"Suck up to the bosses and ignore everyone else, huh?"

Allie pointedly ignored Phoenix's quip, but Stan answered for her, his warm voice tensing. "I'm only the wallet around here, son, not the boss."

He didn't wait for Phoenix to clown back. Greetings concluded, Stan turned on his fancy leather heel and led the pair of them toward the big meeting room, asking Mr. Bennett something or another about his apartment.

Finally—*finally*—Allie swept her folders aside and got to work.

Paging through profiles of fresh PTSD discharges, matching each with work and mental health services, she felt her focus begin to drift. Allie was a little jealous of the veterans who responded to therapy. A touch resentful, even. It had worked for her when she was a kid, back when the nightmares had plagued her nearly every night. For a time, she had embraced the fact that the crimson rivulets and her blood-splattered feet weren't real—they were just regurgitated images from a horror movie she'd watched too young. She had accepted her dreams as dreams.

But then therapy had failed her as spectacularly as everyone and everything else. The Rangers were gone—her second family was gone—and the dreams were back, worse than ever.

And so the great stealth operation of Allie's life had begun.

Home, work, school. Thoughtful friend, office drone, college girl. Her masks changed but the disguise at its root was always the same: normalcy. No one knew the real Allie. No one would like the real Allie. Experience had taught her that time and time again. All she could do was hide until the time came to unleash herself in dark alleys with terrible men on the business end of her fists. Whenever she stopped, the rage—and the nightmare—stirred.

Allie flew through the reports. She had another job to do that day. She was going to make Libby's morning wish come true.

She was going to do something about the Weekend Rapist.

Allie ducked out for an early lunch break with the straight-backed posture and laser focus of someone on a critical mission, not to be stopped or bothered. She encountered no resistance between her desk and the service door.

Checking to be sure that no one was following her, Allie went out of Soldiers HQ and down the narrow back alley, keeping one eye on the door in case anyone stepped out for a smoke break. Most of her hunts involved going undercover with high heels and lipstick, and Allie didn't normally get a rush from information-gathering, but this one was special. This one was different. She wanted to give this job—this unsanctioned, self-appointed job— her full attention.

Pulling her phone from her pocket, Allie took a deep breath and dialed.

Chapter 4

I t rang. Allie paced beneath the fire escape, her heart beating fast, her muscles tense, her throat dry.

Come on, pick up, she thought, drumming her thigh with her free hand.

It hadn't taken much to prod Mila's number out of the university admissions office—just a little confidence and a big fat lie about working for the NYPD. But the number was meaningless if Mila didn't answer.

Allie had resigned herself to leaving a message when the tone cut off midring to a cautious "hello."

"Is this Mila Turner?" Allie's adrenaline surged, but she kept her voice cool and even.

"Um, yeah. That's me," Mila said. Hers was a bit of a southern drawl, soft-spoken and unhurried. Almost definitely an out-of-state student, which strengthened Allie's hunch that the shitbag chose victims who might not be missed for a few days.

Allie slipped on an accent of her own. It was an amalgamation of every clever big-city TV cop she'd watched question a fictional uncooperative witness, and it felt a little funny in her mouth. She hoped Mila wouldn't call her bluff. "Hi, Mila. This is Detective Weeks with the NYPD Special Victims Unit. I was hoping you could answer a few questions."

Mila was quiet for a long moment. "How did you get this number?" she asked, pitch climbing with anxiety.

"I heard you might know something about the recent abductions around your campus."

"Who told you that?"

"I'm performing an on-and-off-the-record investigation, and your name came up."

"I don't want to talk about it, so don't call me again and just leave me—"

"Please don't hang up." Allie rushed to explain. "Just think of it as an anonymous tip, okay? I can't expose my sources, just like I won't expose anything you tell me to anyone. I've been interviewing victims and witnesses since the first abductee came forward."

"Yeah, well. From where I'm standing, you don't seem to be very good at your job."

"I guess I deserved that." Allie's mouth twitched upward. She respected Mila for being able to muster a little fire after what she'd been through. "Look, I can assume you have very little faith in the police, and I don't blame you, but if you keep quiet, we'll share the blame for the next victim."

"I... umm... It's not like I have a lot to tell you."

"Anything you can tell me will help."

"I don't want to place a complaint. I heard how you guys blew off the other girls."

"You won't have to do anything you don't want to do, Mila. Anything you tell me is off the record," Allie added before Mila could lie or hang up. "You won't have to testify."

"Then what do you want from me?"

"I just want to talk. I want you to help me catch this guy, one way or another."

"I won't have to go to court or... or go down to the station or anything?"

"No court, no station," Allie confirmed. "I'll just ask you some questions over the phone. No strings attached."

"Won't that be... I don't know... like... inadmissible evidence or something?"

"How about you let me worry about legalities, and just tell me everything so I can get my hands on this rapist?"

The line was quiet for another long stretch before Mila came through, hardly audible over the ambient sounds of motor and foot traffic. "I... I guess I can tell you what I know about him. But I don't know how much help I'll be. I don't remember much."

"Anything you tell me will be better than nothing," Allie assured her. "Any detail, no matter how small. Why don't you start by telling me what you remember from that Friday night?"

She heard Mila swallow. Allie pinned the phone between ear and shoulder, shifting to prop a notepad she'd smuggled from her desk against her thigh, pencil at the ready.

"Okay, okay..." Mila let out a shaky breath. "So I'd been chatting with this guy online for a while, right? Jason. He seemed real nice—down to earth, not arrogant or anything, and he was actually interested in getting to know me, unlike just about everyone else I seem to meet on dating sites. No inappropriate pictures or nothing like that—"

"Which dating site?" Allie interrupted.

"Uh, Cupid's Arrow."

"That's great info, Mila." Allie scribbled down *new app*. Unsurprising. "Go on."

"I'm rambling, sorry," she mumbled, rushed and breathless. "Anyway, we were supposed to meet in person at a bar, but he stood me up. I had a drink or two, but no more than that. I was *not* drunk," she emphasized defensively, "but that's where it all starts to get hazy. I... I must have been drugged."

"Where did you set to meet?" Allie asked, watching a couple that passed by the far end of the alley, their arms linked.

"A place called Jeffrey's. It's kind of an old-fashioned bar."

Allie knew the place. One of the other women had been taken—and returned—to the same bar. And just like the other abduction locations, it didn't have security cameras, so Allie knew there'd be no catching this creep on tape. "Whose idea was it to meet at Jeffrey's?"

"His. Though I don't think Jason was his real name," Mila added, sadness tinting her anxiety.

"What do you mean by that?"

"Well, just that once I was back in my right mind, I checked the app and he'd deleted his profile. I couldn't find a Jason DuPont who matched his picture anywhere. Guess he decided I wasn't very interesting after all."

Allie jotted down the obviously fake name. Mila didn't seem to have connected the dots that "Jason" had probably been her attacker, but Allie didn't bring it up. "And was anyone hanging around you while you were at Jeffrey's? Did you notice anything suspicious before your memories start to get hazy?"

"I don't know. A few people talked to me while I was waiting. I was all prettied up at the bar, and... you know... boys will be boys. Nobody I could pick out of a lineup."

"Do you remember getting out of there?"

"I feel like I remember someone walking me out the door, but..." Mila paused, and Allie heard another gulp. "I couldn't tell you anything about him, if he was even real."

"That's all right. Tell me what you remember next."

"That's where it goes blurry. I remember a room. There was something on the walls—some kind of padding. I remember thinking I was in an egg carton. I know that sounds stupid..." Her voice caught in her throat. "There was always water on the nightstand. Sometimes a man would talk to me through the door. Maybe two men? I'm not sure of anything. I never saw a soul."

Somewhere off to Allie's right, a car honked three times in quick succession. She cupped her hand around the speaker, hoping she wouldn't miss a word of Mila's story or the way she told it. "What did this person say?"

"He told me to drink, but I figure that stuff was all drugged, because I went under again. I kept waking up and falling back asleep, over and over." Mila's voice wobbled, but she pushed on.

"I'm sorry, Mila, but I need to ask. Did he... Do you remember if you were... umm..." Allie struggled to pick at such a fresh and obviously painful wound.

"I know he raped me. I know it. The next thing I remember is waking up outside the bar on Monday."

Allie knew what it was like to wake up somewhere disoriented and afraid, and she knew what it was like to have someone try to hurt her in that state, but she couldn't shake the feeling there was something Mila wasn't telling her.

"You never saw who attacked you? Never smelled them? Felt them? Interacted with them while you were conscious?"

"You see? You're already judging me!"

"I'm really not, Mila." Allie backed down. Her own memories were boiling insider her, threatening to make her sick. She wanted to promise Mila she would catch this bastard before he could shatter another woman's sense of safety for the rest of her life. She wanted to whisper that she'd kill him. But she only drew a breath of cold air and gripped the pencil tighter.

"Jeffrey's?" she asked one last time, just to be sure.

"Yes." Mila's answers had grown short.

Exactly like the other three, a few minor details aside. The guy's MO was rock solid, and Mila's story only further convinced Allie that he knew what he was doing. "Is there anything else you remember?"

"No," Mila said, soft and damp-sounding. "And I'm done talking to you about this."

Allie straightened against the building wall, shifting the phone back into her hand. "Thank you for speaking with me. You've been very helpful and I'm sorry if you—" She didn't have time to finish her apology before Mila hung up.

Stuffing her phone into her pocket, Allie stared down at her notes. *Jeffrey's* stared back in her scratchy penmanship.

Allie paused, the pieces of an idea fitting themselves together. No new intel besides yet another dating app, yet another fake name. But what if chasing down clues about the perpetrator's identity wasn't the path to tracking him down? What if it all came back to the bar?

What if tracking his MO was the best way to track him?

Chapter 5

S *nap!*
      Shouting.
Screaming.
Blood.

A lake of blood, alive and animate and moving. It reached out to grab Allie's bare feet with tendril fingers, rushing down the grooves between white kitchen tiles. She pulled away, scooting back, ignoring the pain in her thigh, but the blood followed her—it always followed her—pooling around her toes and soaking her in thick, hot crimson syrup.

Allie couldn't scream. She couldn't come out— she *mustn't* come out. The woman on the floor just beyond the edge of the tablecloth had warned them not to, and her unblinking eyes were staring lifelessly, a red hole just between them. She would know if Allie came out.

Allie didn't want to find out what would happen if she did. She mustn't come out, and the baby had to stop screaming. Maybe if she gave her something, she'd stop.

Her eyes snapped open.

It took Allie a frantic moment to realize that *she* was the one screaming. Not the baby. There was no baby. There never was. She wasn't in a kitchen or under a table. She was under the same ceiling as always, its panels lit with the faint glow of morning creeping in from behind the curtains.

This was her bedroom, in her apartment where she lived with—

The thump of footsteps just beyond her door yanked Allie upright, sending another shock of cold adrenaline through her body.

"Allie?" The door creaked open and Libby hurried in, fully dressed, earrings jangling. She looked like she'd been in the middle of lining her left eye, judging from the brown smear at its corner. It was Friday morning, Allie remembered. Libby must've been getting ready to leave for her trip home. "Are you okay? I heard a scream."

"I'm fine," Allie responded automatically, reflexively.

As she filled her lungs with air, everything started to filter back. She'd been up late the last three nights going over and over her case notes, scouring for new clues on social media. She remembered turning off her alarm at four and closing her eyes for just a moment.

She should have known better. She should've known that if she deviated from routine, the nightmare would wake her up instead.

And this time there was a terrible aftertaste. When Allie swung her legs over the bed to stand up, a spike of nausea shot through her, and a second woman's lifeless face flashed through her mind, a second concaved skull.

It was the woman from her last mission. The civilian. The target's wife. The mother Judd had shot dead right in front of her child.

Judd. That bastard. He'd killed an innocent woman, then he'd killed Allie's soul—and, in return, she'd killed him. Now she had two dead women crowding her dreams every time she closed her eyes.

"They're not real, honey," a third dead woman whispered in her memory. It was Olivia, her adoptive mother, and the only mother she'd ever known. *"The woman's not real, and neither is the baby. It's just that horrible movie. Oh, sweetheart, I wish we could go back in time and yank the damned thing out of the VCR."*

Another wash of nausea doubled Allie over. She grabbed her ribs and swallowed hard to keep it down.

"Holy heck, babe. Do you need me to get you a bucket or something?" Libby padded closer in the dark, peering worriedly at her. She plopped down at the far end of the mattress, looking like she wanted to drape an arm around Allie, but didn't know how. "It's okay if you throw up. I won't get grossed out, I promise. I know you've been sick the past few days."

Crap—she'd noticed Allie hadn't been sleeping much. She was going to have to be more careful. She was going to have to fit her mask on even tighter.

"I think it's just stress. Midterms," Allie rasped weakly. It was a stupid, stupid lie, but in her foggy, flighty state, Allie couldn't come up with anything better.

Libby scrutinized her from the end of the bed. Through the dim light, Allie could make out the soft edges of her face, her shapely eyebrows pitched downward in concern. "Maybe I shouldn't go. I'll stay here this weekend," she said, folding her arms. "I'll see my parents over Thanksgiving anyway, and I'm sure they'll—"

"No." Allie interrupted her too quickly, hating how loudly she said it. She fumbled around for an explanation—any reason to convince Libby to keep her weekend plans. If she were there, it would be much harder for Allie to go on the hunt. "You don't get to see your dad that often. He's gonna be home. You should go."

Libby softened at the mention of her father. "Are you sure? This is the second time in a week you've had a nightmare. I'll stay if you want. There's like a fifty-fifty chance Dad'll have some work thing turn up anyway," she said glumly.

From what Libby had said, her dad's job was a stream of constant travel. Especially now, during college, it was hard for her to spend as much time with him as she wanted. Allie recognized Libby had family baggage, but at least her parents loved their only daughter. Olivia had tried to love Allie, even as the cancer ate her up, but Logan sure hadn't. Still didn't.

"All the more reason for you to go," Allie urged. "I'll be okay. A quiet weekend to myself might do me some good."

That seemed to decide it, because Libby stood up and wandered over to the door, resting a hand on the frame. "You know you can tell me if you want me to stay, right?"

"I know," Allie replied. "I'll be fine. It was just a dream."

If only it were really that simple.

Libby swiveled and took a big step back in, concern knitting her brow.

"Don't hug me, Libby," Allie snapped. It came out too harsh, so she weakly added, "In case I really am sick." She added a smile so as not to hurt Libby's feelings.

"If you say so. Take care of yourself, okay? And go back to sleep."

"You have my word."

Allie lay back down obligingly, folding her hands over her stomach. Libby stood there for only a moment more before reluctantly ducking out.

She waited until she heard the front door close before she got out of bed. Then she waited an extra five minutes before setting herself up on the couch to continue her investigation.

Over the course of the week, Allie had managed to contact four other women who'd been attacked. They'd been leery at first, but—like Mila—as soon as "Detective Weeks" assured them they wouldn't be required to testify, each had willingly shared what little she remembered. Every detail strengthened Allie's understanding of the shitbag's MO.

He'd picked out each victim on a hip, shoddy new dating site, set up a date, and told her to wait for him at the bar, feeding her some bullshit line about finding the most excited girl there. Then he'd drugged and dragged every woman off to a place some described as a "sex dungeon." The egg carton padding Mila had mentioned made it sound more like a soundproof room to Allie. That meant he had a dedicated location, since she couldn't imagine he'd lug all that soundproofing around every weekend without someone noticing.

When the weekend was up—when he was sated —he'd returned his victims to the same bar. Each had reappeared afraid, disoriented, violated, and with nothing useful to tell the police.

It was a disgusting procedure. It was nefarious, it was evil, but Allie was a little impressed. His routine was practiced. It was calculated. It was smart, and Allie ached to be the one who took this fucker out. She was itching to beat all of that calculation and malice right out of him—spread it all over the pavement outside the bars he frequented—

"Wait!" Allie said aloud to no one.

The perp's MO was so calculated and so practiced, he'd hit some bars more than once, including Jeffrey's. Nobody was perfect. Maybe he was getting complacent with his routine. Maybe, if he kept to his habits strictly enough, she could predict where he might strike next!

Allie opened a city map on her laptop. Her pulse sped up as she placed pins, one for each abduction, and as the victims who hadn't reported were added to the map, a pattern unfolded before her. A five-spoked wheel of red pins, one Friday after the other, proceeding chronologically around the circle in a neat order. There it was.

Jeffrey's had been the last hit. If he stuck to his wheel, the next would be a seedy bar called After Hour, and he'd be out hunting tonight.

So would Allie.

Chapter 6

"Would he like red or green better?" Violet held up one top against each shoulder, frowning at her reflection in the floor-length mirror.

It shouldn't matter what her date liked. She should go with what *she* liked, but she was so indecisive, she just wished someone would make the decision for her. She wasn't usually so concerned with looks—she'd never been much to look at anyway, so why bother? But tonight wasn't a normal night.

She just wanted this to go well. Her first date with Carl had to be perfect.

She spun around to her bed, where her brown tabby cat was stretched out across the rumpled covers, watching her with a sleepy attentiveness.

"What do you think, Caesar?" she asked, showing him the two fanciest shirts she owned. "Red or green?"

Caesar didn't look at either hanger—just blinked sleepily at her.

"You're no help," Violet sighed fondly. She tossed the green blouse to the bed, turning back to her reflection to hold the red one up again. Red was supposed to be a romantic color, right?

She visualized how her date might see her in crimson. She imagined the sounds of the bar, the low light, and finally sitting next to him. It felt right and a smile spread across Violet's face.

She had a feeling about the red top, just like she had a feeling about Carl.

Three states from home with only one New York friend to speak of, Violet had tried the online dating thing, but the disappointments were wearing on her. She wasn't conventionally attractive, she wasn't knowledgeable about makeup or clothing, and she knew she didn't make a memorable first impression. She also knew that men online were shallow, but every time someone lost interest when they saw her picture, her heart cringed.

She'd changed her profile picture to a photo of Caesar. It only worked until a guy asked for her photo, inappropriate or otherwise.

Carl was different. She'd known he was special when the first thing he'd said to her was that her cat was cute. He'd never asked for pictures, he'd never sent her messages that made her uncomfortable, and he'd never pressured her into going out before she was ready.

Even on the eve of their first date, Carl insisted he didn't care what she looked like. Violet smiled again at the memory of his last message.

"Just sit at the bar and I'll find you :) I'll pick out the most excited girl there," he'd written. "Can't wait to meet face-to-face!"

She'd studied his profile photo for a long time. He was casual, candid, and a handsomer man than she'd ever dreamed of being with, though she liked him for his humor and manners more than his looks. She hoped one photo would be enough to recognize him tonight.

Violet pulled the crimson blouse over her head, adjusting it over her shoulders and smoothing it over her chest. She didn't bother with another look in the mirror.

"You behave yourself," she told Caesar, giving him a scratch under the chin and dropping a kiss on the top of his head. "I'd ask you to wish me luck, but I don't need it. Tonight's the night! I'm off to meet the man of our dreams!"

Chapter 7

The sky blackened; the streetlights glowed. It was time to transform.

Allie had learned long ago that once she slipped into her battle gear, it was difficult to think of anything else. She did not allow herself to prepare until the clock struck nine.

Her undercover kit was shoved in a discreet corner of her closet. When it was time, she pulled out the duffel bag, then dropped it onto her bed and roughly unzipped it. Her appearance was her armor: an arsenal of lipstick; a black pencil dress, lowcut and tight in all the right ways to attract the wrong kinds of attention; wigs of various colors and styles; and a pair of six-inch black heels.

She put on the brunette wig, adjusting the bangs just so across her forehead.

Allie didn't need weapons—she'd spent her adult life and a decent amount of her adolescence honing her hand-to-hand combat skills. *She* was the weapon. If the Weekend Rapist was looking for excitement tonight, she'd give him more than he'd know what to do with.

She touched up her lipstick. The bright crimson spread across her bottom lip made her think of blood—women's blood—spilling across the kitchen floor. Swiping a nail around the corner of her lip, using only a compact mirror to guide her, Allie sharpened the line of lipstick with the diligence of a Ranger reassembling her rifle.

Judd had shot a frightened mother down in cold blood. And Allie stood there, frozen, while she'd bled out in front of her child.

She swept the ends of the wig away from her neck, her fingertips brushing against the exposed skin of her throat, where her own blood thrummed steadily. A second memory burned at the back of her tongue.

Her fellow soldiers had turned on her in an instant, choosing to believe Judd's innocence even when Allie's neck, purple and bruised, had borne the proof—that he'd cornered her in an empty tent and attacked her. Nothing she said had convinced them. None of their lauded bonds of brotherhood had mattered when she was the one who needed help.

She adjusted the hot-pink strap of her bra, letting it peek out from the shoulder of her dress like maybe it had slipped.

The only hands she'd ever welcomed on her body had been Matthew's, and he'd turned his back on Allie with the rest of them. Almost two years had passed since she felt like the floor opened up under her. Two years since a dull-faced lawyer told Allie that her own boyfriend didn't believe her—that he was prepared to testify to her guilt—that he already believed she was a killer, deep down.

That brotherhood of men had taken everything from her, and thus she vowed to do everything she could to prevent any more women from being traumatized and shamed into silence. Trauma and shame were the Weekend Rapist's forte, but not for long. Not if Allie could help it.

With heels in hand and a purse stuffed with extra wigs—in case the intended victim tonight wasn't a brunette—Allie padded toward the bathroom, unease squeezing at her guts for the first time. She took a deep breath in, then let it out. Flicking on the light, she stepped in to assess her disguise.

Her breath stalled in her throat as she took in the black-clad figure looking back at her. Staring fixedly at the pink bra strap, Allie gave herself a moment to prepare before sliding her gaze upward.

She tensed as her eyes passed over the curves and planes of the face in the mirror. A pang of familiar fear clutched at her—the same pang that had haunted her mirror since Allie had grown into the woman she was. It wasn't quite as awful looking at her reflection when she was this gussied up.

Between the wig, risqué dress, and makeup, she looked like someone else entirely.

Still, it wasn't easy to look herself in the eyes.

Pulse fluttering in her chest, she teased her sideswept bangs, just the right balance of primp and disarray. The deadliest hunting costumes were casual and a little sloppy—the complete opposite of the molten rage boiling up inside of her. She watched her hands touch up her makeup, feeling as if they belonged to someone else.

When she was satisfied—no, when she was armored up—Allie shoved her feet into the high heels and clattered downstairs to catch a cab. Tonight, she'd beat this bastard to his mark.

• • • ● • ● • • •

After Hour wasn't the noisiest bar Allie had ever hunted, but it was still a Friday night, and the barflies were out in full force.

She paused just inside the door, near the tacky jukebox up against the wall. Allie felt less than certain After Hour was indeed the right place, and she'd no idea what sort of person she was looking for. Tall, short, dark hair, light hair—*Jason DuPont* was as fake as his profile photo. What was the shitbag's go-to line for setting up these doomed dates? He'd look for the most excited girl sitting at the bar.

If it was good enough for him, it was good enough for Allie.

Scanning the old bar stools, her eyes locked on to a young woman—college-age, dressed up in a crimson blouse with her dark hair all done up, looking toward the door every few seconds. She didn't have a drink in front of her, so she must have just arrived.

Allie clicked over to the bar, claiming the stool beside her and dropping her large purse on the floor with a heavy thump. The girl startled, surprised to see someone suddenly in the hitherto empty seat, but despite her wide eyes and parted lips, she didn't say anything.

"Don't you look nice." Allie made a show of looking her up and down. "You meeting someone?"

"Yeah, I am. Is it that obvious?" A blush rose on her cheeks, and she looked down, tucking a lock of dark brown hair behind her ear.

"You keep eyeballing the door," Allie explained. "I figured you must be waiting for someone."

"He's not late or anything." The girl seemed a bit defensive. "I'm half an hour early, that's all." She leaned her elbow on the bar.

"You must be excited if you showed up this early." Allie let herself trail off, fishing for a name. "I'm Lilly, by the way."

"Violet," the girl offered. Easy as pie. "I'm waiting for the man of my dreams."

"Ooh, so you're waiting for your *destiny*." Allie tittered behind her hand. "What's he like? Have you known him long?"

Violet fiddled with her sleeve, a shy smile spreading across her face. "We met on a dating site, but he isn't like any of the other guys I've met online. He's nice, and funny, and really polite. I think he's a little old-fashioned."

"You've never met him in person before?"

"No. This is our first date." Violet smiled wider, excitement lighting up her whole face. "He doesn't even know what I look like."

Allie thanked her lucky stars she'd gone with the brunette wig. "And how are you two planning to find each other if you've never met?"

"The usual way, I guess. I have his picture."

"Adorable. A photo swap."

"Not exactly a swap. I'm not very photogenic, and I don't like sharing photos..." Violet's fingers curled against the worn wood of the bar top. "Carl said he'd find me if I sat at the bar. He said he'd pick out the most excited girl here." She smiled shyly again.

Well, that fucking clinched it, didn't it?

Now Allie just had to get Violet to scram so she could take her place and trick the Weekend Rapist into trying to take her instead. She'd string him along until he realized too late that it was him who'd fallen into the trap.

"He sounds delicious and I, too, have a few minutes to kill. Would you mind if we killed time together?"

"Um, okay." Violet seemed reluctant.

"So go on. Tell me more about this Carl," Allie said, slipping a note of suspicion into her voice. "Describe him to me."

Violet swallowed. A nervous wince darkened her smile—she must've picked up on Allie's change of tone—but she was too excited about her date to stop talking. "Um, well, his profile picture was a little small, but he's got black hair, kind of short and buzzed along the sides." She mimed a close-cut shave against her ears with her hands. "He seems pretty tall. A little outdoorsy?"

Not even close to the way the other victims had described their dates, but that was to be expected. Allie's eyes narrowed further. "What's his last name?"

"Um, Greene?"

Allie knew time was running out, so she feigned a loud laugh, pretending Violet had just told a hilarious joke. Then she leaned in close, as if to tell her good friend a secret.

"You listen to me and you listen to me good," she whispered. "Carl Greene is my boyfriend and the father of my child."

"Wh—What?" Violet tried to lean away, but Allie grabbed her wrist, pinning it to the table. Her grip was gentle but jarringly swift. If anyone happened to glance over and see Allie's hand on Violet's, they would've seen nothing more than a heartfelt gesture of affection between sisters.

Violet, however, surely felt the ridges of Allie's fingernails gently curling into her wrist bone, one by one.

"Stay quiet!" Allie hissed. "Don't you dare make a scene. If you act natural and stay calm, I won't kill you for going after my man." She dug her nails hard into the soft skin, flashing a big, affable smile for the rest of the bar.

"Wait, I—" Violet stammered, still too loud. Allie squeezed harder, and she corrected her volume. "I didn't know! I swear I didn't know!"

"You're going to help me out a little if you want me to believe that."

"It's true. I had no idea!"

"Then all you need to do is tell me everything Carl said, and you can go."

Pale-faced, Violet spilled it all. She recited their entire chat history, explaining again how he was okay with not having her picture, and how they'd discovered they were both out-of-towners. Once Allie got a sense for what Carl knew—all the while leaning against the bar, smiling and nodding, as if the two of them were just girlfriends chatting it up —she was ready to take Violet's place.

"What time are you supposed to meet him?" Allie asked.

"Eleven." It was a little past eleven already.

"It was nice talking to you," she said amicably. Violet stiffened as Allie leaned forward to give her a hug. At the last moment, she turned a cheek to mutter in her ear, "Now go home and mind your fucking business, okay? And if you ever talk to him again, I'll hunt you down."

As soon as Allie released her, Violet gathered up her purse and scurried out. Allie watched through the bar window as she dashed across the street, casting many anxious over-shoulder glances, until she was finally free of Carl's vengeful girlfriend.

Good, Allie thought. She might've felt bad for ruining a dream date if she wasn't so sure that all romance unavoidably ended in disaster, big or small. The poor girl had to learn sooner or later, and better she do it now—when she had someone to save her from catastrophe—than to fall into the clutches of someone who'd break more than just her heart.

Allie took a last deep breath, cleared her mind, and assumed the role of Violet.

It was easy to slip into such roles by now. Perched at her post, hunkered against the bar, Allie subtly kept tabs on the other patrons, wondering if one of them might be her target. She'd been sitting restlessly for twenty minutes when a short man in a leather jacket approached her.

"Are you here waiting for a blind date, by any chance?" he asked, leaning his forearm against the bar.

Allie tensed, ready to spring into action. *Not now*, she told herself. *Not yet.*

"Well, that depends. Are you Carl?" She tilted her head innocently, examining every detail of his face. His cheeks were covered in stubble, a color between blond and brown, and his hair was laden with product. He also had one of the most punchable smiles Allie had ever seen—and that was saying something. Was this him?

"I sure am, gorgeous. Did it hurt when you fell from heaven?"

Allie paused, stuck between wanting an excuse to break this man's nose and her inability to believe this tool was an evil mastermind. His behavior didn't match her guy's MO at all. Approaching the victim, identifying himself as the man she'd supposedly met online? She didn't even have a drink in front of her yet.

Most importantly—none of the girls she spoke with remembered what their date looked like. They could only remember being roofied and herded out of the bar.

This couldn't be him, could it? There was one easy way to find out.

"If you're really Carl, then you must know my name. Do you?" Allie demanded.

"Uh..." His jaw flexed as he clearly tried to make something up. "Sarah?"

"Go away." Allie scowled, but Did It Hurt When You Fell From Heaven Guy slid onto the stool Violet had just vacated.

"All right, angel, I admit it. Maybe I'm not the guy you were supposed to meet, but what if I'm better? You've been here for a while and he hasn't shown up. I'd never make you wait like this, baby."

Allie rolled her eyes. The perp was expecting Violet to be sitting alone, looking miserable and lonely after she'd been stood up. This guy was blowing her cover!

"I'm waiting for someone, and you're not him. Now leave me alone!" she said loudly enough for at least half the bar to hear.

"Come on, just give me a chance! I may not be your blind date, but you blinded me with your beauty."

She wanted to punch him. She wanted to punch him so badly, but she couldn't risk compromising her mission by slugging some random guy who thought he was being smooth by pretending to be someone else's blind date.

"I'm waiting. For someone else," she ground out, low enough for only him to hear. "And if you know what's good for you, you'll back the fuck off right about now."

"Hey, jeez, I was only trying to compliment you," he whined before slinking off to mope at a corner table.

Left alone at last, Allie settled in to wait for her real target. She ordered a drink—rum and Coke, with a straw—and took a sip to wet her throat while she knew it was clean. The minutes crawled by. Every tick of the clock wound the spring of Allie's trap tighter and tighter still.

It was approaching midnight when she decided to try a different tactic—one the Weekend Rapist, if he really was there, couldn't ignore.

After scooping her bag from the floor and plopping it next to her drink, Allie fished out her phone and headed for the bathroom. There, she locked herself into the corner stall, sat on the toilet lid, and scrambled to call up the necessary app. The camera hidden in her bag woke up.

Allie watched her glass, cleverly centered in the camera's frame.

She didn't usually worry about such high-tech strategies. The previous three hunts had been pretty straightforward—Allie prowled around for creeps, beat the shit out of them, and that was that. She was glad she'd sprung for the wireless camera this time. This one was her most involved investigation yet.

She didn't have to wait long to see movement near her abandoned seat. A neatly dressed man with shaggy blond hair and a bushy mustache slid into the seat next to hers. He leaned his elbows on the bar, casually glancing left and right, as if waiting for the bartender. Then—as he reached up to readjust his thick glasses—the man deftly pulled something out of his button-up sleeve with his fingers, and dropped a small white pill into Allie's drink.

"Bingo," she whispered to herself.

Chapter 8

M inutes after the strange man left, Allie returned to the bar. She hopped onto the stool, crossed her legs, and picked up her freshly poisoned drink.

Swirling the glass in her hand, Allie subtly scanned the bar, looking for the shaggy head of hair. She found her suspect lurking alone in a dark corner, almost hidden in a booth. He was watching her, but Allie made sure her eyes didn't linger. Instead, she turned to gaze forlornly at the door instead, as if waiting for her absentee dream date.

She fit her lips to the straw and hollowed her cheeks like she was taking a long, deep drink. Then she set the glass down on her napkin, using her body to shield it from Carl's view as she tipped it just enough to spill a little down the side, letting the recycled paper napkin underneath soak up the dark liquid.

Allie had already deduced the perp would wait for his target to drink herself to blackout—until she couldn't remember anything, especially not a stranger's face—and then usher her from the bar right before she collapsed. If everything went according to plan, all she had to do now was wait.

A few tense minutes passed while she pretended to nurse her drink, all the while acting progressively tipsier, swaying as she leaned over to check her phone or her purse.

Allie was wondering when the hell Carl was going to make his move when, out of the corner of her eye, she saw the mustached man get up. She pushed her purse in front of her drink and cola-soaked napkin before he arrived.

"Is this seat taken?"

Allie listlessly turned her head toward him, as if she were feeling the effects of the drug. "Umm... no. It's... umm... no."

The man took the stool next to her, folding his arms on the bar. His buffalo check button-up was tucked smartly into dark jeans, and now that he was up close, the authenticity of his bristly mustache made her take a second look. It was probably a high-quality fake. Allie expected a disguise, but this elaborate costume suggested he had significant financial resources, especially if he was changing his appearance every week.

Very interesting.

"So are you here all alone, or...?" He trailed off, politely leaving the obvious unsaid—that she'd been stood up.

"Well, that's none of your business, is it?"

"I'm sorry. I couldn't help noticing you've been sitting here by yourself for a while."

"Good for you." Allie hung her head.

"I'm not trying to offend you or anything. Just wanted to make sure you're okay. Are you?"

"Am I what?"

"Okay?"

"Jeez... I dunno... I was supposed to go on a blind date. He didn't show up."

"I'm sorry to hear that," he sympathized.

"That does it. I'm done with men. I'll live the rest of my pathetic life with my cat."

"That sounds like one lucky cat to me." The guy smiled harmlessly. "What's your kitty's name?"

"Caesar," Allie hiccupped, and let out a muffled sob. "He's my best friend. I don't need anyone else."

"I know how you feel. But if I may... don't let this guy turn you off dating altogether. You just have to wait for the right one. My wife and I met on a blind date, you know?"

"You did?" Allie lifted her head, all inebriated innocence and watery eyes.

"Sure. And we've been together for fifteen years now. Got three kids too."

"Wow. That's a long time. And a lotta kids."

Allie wondered if this wife-and-kids routine was part of the reason why none of the girls seemed to remember being approached by a family man. Maybe it just hadn't seemed important, considering what had happened right afterward, which made them dismiss running into such a stand-up guy.

"You're nice," Allie slurred. "What'd you say your name was again?"

"Carl."

Thrown for a loop, Allie nearly lost her grasp on her dazed act. She thought for a moment he was admitting to being her blind date, but then it occurred to her—his game was to endear himself to his victim by just-so-happening to share the no-show's name. In their compromised states, it might've been just enough to get them talking more.

She recovered quickly, using her surprise to exclaim, "Carl? Really?!"

"Yeah, why?"

"That was his name! My date, I mean." She rested her elbow on the bar, mimicking Violet, sinking her chin deep into her hand. "*Carl*."

"Different Carl, I swear." He chuckled convincingly. "On my life."

Leaning in a little closer, Allie examined him through exaggeratedly narrowed eyes. "Well, you don't look anything like his picture, so I believe you. I'm Violet, by the way."

Was that a glint in Carl's eye, or was Allie imagining it?

"It's nice to meet you, Violet."

"It *is* nice to meet me." She faked pouting. "I am a really nice person."

"You are." Again, he chuckled. "So what are you doing still hanging around here? Wouldn't you rather go home and talk this out with a friend or something?"

Allie's rage spiked. This must've been how he made sure victims wouldn't be missed too soon.

"I live alone," Allie lamented. "I'd just be by myself all night."

"Ah."

If Violet had ingested the roofie, she'd have been close to losing consciousness by now. Allie sleepily scrutinized Carl's face for a few long moments. "Wait... wait... Who're you again?"

"Listen, you seem like you're quite a few in. How about you go home, huh? Go to bed. Forget about that other Carl."

"Home sounds good," Allie murmured, leaning her weight on the edge of the bar. Carl called for the bartender and quickly, politely settled her bill with a folded twenty.

Even as Allie slumped over the bar, she felt the thrill of the chase building inside her gut, spilling into her limbs and making her fingers threaten to twitch. They were itching to ball up and plunge into this bastard's family-man mask, to make him bleed, and hurt, and pay. Allie had only killed the first man she'd hunted, but she wouldn't hold herself back if this hunt took a lethal turn. She waited for him to gather her things for her—weakness on the outside, a tempest on the inside, the sound of blood roaring in her ears.

Soon, she soothed herself. Soon she could let it out. Soon she could quiet the rage that had been howling inside her since that sick military brotherhood ruined her life.

"I'm just about to head out myself," Carl said, hurriedly stuffing his wallet into his back pocket. "My wife will be expecting me home soon. Do you need a ride?"

Allie had just opened her mouth to accept—to begin the final phase of her hunt and finally quench her thirst for violence—when a heavy hand landed on her shoulder from behind, and threatened to ruin it all.

Chapter 9

I knew I wasn't going to get my girl the moment that asshole got involved.

A huge man had appeared behind Violet, his hand materializing on her shoulder. He was muscular, tall, and self-assured—in short, not someone I wanted to deal with, especially not when I was sitting next to a date who was one hard sneeze from knocking out in public. His disheveled hair was sandier than the mustache glued on my lip.

He made me nervous, looking at me like that with beady, beat-your-ass eyes. I don't like to be nervous. I like to make women feel nervous around me, and if this one was going to be a hassle, then I'd just have to cut my losses and return home without her.

"What the hell are you doing here?!" Violet, gawking, seemed just as surprised to see him as I was.

"I could ask you the same thing," the man snapped. He didn't just look like a disciplinarian—

he sounded like one too. "What's going on?"

Violet's eyes flickered back to me, so I made sure to keep my expression cool and collected. There was nothing wrong, my gaze said. This was not an infuriating or alarming development.

I may or may not have also needed the reminder.

"I'm just—just—meeting with someone," she stammered.

"Oh?" He turned his stare on me, his hand still perched protectively on Violet's shoulder. She hadn't shaken it off or recoiled.

Oh, shit. I was probably looking at a boyfriend.

Violet had seemed genuine online, and I hadn't mentioned my wealth while masquerading as Carl Greene, but it wouldn't be the first time a girl tried to play me for gifts. Time and time again, she'd claimed she wasn't much to look at, yet she was absolutely gorgeous. Dolled up just for me, as though she knew exactly how to make me want her—to make me want to punish her for going around looking like she was fair game. This girl didn't have self-esteem issues. She looked more like a case of daddy issues.

Something didn't add up.

"And who might you be meeting?" His stare was quickly darkening into a glare.

That did it. Forget Violet; the whole weekend of fun had to be called off now. I had to get out of After Hour—put as much distance between the little minx and me as I could before she wiped out.

There was a good chance this guy was going to remember me if she collapsed from her barstool, even if the girl wouldn't.

I was going to get out of this one by the skin of my teeth. By my immaculate mustache hairs, to be exact.

"Do you know this guy, Violet?" I asked, willing my voice to stay smooth and my brow to stay dry.

The man frowned deeply. "Violet?"

I studied her face, trying to get a read on that quickly fading mind of hers. Contrary to her acquaintance's—and my—confusion, she didn't seem bothered in the slightest. In fact, her big, brown cow eyes suddenly seemed much too sharp and attentive for my tastes. Perhaps the shock of seeing her friend had rallied her. Was that even possible? In all my years of experience with flunitrazepam, I'd never seen a girl bounce back like this. I'd no idea how long I had before she crashed. I guessed five minutes, tops.

"Carl, meet Daniel. Daniel, meet Carl." She made the unnecessary introductions.

"Well, then." I didn't wait for anything else to happen—I couldn't—I was running out of time to make my escape. "Why doesn't Daniel take you home instead, since you seem to know him?" I stood to go. "My wife is expecting me—"

"No!" Violet bayed, snatching my sleeve with strong fingers. Her grip slackened immediately. "I'll go home with you, Carl."

She said my pseudonym with a kind of emphasis, and in my rising state of unease, I couldn't tell if it was the drug or something else that made her say it that way.

"I think it's best if I just go." I tried to shake her off, but Violet's grip tightened again, and damn—now it was a bear trap.

"Calm down, Carl. It's just my boss and he was just leaving. Weren't you, sir?"

Violet's boss looked between us for a long moment. His gaze finally landed on her, not me, as I had expected. "Are you sure you're okay?" Daniel asked, sounding perturbed.

"*Yes*," she assured him. "I'm having a fun night out. Carl's gonna take me home now, and then I'll see you at work on Monday. Okay?"

He paused for a very long moment indeed, and then leaned down to cup his hand against his mouth. He whispered something into her ear and she giggled, but whether it was a reaction to his words or the tickle of his breath, I couldn't say.

"I know, you big dummy!" She reached up a noodly wrist to smack at his arm. "Now get out of here! Go on. Shoo!"

Hesitantly, the man left the bar, falling back to settle in a booth set against the wall, his eyes still trained on Violet and me.

Their gestures—his whispering, her playful hit—hinted at some kind of intimacy between them, performative or otherwise. The idea I'd probably been duped by this stupid, devious woman boiled my blood, but there would be no exacting my revenge now, and there would be no finding out whether Violet was a manipulator or just a flirt.

This was bad. I should have listened to my gut.

"If he doesn't take the hint that I'm not into him soon, I'm gonna have to get HR involved." Violet's dull brunette hair fell back into place as she twisted around to face me, rolling her eyes. "I'm sorry about that. Will you still give me a ride?"

At this point, I was beyond being disappointed about my spoiled weekend. My identity was at risk, and this had all suddenly become much, much too complicated for my liking, so I kindly declined.

I do a lot of shady things, but I don't do complicated.

Chapter 10

Daniel Bennett slid back into the booth, watching Dex Riklis like a hawk. He wasn't going to get away with hurting this one. Not on Daniel's life.

What the hell was Grecco doing sitting on a barstool next to the Weekend Rapist anyway, pretending to be drunk or drugged or both? Why was she going by Violet? What was with the getup and the cheap wig?

Whatever she was doing, nothing good could come of it.

"Oh, come on. Pleeeeease," Grecco pleaded when Dex didn't cave right away. He glanced over toward Daniel's booth for just a moment, licked his lips, then opened his mouth to reply.

Grecco was undercover. She had to be. It was the only explanation that made sense—she'd been faking sips of her drink, and when Daniel had whispered that "Carl" was actually named Dex, she snapped that she already knew and called him a dummy, probably to keep her act. But she was making such a mess of it all, maybe this was something else entirely.

Daniel wasn't going to let either of them out of his sight, no matter what Grecco's bizarre game might be.

And why was Dex still there? Why was he still playing this sloppy little game? Pretending to drink was clever, but Daniel could see the cola-soaked napkin under her glass from his seat. Who did she think she was fooling with that party-store wig? If Dex was really buying into Grecco's halfhearted disguise, well, then the Weekend Rapist was dumber than Daniel thought.

"I can't. Like I said, my wife will worry." Dex stood up, shaking his head.

"I thought you were one of the good guys, but here you are, leaving me all alone. How will I get home?" Grecco whimpered, swaying unconvincingly, catching herself against the bar.

"It really was nice to meet you, but I have to go now and—"

He got half a step away before Grecco's hand shot out, snagging the shoulder of his checkered shirt in her fist, and dragged him down to her level. Daniel couldn't hear what she whispered to him, but based on how pale Dex went, it was obviously a threat. She was making her move, whatever it was.

With a little extra encouragement from Grecco's fist in his shirt, Dex sat back down. Then she lifted her half-full glass, her fingers suspending it like a spider, and offered it to him.

Her voice was low, and Daniel would have lost it in the jukebox music if he wasn't straining to hear. Grecco's eyes locked on to Dex's as she innocently asked him, "Finish this for me?"

Unbelievably, hesitantly, he took the glass from her and lifted it to his lips.

She must have threatened to expose him with something more concrete than just an accusation. It was the only thing Daniel could think of that might make the son of such a wealthy, well-connected politician obey a girl he drugged at a bar. Over the years, Riklis Senior—Senator Riklis, that is—had bailed his only child out of serious legal trouble more than once.

Daniel wouldn't be surprised if the senator already knew about Dex's weekend habit.

And now Grecco had him drinking his own roofie cocktail. He drank it all, taking one gulp after another while she watched. When the glass was dry, he gasped once, loud and miserable, then set it gingerly on the bar.

Daniel watched eagerly as they sat in silence. Grecco must have been waiting out his roofie, just as Dex thought he'd been doing, but for what purpose, Daniel couldn't say. After about ten minutes—though it felt like much, much longer— Grecco stood to collect her purse, drunkenly pulling Dex up too. Taking his arm, she leaned heavily into him as she made him walk.

Daniel had to admit: he'd enjoyed watching Dex choke down his own roofie more than he should've. He waited for them to reach the door before he stood up, leaving his nearly untouched beer behind.

Grecco may have bungled the rest of her operation, whatever it might be, but this part? This part she was acing. Unless you'd been watching all night, as Daniel had been, a bystander never would've thought that Dex—who was looking a little unsteady now, himself—and Grecco weren't just two drunks leaving a run-down bar, leaning on each other for support. Most people wouldn't blink an eye at a posh thirty-something with a woman dressed like that on his arm.

He followed the pair at a distance, trailing Grecco as she steered a wobbly Riklis onto a quiet side street, down the sidewalk, and toward an alley.

Now the sheep was dragging the wolf into her den, giggling loudly enough for Daniel to hear. Maybe Daniel would've been a little more captivated by her strategy if he wasn't so concerned she was about to do something reckless.

He trailed them to the dark alley mouth, leaning casually against the bar's grimy siding, like he might be waiting for someone. By that time, Grecco's demeanor had changed completely. She was no longer stumbling or hanging on to Dex, but marching him further into the shadows. There was the no-nonsense, straight-to-business behavior Daniel expected from an ex-soldier. Whatever she was planning to do with Dex, she was likely to do it soon.

Dex was fighting back now, but his sluggish body couldn't muster enough panic or strength. He squirmed on her arm like a hooked worm—until Grecco swung around, driving her fist directly into his nose.

Daniel didn't make a peep. He stood stock-still, watching, learning.

Dex yelped, clutching at his face. Without letting him recover, Grecco hit him again, staggering him into the side of the alley. Then she shoved him against the wall and thrust her fist into the soft points of his stomach again and again.

Daniel listened to the meaty thuds of Grecco's fists beating whimpering Dex Riklis to a pulp. She was cool and in absolute control. She didn't yell or lash out. She just aimed, hit, and took aim again. Daniel knew she was an ousted Ranger, but he never imagined that dour, distant Allie Grecco might be concealing this reckless rage. Apparently, she disguised herself in more than just lipstick and a wig.

A yellow cab shot by on the street. Daniel flattened himself against the siding, scanning for anyone who might've seen them enter the alley. Christ, she hadn't even looked for witnesses.

In a perfect world, Daniel would've taken out Dex the old-fashioned way. But a skilled operator —and he *only* sent skilled operators on this kind of work—would've known better than to pulverize a high-profile senator's son in a bar alley. Yet there was Grecco, swinging a metaphoric sledgehammer around willy-nilly in red lipstick and high heels. Daniel got the feeling she knew what Dex had been up to, but there was no way Grecco knew who he really was, no matter what she said. If she did know, she was playing it fast and loose with her safety, a thought that twisted his stomach into even uglier knots.

He needn't have bothered trying to stay hidden from her. Grecco was so lost in wailing on Dex, she probably wouldn't have noticed if he'd skipped past her, whistling a tune. Daniel was intimately familiar with that rage—the desire to throw yourself up against something, anything—to relieve the pressure building inside. He'd seen it countless times before.

He'd been there, once.

Daniel left his hiding place. He approached the fight—if you could even call it that—walking straight through a puddle with his hands in his pockets. Dex was on the ground now, curled like a shrimp in the gloom. His nose jutted at an unnatural angle, and it gushed blood over his split lips, mottling that garish fake mustache, now holding on by a single dab of glue. He hardly seemed conscious as Grecco kicked him in the ribs, over and over again.

It went on like that until Dex stopped sobbing. He fell quiet, and Grecco loomed over him, the heel of her stiletto poised above his throat.

"Stand down, Grecco."

Her head snapped toward him, eyes wide and wild, catching the dim light from the street.

She was breathing heavily, sweat bleeding through her makeup, a look of all-consuming fury on her face. In that instant, she looked like an animal in a club girl's skin. But she still couldn't disregard an order.

Allie Grecco was still a soldier, through and through.

Daniel knew all too well what could happen to soldiers who'd been set adrift. He'd seen the rapid decline and deaths of those who'd been tossed out of the field, given no help resettling into civilian life, no plan to let go of the lifestyle that had been drilled into them. Yeah. The front-end desk job at Soldiers wasn't going to cut it. She was a textbook candidate for the back end, that much he couldn't deny.

"Sir?" She looked to him for instruction.

That settled it. He'd have to talk to the General about her.

"Leave him," Daniel said flatly, nodding toward Dex on the pavement, near death but still breathing. He turned to make his way back out to the street. "We'll talk more on Monday," he said over his shoulder.

He only got a few steps before Grecco's voice made him pause. "What about... You aren't gonna ask me about all this?"

He threw her a glance over his shoulder, but said nothing more.

Daniel didn't have to turn around a second time. Halfway back to the light of the sidewalk, he heard a pair of heels clicking away in the opposite direction, leaving Riklis where he lay.

Chapter 11

Allie didn't know what to think of her run-in with Mr. Bennett. Two days later, she wasn't any closer to figuring him out.

Or figuring out what any of this shitshow meant for her. Had she lost his respect? Was she fired? Was he gonna report her to the police?

Allie flung open her kitchen cabinet, crouching to peer inside. Where was the damned pan?

She'd been so consumed by what-ifs, Allie had cut her morning run short, unable to focus. The lack of physical release left her jittery and unbalanced. As she noisily rifled through pots and dishes, grim possibilities raced through her head, making a mess as they went, and so Allie made a mess of the kitchen too.

She liked her job—she needed it—and the thought of losing the structure and familiarity of Soldiers for Hire sent her into a near panic. She respected Mr. Bennett too, and the idea of disappointing him so severely troubled her more than she liked to admit. But being turned in? Well,

Allie had never really been too concerned about that. You had to have a half-worthwhile life before you could cry about losing it.

And if she did get dragged off to prison, it's not like anyone would miss her. Anyone except—

The creak of a door froze Allie just as she was about to slam the cabinet shut. There was Libby, standing in the threshold, squinting her eyes in the gray morning light that seeped through their kitchen windows.

"It's Sunday," she griped with a rare unsuppressed frown. "What on earth are you doing, babe? It's not even seven..."

Libby must've returned from her parents' house late last night, but Allie was so caught up in her frustration, she'd forgotten. "Um, making breakfast?" she offered pathetically.

Libby's gaze moved from Allie to the cabinet, then back to Allie. "Did something happen while I was gone?"

"Logan called me yesterday," Allie lied.

"Oh." Libby's grumpy expression softened, and she padded across the wood floor to lean on the kitchen island. Allie had shared just enough about her adoptive father and his years of abuse to justify the occasional tics of paranoia and sadness she couldn't quite hide. "Why do you keep answering his calls? You know he just wants to argue, don't you?"

Allie closed the cabinet carefully, then stood up to lean against the counter, facing Libby. "We didn't fight about anything specific. Just having to talk to him ruined my whole weekend." That much wasn't a total lie. She hated talking to Logan— though he never called.

Libby propped her elbow on the island and made a sleepy, sympathetic hum. "I'm sorry, Allie. I know you can't stand him." It was an understatement, but Libby was prone to understatements, so Allie didn't correct her. "What were you looking for? When you were taking your anger out on the cabinet, I mean."

Allie was relieved to put such a painless end to Libby's daily dance of *finding out what's really bugging Allie*.

"The pan. I wanted to fry up some eggs."

"Try the dishwasher."

Allie popped it open, glancing inside. Lo and behold, there was the pan.

By the time she'd pulled it out and hip-bumped the dishwasher shut, Libby's frown was back. "Didn't you cook at all this weekend? Tell me you didn't live off chips and coffee while you were sick..."

"Uh, no," Allie mumbled. It was hard enough hiding the fact she'd been hunting down criminals, never mind Libby interrogating her about her junky eating habits. She said the first thing that came to mind. "I started feeling a lot better, so I went out."

"You got Chinese without me," Libby groaned with mock betrayal, cat-stretching both arms forward across the island until she could sleepily thump her head down. "I haven't had lo mein in forever..."

Allie clicked the dial on the stovetop, heating the pan, then opened the fridge to pull out the eggs and butter. "Just bar food. Just to get out of the house after Logan called."

She paused with her hand on the egg carton, its shape reminding her of Mila, of the way her voice broke when she told Allie about the monstrous prison room. Mr. Bennett had given her a clear order to disengage. But thinking about it now... she regretted not ending Dex right then and there.

In a way, it was Mr. Bennett's fault she'd been so restless and irritated throughout the weekend. He'd stopped her from finishing off Carl/Dex with a stern command he must've known she couldn't disobey. And then he'd left her there with that enigmatic "we'll talk on Monday." Allie had barely slept since. Her inner demons were still clamoring for the kill they'd been denied. She knew the nightmare was waiting to drown her with its red lake.

Libby could never know about Friday night. But maybe it would ease her mind if she could, like always, try to talk it out in half-truths.

"I ran into my boss there. It was weird. Do you want eggs?" She flicked open the carton.

"Yes to the egg proposal." Libby's head popped off the island, red hair mussed with sleep. She'd perked up at the prospect of breakfast—or maybe the promise of gossip. "And weird how?"

"Well, I didn't just see him. He interrupted a conversation I was having with someone."

"Hold the phone," Libby squawked. "Forget your boss. I wanna know just what kind of conversation you were having. Who's the guy? *Was* it a guy? What does he look like?"

"I'm serious, Libby. It was super weird. I've never seen my boss outside the office, but he was acting all protective and clingy. He wouldn't take a hint. I had to send him away. I literally shooed him!"

"Back to my questions. Were you talking with a man or a woman?"

"How is that relevant?"

"Humor me."

Allie found herself a little thrown, but answered anyway. "It was a man."

"Now, I don't know your boss..." Libby crooked her arm, perching her cheek in her hand. "But he might've been jealous. Do you think he's got a bit of a thing for you?"

Allie hadn't even considered that. "Oh, no. You think he's into me?"

Was he into her? Mr. Bennett had never given Allie the impression he was interested in anything other than Soldiers for Hire, but maybe she'd misread him. It wouldn't be the first time she'd misread a man and his intentions.

She cracked the first egg against the side of the pan a little harder than she needed to.

Was Mr. Bennett the kind of person who'd try to control her? Blackmail her into sleeping with him in exchange for not calling the police? She didn't think so, but if he tried to pull something like that —if he betrayed her too—it would be time for Allie to test herself against an opponent on her level instead of amateur creeps. If it came to that, she wouldn't hesitate.

The first egg hit the hot butter with an aggressive sizzle.

"I dunno, maybe he does have a bit of a crush on you," Libby mused. "If he was kinda drunk, it might explain why he was acting like that when he ran into you outside of work."

"He didn't seem drunk." Allie remembered the sharp and serious spark in his green eyes as he'd leaned in to whisper the Weekend Rapist's name. How had he known? What were the chances he'd swoop into After Hour, out of all the dives in NYC, at exactly the wrong moment? Had he been watching her the whole time? Had he followed her there?

A chill crawled up Allie's spine. She could think of only two explanations. Either he really was interested in her, or there'd been a third hunter there in the bar that night.

Maybe Allie wasn't the one he'd been tailing. Maybe Mr. Bennett had been at After Hour for the exact same reason she was.

Dex.

Libby chewed absently on her lower lip as Allie cracked the rest of the carton into the sizzling pan. "I suppose I can't blame him for looking out for you, but you're right. That's weird."

The conversation fell into the spits and pops of frying eggs.

"Or…" Libby paused for a few seconds. "Maybe he was at the bar because he's in an unsatisfying marriage and is looking to have a sordid affair," she amusedly suggested out of the blue, waggling her eyebrows, trying to lighten the mood. "Or maybe he's secretly gay, looking for someone to hook up with before he gathers the nerve to come out?"

"Libby!" Allie scolded, giggling. Libby giggled along, but Allie was already lost in her thoughts again. It was killing her, not knowing if Mr. Bennett was an ally or an enemy.

She was just going to have to wait until tomorrow to find out.

Chapter 12

"And she listened to you, right? She left Riklis alive? Tell me she walked away, because 'dead senator's son à la mode' is the kind of mess I'm not sure we can clean."

"She did," Daniel confirmed. "Though he was badly hurt and out cold by the end."

"Good, that's good. We don't want that kind of trouble." There was a long pause as the General considered everything Daniel had told him about his midnight encounter with Grecco and Dex Riklis.

Daniel allowed his attention to wander, slackening his grip on the cell phone and refocusing on the television screen. The commercial break had ended, which meant he'd missed a few minutes of *Queen's Bridge*, and a tiny pang of frustration rankled in his gut—though he'd die before admitting he watched soaps. If he kept the volume low, the General never had to know he was spread out on his couch, soaking in his favorite TV drama, working his way through a box of macaroons.

"Maybe Miss Grecco could benefit from our particular brand of help."

"I don't know." Daniel felt his mouth start to thin, and quietly lowered a bitten cookie to the box on the side table. "She was wild, driven, just like all the rest, but... Do you really want to put her in the hot seat?"

"Why? Because Allie's such a soft, blushing maiden?" the General teased. "What's your real reason for second-guessing her, Daniel? Do you have some ulterior motive for wanting to keep her at her desk?"

"I do not."

"Then why shouldn't we consider recruiting her?"

"Because she's a loose cannon," Daniel retorted. His sour voice sounded more immature than he liked—and he did not like it at all.

The General should've known better than anyone that Daniel didn't do ulterior motives. Not that kind. Not anymore, anyway. After everything that had happened, after everything he'd been through, and after everything he'd lost, he was sure he'd never feel that sort of attraction ever again, and he didn't care to.

"Relax, relax, I'm just yanking your chain." The General laughed. "How is Allie different from anyone else we've invited to the back-end operation? They're all loose cannons to start. They all need help—which is still the reason why we do this, if I'm not mistaken. I'm not mistaken, am I?"

"That's different," Daniel insisted. "I know what to expect with guys. Grecco is..."

He paused, considering his next word carefully. On the screen, Delilah twisted away from the camera as her husband confessed to his romantic involvement with one of his nurses. Daniel knew they'd forget all about their traumas by season six, as people so often did on TV. Real life didn't work like that. It couldn't.

"She's what?" The General's question jolted him out of his head.

"She's a unique case," Daniel concluded, hoping he wouldn't be pushed to elaborate.

He'd never invited a woman to join the inner circle—the hidden back-end operation—before. The front end, sure, and so far, they'd all responded to more conventional treatments. Daniel had read many times that PTSD tended to turn inward on women rather than out. There were also fewer of them than their male counterparts, and he'd never needed to consider it before.

The fact she was a woman shouldn't matter, right? A soldier was a soldier, and Daniel didn't doubt Grecco's capability—the scene in the alley had more than proven it. Yet there was something distinctly *off* about her that made him hesitate to send Grecco into harm's way.

Maybe it did matter. Only a little. But 'a little' was far more than Daniel cared to admit.

"If you ask me, I don't think Grecco is much of a special case at all," the General said.

"Look." Daniel began to protest, but found he'd already run out of excuses. He knocked his knuckles against the smooth leather arm of the couch as he gathered his thoughts. "It's not that I don't respect her. I do. I just have reservations, all right?"

"Well, you're allowed your nebulous reservations, but if the back end might be good for her—and I firmly think it would be, just so we're clear—then my vote is to give her a whirl."

"You're right." His funny feeling aside, Daniel couldn't deny the logic of at least testing Grecco. He rubbed his forehead. "I'll tell her tomorrow, and I'll start the assessment."

"Glad to see you've come around. We'll talk then," the General said, his smile audible, and said goodbye.

A second later, the elevator—the private elevator —to Daniel's penthouse apartment dinged. He dove for the remote, mashing *channel up* just as the stainless-steel double doors slid open, and Phoenix moseyed in.

"How did you sneak past the front desk check-in?" Daniel demanded, snatching his phone from the couch cushion where he'd dropped it. "*Again?*"

"I have my ways." Phoenix gave him an infuriating smirk and his usual answer, letting the doors slide shut behind him. His gaze wandered around the tidy, spacious apartment; lingered on the barren, clutterless mantel; and then, with a flash of amusement, landed on the widescreen TV mounted over Daniel's fireplace.

"Women's hockey?" Phoenix asked, screwing up his nose.

Daniel looked to the screen, where *Queen's Bridge* had been replaced by two geared-up players jostling across the ice. "Hockey's hockey." He shrugged.

Phoenix sauntered to the couch, leaning over the back to pluck a macaroon out of the bakery box. "What are you talking about? This isn't hockey! You know they don't let them fight, right?" Daniel frowned as Phoenix popped a tiny pastry into his mouth. "So who were you on the phone with?" he asked through his commandeered macaroon.

"The General."

Phoenix swallowed. "Ah, yes, the famous general. The general we are apparently still pretending is not your imaginary friend."

"How many times are you going to make me go through this every day?"

"Only until you finally drop this embarrassing bullshit and admit 'he' is your scapegoat for making us work overtime," he teased, climbing over the back of the couch and flopping down between Daniel and the pastry box.

"Oh no," Daniel said, making room. "You're on to me. What on earth will I do now when I want you to go on a mission in the middle of the night? Who will I blame?" he added, though knew not to expect any response, and—funnily enough—he didn't get one.

They were quiet while Phoenix righted himself on the cushions. The roar of the crowd drew Daniel's attention back to the game as two players pummeled each other with their oven-mitt gloves. Their teammates dragged them away from each other, and the referee skated in to hand out the penalties.

"See?" Phoenix gestured idly toward the screen. "How could anyone call this hockey? If that's hockey, they should just let 'em fight."

Chapter 13

It was fairly quiet in Daniel and Phoenix's favorite sandwich place. They'd beaten the lunch rush by half an hour. Tucked into their usual booth in the back, Daniel unwrapped his sandwich from its paper sleeve, but didn't pull it out just yet.

"Hang on. Let me get this straight." Phoenix tilted his chin toward his collarbone. "Grecco—a raging lunatic? I can't even imagine what that looked like."

"Oh, you have no idea! Once she got him where she wanted him, it was like she'd done it a thousand times. And maybe she has. She really put on a show." He picked up his cup to pantomime. "She pretended to drink the roofie, tottered around like she was one step from hitting the floor, then somehow managed to get him to down the rest of her glass. She hung on to him until she could get him alone... I'll admit: it was smart work for an amateur."

The sandwich shop was never packed, which was precisely why he liked it so much, but Daniel was careful not to say the name *Riklis*—just in case someone was listening in.

"Did he at least put up a fight?"

"He never got a chance. Once she had her claws in her target, there was no deterring her. She would've stomped him if I hadn't stepped in." Daniel stared into his water, tilting his wrist to shift the ice cubes around. Phoenix was waiting for him to finish, so he took a quick drink, then pushed his cup far enough away that he wouldn't be tempted to fiddle with it. "Yeah. Overall," he confessed, "it's safe to say that her performance impressed me."

"Daniel Bennett? Impressed?" Phoenix's jaw dropped in a mocking gasp, and he slapped a hand to his chest as if he were clutching at pearls.

"Come on, man, I'm serious. I need your advice."

"So what's the problem?" He plucked a buffalo chip from its bag and used it to point at Daniel. "If she's so impressive, just give her the test and see if she lives up to the hype."

The ensuing crunch derailed Daniel's train of thought before he could get lost in it again. Was he the only one with reservations about Grecco? First the General, now Phoenix. He was zero for two.

"Well, we're planning to," Daniel said. "But doesn't that—I don't know—worry you at all?"

Phoenix swallowed another mouthful of chips. "Testing her? Nah. And even if she doesn't pass, I don't think she'd blab. Grecco doesn't seem like the talkative type."

"Not like you."

A smirk curled across Phoenix's mouth. "Definitely not like me," he agreed, humming in amusement. "I dunno why you're even asking me. My professional opinion never mattered to you before, so what exactly do you want me to say?"

"I want to know your personal opinion."

"About Grecco or about recruiting Grecco?"

Elbows on the table, Daniel folded his hands over his untouched sandwich. "Recruiting Grecco."

Phoenix frowned, leaning back into the booth cushions. "Well, we've never had a girl in the back end before," he said thoughtfully. "You don't think that would change anything, do you?"

"It shouldn't, no. But it might be a bit of an adjustment for some of the guys."

Daniel hated to admit it so much, he almost hadn't—not even to himself. But he was one of them. He was, to his dismay, one of *the guys*.

That burbling feeling he'd been wrestling with all morning wouldn't stay quiet, and Daniel had no choice but to accept it for what it was. The thought of being personally responsible for sending a woman to her death made him deeply uncomfortable. It shouldn't matter—a life was a life, and a soldier was a soldier—but it did. And Allie Grecco wasn't a typical soldier or a typical woman, at least not in regard to her trauma symptoms. Things were going to change if she passed the test. Daniel had never been good at change.

"I get the sense that whatever Grecco's dealing with, it's different from what we usually see. It's more than battle shock." Daniel scrubbed his jaw, frowning, remembering the ravenous look on Grecco's face when he'd stopped her from spearing Dex's windpipe with her heel. "I've never seen so much fire behind someone's eyes, and I'm wondering if Grecco's problems run deeper than her military history. Beyond our area of expertise, I mean."

Phoenix flashed him a Cheshire grin. "Fiery eyes, huh? Sounds like you've got some kind of weird crush."

Daniel's frown deepened. "Oh, give me a break," he said flatly. Phoenix knew better than anyone that romance was behind him now. The only thing in his future was Soldiers.

"Well, here's my personal opinion, since you wanted it so bad." Phoenix bit into his roast beef sandwich, dropping a hail of lettuce and onion onto the wrapper. He chewed obnoxiously as he spoke. "Grecco's a killjoy, but if she's really as good —and as unhinged—as you say, wouldn't you rather have her somewhere we can keep an eye on her?"

"I suppose you're right. And I guess we can thank her for benching our perp. I can't imagine he'll be up for a night on the town any time soon. Looks like she stuck his face in a rock tumbler." A mean little smile pulled up one corner of Daniel's mouth.

Phoenix choked on a too-big bite. "Anything about it in the news?" he rasped, hammering his chest, coughing to clear the dregs of sauce from his throat.

"They're saying he was mugged. I'm guessing he'll stay inside for however long it takes to lick his wounds."

"Did she get him that good?"

"Better than good. Guy's nose is in splinters."

"Well done, Grecco. Finally, someone had the balls to give that prick a little taste of his own medicine."

Daniel gave him a somber nod. "That she did."

"If you ask me, she could have roughed him up a bit more, uh, *permanently*."

"Absolutely not. It was already reckless. Killing him would have been suicide."

"I disagree and you know it." Phoenix paused long enough to steal Daniel's unused napkin and dab his mouth. "Hell, I've been dying for a chance to let loose, and you won't even let me hit 'em. Now a desk jockey clobbers a high-profile daddy's boy in an alley—a frickin' bar alley—and look: nothing bad came of it. Thank god Grecco didn't ask for your permission. If you ask me, she should've knocked the brains out of his head. Finished the job!"

"Nothing bad came of it *this time*," Daniel corrected, finally picking up his sandwich.

"Does anything else need to be done about him?" Phoenix—who was already halfway through his lunch—looked on as Daniel chewed, his bites far more thoughtful and reserved. "I mean, this isn't gonna stop him, will it?"

Daniel chuckled, a note of bitterness darkening the pleasure. "Let's just say Daddy can't pay this kind of pain away. Grecco bought us a month at minimum. And if this doesn't convince him to hang up his hat, well, it'll be easy to identify him next time. He'll be the guy at the bar who looks like he just stood up a werewolf."

Phoenix laughed too. "I wish I coulda seen it. Hey, there wasn't a picture of that ugly Richie Rich-looking motherfucker on the morning news, was there?"

"No," Daniel replied, a little disappointed.

Phoenix let out a crestfallen groan, but it didn't take long before he perked up again. A noisy breath escaped him that sounded remarkably like a giggle.

"Man," he mused, and sighed, and—like it had never left—the toothy grin was back. "Grecco is in for the surprise of her life tomorrow morning."

Chapter 14

Wherever Avery was, it was dark.

She wasn't sure how long she'd been locked in there. Maybe weeks, maybe months. If she flattened her palm against the tip of her nose, she could just decipher the silhouette of each finger, but that was it. Avery couldn't see a darned thing more.

Was it all her fault?

If she had done something different—said something different—felt something differently—would she be at home right now? Would she be curled up with a tall stack of court documents and a taller glass of strawberry milk, bathed in the light of her desk lamp, without a thought in the world about darkness? It scared her to admit she didn't know.

Sitting up from the pile of blankets she'd slept in, Avery ordered herself to focus, searching each detail of her last day of freedom for what must have been the thousandth time.

She'd met her boyfriend at a bar—her ex-boyfriend now, she supposed—and left madder than she'd been in a long, long time. The grief and the betrayal had bubbled up in her throat as she drove. Maybe that was her first mistake: she should have known better than to let her guard down around a rich white man like him. But he had been so sweet at first, so funny, so disarming with his lopsided grin and awkward little laugh. She was so sure he'd brought her out that night to invite her home for the holidays.

And then he'd thrown the truth in her face. He was never going to bring her home. His parents, he'd said, wouldn't understand.

A girl like you is what he'd told her. But Avery knew what he meant. A Black girl.

It was so stupid, so childish to cry over a man while she was drowning in the darkness of a dungeon, but the tears came anyway, rolling down her face and into the pile of blankets she couldn't see.

The breakup had blindsided her. Rage hit first, then the sadness. Avery had shouted at him to never so much as say her name again. Then she'd stormed back to her car, desperate to escape before he saw her crumble, and screeched away from the curb. Maybe she should have pulled over and caught her breath. Maybe that was her second mistake.

She couldn't remember the details of the accident—just the awful crunch of metal smashing into metal.

Then *he'd* shown up.

And then she'd snapped.

She couldn't say how much time had passed between the accident and the moment *he* brought his holier-than-thou act in her face, but it couldn't have been long. She remembered getting out of the car. She remembered his false sympathy, his mask of trustworthiness. She remembered exploding when he'd put his hands on her. She didn't recall hitting her head, but she could feel the bump behind her ear and a splitting pain that kept her dizzy in the dark. She definitely couldn't remember exactly how it was he'd kidnapped her.

Kidnapped her. Abducted her. Disappeared her. She supposed men like him did it all the time.

Avery drew a deep breath and wiped her face in the blanket, willing herself to calm down. He hadn't even allowed her enough light to keep track of time with scratches on the wall or something like that. What on earth was wrong with him? He knew who she was—half of New York knew the name *Avery Burke, Esq.* after she'd taken down two corrupt prison wardens in as many years. He knew what she could do to him once she got out.

Did that mean he wasn't planning on letting her out?

The slide of a deadbolt snapped Avery out of her memories. She braced herself, scrambling up the wall behind her. The knob twisted audibly, and Avery shielded her eyes in anticipation of a blinding wash of bright light. It flooded the room and drowned her head with pain.

The door creaked wide. Cutlery clinked on a plate.

She didn't have to see to know he was replacing her empty dishes with a hot meal. The consistency with which he fed her was her only method of tracking time.

As the light seared her, the plate filled with what smelled like ground beef, but her captor didn't say a word. Neither did Avery. Not anymore. At first, she'd made sure to let him know what she thought of him and his poor choice of action. Afraid, disoriented, and mad as a hornet, she'd threatened to ruin him. She'd vowed to go to the press, to get him fired, to drag him to court. But nothing she said seemed to make any difference.

She had no idea what was going on inside his head. He fed her often enough that she never went hungry, he gave her water, and he wasn't torturing her—apart from the imprisonment. But if he was capable of locking a woman in a dungeon, who knew what else he'd find it in himself to do? For what purpose was he keeping her alive?

When the door closed again, Avery opened her eyes, still seeing spots in the dark. She didn't want to risk making it worse.

Talking to him had been her third and worst mistake. She hated knowing she failed to make him realize his errors, and she couldn't stand his silence. But she should have at least pretended to cooperate. She should've shut up and soothed him, appealing to his guilty conscience. She should have lied, swearing she understood him and felt sorry for him and didn't have any interest in revenge. She should have promised that if he let her go, she would never tell a soul. Then she could have turned on him the moment she was free.

Now he wasn't talking to her anymore. Now a release deal was off the table. Now she was stuck. Now she might never go home.

Avery sank down the wall, shuffling on her hands and knees toward the smell of warm meat.

She should have accepted his outrageous bargain. She could have scooped her family up and moved them all across the country, found work somewhere else, and spent the rest of her life trying to be okay with letting this one outrageous wrong go unpunished. That happened all the time, didn't it?

At this point, she would have given him anything just to hear Mom's voice. Just to tell her friends to be strong. Just to let them know she was alive.

Just to be able to see more than her fingers.

Chapter 15

Walking past the front desk with her head down, Allie didn't even notice the secretary's hello.

She shuffled through the office, clinging to the unlikely hope that she'd make it to her dismal little cube undisturbed, where she could then hole up for the rest of the day. Maybe—if she were lucky—Mr. Bennett had forgotten about Friday night.

There was no way Mr. Bennett had forgotten about Friday night.

Allie was supposed to be in class on Mondays, but she'd decided to skip in favor of honoring his cryptic order to talk. She couldn't imagine telling her boss she had a minor scheduling conflict after the weekend they'd had.

Worse still, Libby was suspicious. Allie had mumbled a weak half-truth about a mandatory meeting, and Libby had mumbled back a promise to share lecture notes. Maybe she wasn't suspicious so much as worried. Allie, who wasn't used to being worried about, hadn't a clue what to do to appease her.

Following the wall, Allie turned a corner, and her gait faltered. There was Mr. Bennett—leaning in his office doorway, stern and serious, sharp eyes pinning her in place. He beckoned her over with a joyless curl of his finger.

In the time Allie had known him, Mr. Bennett had always been a cool, collected, authoritative presence. Trying to search his face for clues about his emotional state yielded nothing beyond the fact he was displeased. His brows were pitched dangerously low, his eyes gave away nothing, and his mouth was a thin line. But that was a typical Mr. Bennett expression. If he *was* boiling mad, at least he wasn't tomato-red with fury, like Logan always was. Like Judd had been.

Actually, she might have preferred the rage. Allie knew how to withstand brute anger. Mr. Bennett and his blank slate of a face were unfamiliar territory.

"Good morning, sir," she said, swallowing hard as her feet marched over to him. He didn't reciprocate. He merely stepped aside to let her in.

Whatever that face meant, Allie was about to find out. She steeled herself, and strode in.

In the almost two years she'd worked at Soldiers for Hire, Allie had never been inside Mr. Bennett's office. She was struck by its smallness and cleanliness. His desk sat in the middle, as spotless and barren as his shelves; the folders piled on its edges were the only indication someone worked there. It was a lot like Allie's cube in its utilitarianism. And in that it looked more like a furniture store display than a real person's office.

Mr. Bennett closed the door behind her, and Allie felt the hair on the back of her neck stand up. Now they were alone.

She didn't trust men when they had her alone. Military men, especially. She hated knowing she was on the wrong end of a power imbalance. If Mr. Bennett forced her hand and she had to fight her way out of this office, she sure as hell would.

He didn't say anything right away. Mr. Bennett simply sank into his fancy office chair, then gestured across his desk to indicate the noticeably simpler guest seat. "Sit," he said.

Cautiously, Allie obeyed.

He folded his arms as she settled in. When he leaned back, his face as unreadable as a sheet of iron, the suffering creak of the chair seemed endless.

"So," he finally said, "tell me about Friday night."

That was an okay question—Allie could handle that. She'd thought about her response all weekend. She'd tell him a partial lie that would hopefully get her out of whatever trouble she might be in.

"Well," Allie began, shifted forward in her chair, and cleared her throat as demurely as she could bear. "I had some things on my mind, so I went out to forget about them for a while."

"So you just happened to be at After Hour? You just happened to meet up with Dex?"

"Yeah. I thought he was just some random guy. When I caught him spiking my drink, I decided to handle it my way."

"Your way? Was that your way of dealing with... life?"

"Look, I beat the shit out of a shitbag. What's wrong with that?" If he was a halfway decent person, Mr. Bennett wouldn't fault a woman for stopping her own rape, no matter how she chose to do it.

His expression stayed neutral, sober. Allie knew he wasn't buying it.

"You weren't worried about putting yourself into a dangerous situation with a probable rapist?"

"That's a good one." Allie laughed darkly. "No, sir. I wasn't worried. I'm not sure how much you know about my training, but I could probably take out anyone who tried to take advantage of me, let alone that weak excuse for a man." She gave him a pointed look, and to her surprise, he laughed back.

"And you sure did." It was a genuine laugh—like nothing she'd heard from him before. It might have thrown her if she wasn't already so prepared for a hundred different what-if scenarios, but his chuckle died away quickly, and the serious look returned. "Do you have any idea who that man was?"

"An asshole."

Mr. Bennett's mouth did a funny little twist. She couldn't tell if it was a suppressed smile or a glower he was holding at bay. "Cut the crap, Grecco. Tell me the truth."

The authority in his tone left no room for doubt —she needed to give him the real story, since he wasn't about to ask for it again.

"We both already know the truth: that man is a rapist and a liar. What else matters? I followed him there to stop him from picking up another victim."

Was it Allie's imagination, or did Mr. Bennett's eyebrows raise just the slightest bit? "And his identity? Do you know anything about who he is?"

"He's Dex, I guess."

"Just Dex?" Mr. Bennett prodded. "You don't know his last name?"

Allie was starting to get annoyed with this directionless grilling. She clenched her fists in her lap until they felt like rocks. "I already told you, it doesn't matter."

He snorted. "Oh, it does. That was Dex Riklis you beat to hell in that alley."

"Whatever." *Riklis* bounced about in her head, oddly familiar, but Allie couldn't quite place it. "I don't care about the details. He deserved a beating, and that's what I gave him."

Mr. Bennett frowned, leaning forward to rest his elbows on his desk. "So you knew he was a serial offender and you followed him to the bar. How did you find him?"

Allie recounted how she'd identified and interviewed students who hadn't gone to the police. She told him how she'd tracked down Violet at the bar, extracted information from her, and taken her place. She explained how she used that information to identify Dex, and how she'd caught him drugging her drink on the camera hidden in her purse.

"I figured he'd find an unattended glass irresistible," she finished. "And I was right."

She definitely wasn't imagining it. Mr. Bennett's eyebrows were sitting higher on his forehead than they'd been a moment ago. He was *impressed* by what she'd done. At least he didn't look like a guy who was two seconds from calling the police.

"What can I say, Grecco?" She breathed a small sigh of relief as Mr. Bennett sat back in his chair. "That was a wild and dangerous thing you did. But..." Allie tried not to tip out of her seat while she waited for whatever came next. "Your detective work was decent. Your right hook looked pretty decent too."

"Thank you, sir."

"What was not decent, however, was your fieldwork."

Allie scowled. "What do you mean?"

"I mean you almost killed Dex Riklis in a dingy alley where just about anyone could have seen you, for one."

"You mean I almost killed the Weekend Rapist in a dingy alley." Why was he so caught up on this guy's identity? "He's a piece of shit, and if you hadn't stopped me, he would never hurt anyone again."

"So I'm right. You were going to kill him." He said it so matter-of-factly, Allie would've been rattled—if he hadn't looked equally nonplussed when they'd met face-to-face in that very alley, while her stiletto was poised against Dex's throat and the rage rolled off her like waves.

"Yes," she admitted. There was no sense in trying to deny it.

"Dex Riklis is the son of Senator Riklis," Mr. Bennett said, and in that moment, his already somber face turned grave. "Is the name ringing any bells now?"

Senator.

The realization of what she'd almost done sucked her in like a toy boat in a rapid. Allie sat in place, arms leaden, trying to keep her chin above the whitewater.

Well, shit.

"Yeah," she said meekly, sinking into the chair. Her head spun as it filled with visions of herself, handcuffed, head down as officers rushed her past a crowd of reporters. It was only just dawning on Allie how thoroughly Mr. Bennett had saved her ass.

"Do you know what Soldiers for Hire does?"

"I do, sir." Her cautious stare met his curious one. What kind of question was that?

"And what *do* we do, Grecco?"

"We help soldiers," she answered glumly. Allie struggled to focus as her heart threatened to ride a wave of bile into her throat. "Ex-soldiers who can't get back to their lives."

"And are you one of those soldiers? Do you need help getting back to your life?"

It knocked her more off-kilter than any question he'd asked so far.

Judd, too, had suggested as much—that Allie couldn't cope. He'd said so that night in the medical tent, hours after she'd frozen during her first combat mission. He'd bellowed at her that she didn't deserve her tan beret, that women didn't belong on the battlefield. Mr. Bennett wasn't bellowing, but the notion still set her dignity ablaze like a match dropped into an oil drum. A small part of her—a part she didn't want to listen to —suspected they were right. That she couldn't cope. That she needed the kind of help you can't get in an office.

"You're making a big deal out of nothing," she shot back, but the break in her voice gave her away. "The cops were fucking up, so I stepped in. I have the skills, and I didn't think anyone else was going to know about it. That's all."

Mr. Bennett was quiet for a long time. Too long. The longer she sat under his gaze, the more her confidence crumpled, and instinct flailed for her to scrounge up a better excuse. He couldn't have known about the other hunts, could he? And he still hadn't explained what he'd been doing at After

Hour. She rifled through her thoughts for something, anything, to launch at him, just to knock his interrogation awry.

"I know about the OTH, Grecco," he said before she could strike, drying up the accusation on her lips. "I know you killed a fellow soldier."

"Judd Abbott was no fellow of mine, sir."

"I couldn't care less if he was your one and only love or your sworn enemy, Grecco."

"You don't?"

"No. I've read your file, and not that polished file released by the court. I've read the sealed court-martial records, your medical records, and your statements. Abbott sounds like a piece of shit, but like I said, I don't care about any of that."

"Then what is this about, sir?"

"All I need to know is if you're going to do this again."

"Well—" Allie cut herself off. How was she supposed to answer? The truth—the full truth—was a resounding *yes*, but did she want Mr. Bennett to know? If he realized she carried this howling maelstrom of anger and hurt inside her—if he found out the bloodshed was an outlet, a lifeline—he'd stop her.

Or he'd try.

"Tell me," he said before she could offer him an answer of any kind, "are you a front-end soldier, or do you need something more?"

Allie didn't want to think of herself as someone who needed help at all, but unfulfilled rage was still smoldering inside her chest. And the prospect of *something more*—something more appealing than another failed attempt at therapy—had her hanging on Mr. Bennett's every word.

Chapter 16

D aniel knew talent when he saw it, but he also knew when someone was looking for trouble.

"Something more, sir?" Grecco asked cautiously, taking her time.

He'd been that kind of person four years ago— the Grecco kind. Manic, desperate, with no thought of the future. While he didn't yet understand her reasons, he did recognize the signs.

She was on the back foot now. He could tell by how she was sitting a little smaller in the chair, her shoulders curled in. The unfailingly reserved, prickly logistics manager was unthreading before his eyes.

"I have a proposition for you," he began, speaking slowly to ensure she took in every word. "But before we get to that, I need to learn a little more about you, Grecco."

"Like what?"

"First, I want to make it clear that if I hadn't stopped you from killing Dex Riklis, you would have been arrested, you would have gone to prison, and I can guarantee that Senator Riklis would have had you killed there. After your name and face had been splashed over every newspaper headline in the country, of course—right under the words 'serial killer,' considering the reason you were discharged."

"I..." Grecco looked shaken. She clearly hadn't expected Dex Riklis to be anything more than just a villain, if not a common one. The possibility of political danger probably hadn't even crossed her mind.

"You were sloppy," Daniel said after it was clear her sentence would never come to an end. Grecco exhaled through a blend of disappointment and defensiveness, but her frown never faltered, not once. "You were in public. And threatening the victim? What would you have done if Violet hurled her drink in your face and screamed? Your cover would have been blown, and if your target suspected detectives were sniffing around, he would've changed up his act. Your wig was cheap, your bet that Dex wouldn't wail for help the second you grabbed him was idiotic, and if you want the cherry on top: I could tell you weren't really drinking from halfway across the bar. You have the drive and talent," he offered, cutting her the tiniest wedge of slack, "but you are sorely lacking in tact and restraint."

Across his desk, Grecco was gazing down at her lap, where her palms now lay faceup. When she looked up, there was a lone flame of wildfire in her eyes, a muted version of the one he had seen on Friday night. He hated to admit he liked it.

"So what if I was a little sloppy? I would have taken a serial rapist off the streets. Isn't that enough?"

She was sorely lacking in self-preservation too. It tugged on Daniel's sympathy to see a former soldier so flippant about her life, now that it was hers again. Or at least it should have been hers.

"Tell me about your discharge," he said, evenly if not kindly. When Grecco looked like she might snap again, he clarified. "I need to know the details if we're going to proceed. Think of it as a background check. I have to make sure you're not just doing this for fun."

"You saw the records. You read the files. You know what happened." Grecco puffed up in her seat, straightening her spine and lifting her chin. His explanation had tempered the fire burning low behind her brown eyes, but only just. "You know they threw me out. You know I killed a"—her upper lip curled into a sneer—"fellow Ranger."

"Exactly. I know what happened, so why just an OTH?" Daniel asked. "Why not a dishonorable discharge? How did you avoid an arrest?"

"They offered me a deal. No criminal charges or DD if I took the OTH."

"And why would you take that?"

Grecco's shoulders rounded again, her core hunching. "It was my only option. They threatened to blast me all over the news—kind of like how you just threatened, by the way—and I guess they could've. They told me it was best to let Judd come home a deceased hero." Her sneer thickened into a snarl as she stared down the edge of the desk. She obviously knew it was a load of crap.

"Grecco." Daniel waited for her to meet his gaze again. "I know how to put one and one together, but I need to hear you say it. I need to know why you killed him."

There was another flare of heat in her eyes, milder than the last, like an ember that refused to go dark.

"It was my first overseas op. I saw Judd—Abbott," she corrected, swallowing the lump in her throat. Daniel watched that sour taste move all the way down. "I watched him shoot a civilian. A mom. I—I didn't react well. I don't remember passing out, but when I woke up, I was alone in the medical tent. Abbott came in. We argued." She was quiet for a long moment. "Things got worse. We traded blows and he tried to rape me. I guess he didn't expect me to fight back, because he looked so surprised when I did. His fingers were wrapped around my neck... I couldn't breathe. I knew I was either going to let him kill me or turn the situation around. I chose the latter."

"Meaning?"

"I choked him to death, sir."

"I see," Daniel said softly. He only gave her a few seconds to rest. "What happened next, Grecco?"

"Nobody believed me when I told them it was self-defense. They claimed I could've restrained him if I wanted to. Maybe I could have. I don't know anymore. I don't care and neither did any of my so-called 'fellow' soldiers." She gave him a look so sharp it could have broken skin. "Is that enough detail on the matter?"

Daniel nodded slowly, conceding. The bitterness and hurt written all over her face made it clear she wasn't going around mauling people to get her jollies, and that was all he really needed. Anger flared in his chest to know someone who was supposed to be her brother had attacked her. It settled into a burning coal somewhere beneath his sternum as he thought about the other brothers, those who hadn't taken her side. He tried to imagine how it felt when she'd been suddenly set adrift with no one to teach her how to be a regular person again.

Daniel didn't have to try hard. He knew the feeling all too well.

Maybe he, the General, and Phoenix could all be right. She *was* a loose cannon, he *would* prefer to have her somewhere they could keep an eye on her, and she *did* need the help Soldiers for Hire could provide—and not just the front office kind.

Selecting the littlest key from his key ring, he unlocked the bottom drawer of his desk and pulled out a packet of papers.

"This is an NDA," he said, pushing it across the desk toward Grecco. "Carefully read and sign all of the pages, please."

"Are you serious?" Grecco's eyes flicked down to the thick stack, then back up to Daniel.

"I sure am, though I'm not forcing you to sign. I want you on board willingly. If you're not, this conversation stops here."

"I don't even know what this conversation is about."

"And you won't if you don't sign the NDA, will you?" Daniel set a pen down neatly on the crisp first page.

"Ugh." Grecco sized up the pile of papers, then snatched the pen and pulled the document closer.

Daniel stood. "I'll give you some time to read and think it over."

He thought he heard the pop of a pen cap just as he was closing the office door behind him.

It took a few minutes to hunt down Phoenix. He wasn't at his desk, he wasn't in the breakroom, he wasn't at the water cooler. He was hovering in the entryway of Shauna's cubicle, shirking his work and causing her to neglect hers. Daniel beckoned him over with a curt bark of his name.

Phoenix left reluctantly, drifting over to see what Daniel wanted. "Listen," he said, barely bothering to dredge up a convincing excuse. "I was just talking to Shauna about the, uh—"

"We have more important things to care about right now than your on-the-clock wandering. I've got another job for you. Grecco's in my office."

Phoenix's vaguely apologetic expression livened into one of interest. "Do tell! Did her eyes go all buggy?" He widened his as if in solidarity, then leaned in closer, dropping to a whisper. "What kind of face did she really make?"

"I haven't told her the full story yet. I thought you might enjoy doing it, since I'm making you her chaperone."

In the year or so she'd been at Soldiers, Daniel had witnessed countless tense workplace interactions between Grecco and Phoenix. Having him hovering around her would be as much a part of her test as the assignment itself. Phoenix was good at his job, wouldn't be cowed by Grecco's attitude, and there was nobody Daniel trusted more to keep an eye on potential risks. Phoenix had gotten his life back on track after a rocky separation from the military, and probably understood at least some of what she was feeling too. Maybe once they'd worked the juvenile bickering out of their systems, his story would prove to Grecco that the back end was the real deal.

A grin slowly split Phoenix's face from ear to ear. "You're gonna spoil me if you're not careful, Boss," he said, rubbing his hands together. "This'll be fun."

They made their way back to the office. Daniel rapped the door with his knuckles before opening it.

"How are you doing in here?" he asked, sticking his head in to check. "Do you need some more time?"

Grecco spun around in the chair. "No, sir. All finished."

Daniel sighed, making a beeline to his desk and dragging the NDA toward him. He noted how Grecco's eyes tracked Phoenix's every move as he slipped in and shut the door.

"Did you read it?" Daniel asked, arching a brow. Her chicken scratch signature greeted him on every page.

"I read enough. And I'll read the rest later," she said. Daniel didn't even need to read Grecco's face —much less her pulse—to know she wasn't going to.

He dropped the agreement to his desk with a papery slap. As her chaperone, Phoenix would just have to make sure she understood what was expected of her.

Daniel took a seat, and waved him forward.

"Would you please explain to Grecco what exactly it is we do here?" he bid, jerking his chin in her direction. "What we do under the table, that is."

Phoenix strode forward dramatically with his hands clasped behind his back, looking like a high school thespian. By the time he propped himself on the corner of Daniel's desk, letting one leg hang boyishly, he was being scalded by one of Grecco's famous subzero looks.

"You don't like chitchat," Phoenix began, "so I'll keep this short and sweet. There's the front end of the business where we help vets find work, right?"

"Yeah?" Grecco seemed confused.

"But some of us need something more than a shrink and a nine-to-five. That's where the back end comes in." He tapped the side of his nose with a forefinger.

"Something more... you keep saying that. Are either of you going to explain what it means?"

"Gladly." Phoenix dropped his swinging leg, stood up, and took a small bow. "The Soldiers for Hire you know is a front for a vigilante operation that sends PTSD-saddled ex-soldiers after the lowest, filthiest, skeeviest bloodsuckers humanity has to offer." He twisted around to shoot Daniel a smartassed look. "That about cover the back-end brochure, Boss?"

Daniel watched closely as Grecco tried not to have a visible reaction to *front for a vigilante operation*.

"A back end," she repeated, scowling, sitting sternly in her chair. "A back end of what? The law?"

"Not exactly. We beat up bad guys that are too slippery for the law, so it's all noble and good, blah blah blah. You probably care about the 'beating up bad guys' part the most." Grecco hummed and narrowed her eyes, but Phoenix didn't pause.

"We've got a deal with the police chief, so as long as you follow your orders and don't go batshit, you won't be arrested for taking out the trash. If you get in, that is."

"So this is the 'something more' you were talking about?" Her dark stare flickered to Daniel. "Is this accurate, sir?"

"It is."

"And you're offering me a place in this organization?"

"I'm offering a trial run. We test all potential recruits to see if they're a good fit."

"And that's what you were doing at After Hour? Hunting Dex Riklis?" She seemed relieved when Daniel nodded.

He leaned forward to pull a folder from his desk drawer, sliding it across to Grecco over the NDA. "If this is something you want to pursue, I'll assign you a closed case passed to us by the NYPD."

"I'm listening."

"A lawyer—Avery Burke—has been missing for weeks. She's been officially declared dead, but her body was never found."

"If the case is closed, what's my task?"

"Figure out what happened to Avery, and you'll be accepted to the back end."

Grecco eyed the case file suspiciously, hungrily. "Is that all?"

"Yes and no." Daniel trailed off. A tiny part of him dreaded her reaction, but the larger parts were eager to see how Grecco would cope with the bombshell he was about to drop. "All potentials are assigned a mentor. Phoenix will be yours."

"Like hell he is!" She blurted her objection right on time.

"Don't you worry about a thing, sweetheart," Phoenix drawled. He seemed to be enjoying the way she bristled in her chair. "You lucked out. I know everything there is to know about Soldiers. If you pay attention, you could learn a lot from me."

"Sir," Grecco appealed to Daniel, "I've been doing this for a while. I don't need anyone"—she glared at Phoenix—"babysitting me."

"This is the way it works. You solve this case and Phoenix supervises. Those are the conditions of the test."

Across the desk, Grecco scowled, slouched, and folded her arms in a way he could only describe as surly.

"So, what'll it be?" Daniel asked, catching her eye again. "Are you in or out?"

Chapter 17

Night was falling over Brooklyn, and Allie was loitering in another gloomy alley outside another gloomy bar.

The Outlet was far ritzier than After Hour, at least on the surface. It was posh, upscale, and the last place her missing person had been seen alive. Her missing *person*. After weeks upon weeks of dead-end leads and no evidence, she would've just as easily described Avery Burke as a missing body. She wondered if Mr. Bennett was setting her up to fail.

Propped against the side of the bar, Allie kept an eye out for her guy.

She'd spent the last few hours reviewing everything there was to know about the case, which seemed pretty cut and dry. Avery Burke, a twenty-eight-year-old prisoners' rights lawyer—and a rising hero or a thorn in New York's side, depending on whom you asked—had disappeared on the twentieth night of October. A coworker had reported last seeing Avery leaving The Outlet shortly before her car had been found on a bridge spanning the Hudson River, totaled and driverless. The official report posited that she hadn't been wearing a seat belt when she'd crashed into the rail, and her body had been thrown through the windshield and into the water. If that were the case, she might never be found, and Allie had a snowball's chance in hell.

She toed a cigarette butt around the shadowy alley, eyeing the parking lot. More specifically, she eyed Scott Dallas's parked car.

If nothing else, Allie mused, joining Bennett's little secret squadron would be worth the price of admission just to avoid research grunt work. It was nice having a file stuffed with witnesses, car models, telephone numbers, and license plates. Yet everything about Avery Burke's reopened case seemed to point to the same conclusion: a desperate mother just didn't want to admit her baby was gone.

And so here Allie was, waiting to catch the last person who had seen her alive.

As if her annoyance had summoned him, Scott Dallas appeared at the opposite end of the alley, just like she hoped he would, taking the shortcut to the street where he'd parked. The autumn sun idled between the surrounding buildings, taking its sweet time to set, and it was a decent part of town. This guy probably thought he had no reason to worry about the lady leaning against the far wall, minding her own business.

How wrong he was.

Don't go overboard, she told herself. Bennett had made it quite clear she wasn't supposed to let loose on anyone without his express permission. She could handle that, right? Verifying a testimony should be easy street for a former Ranger.

Allie reined in her excitement as he approached. Scott Dallas matched his profile photo perfectly—average height, light brown hair parted to the side. As he came closer, hands shoved into the pockets of his black peacoat and eyes on the pavement, Allie identified the scar slashing his left eyebrow. He was looking down to avoid stepping in anything unseemly with his fancy lawyer shoes.

When he was only a few steps away, Allie pushed off the wall, stepping out to block his path. "Scott Dallas?"

Scott startled, stopped, and looked her suspiciously up and down. "And you are...?"

"A private investigator hired by the Burke family," Allie said, hoping he wouldn't ask for credentials.

The assurance he wasn't about to get mugged didn't seem to relax Scott much. "Not this again," he groaned, pulling his hands from his pockets just to slap them irritably to his sides. "I already told the police everything. Can't you bother them for the details?"

"Oh, I already have." She crossed her arms, watching his tantrum with a mixture of amusement and anticipation. "I want to hear from the source."

Scott rather noticeably eyed the muscles of her forearms, considered it for all of six seconds, and heaved a petulant sigh. "All right, fine. And you'll let me be on my way once I do?"

"Cross my heart." Allie drew a finger across her chest to match.

"Well, if you've read the police report, then you know I didn't see much. I went out for a few drinks after work with some buddies, I needed a smoke break, and I spotted Avery outside. She was stumbling over to her car."

Stumbling? He hadn't used that language in the police statement. Allie humored him and decided to keep it to herself. For now.

"Go on," she prodded. "What time was it?"

"Late. Around eleven."

"And did you talk to Ms. Burke at all?"

"Nothing worth mentioning. Someone else might've, I guess. I didn't stick around to see where she went."

"So you just stood there, watching?"

"Yes. I watched her get into her car and I went back inside. That's it."

"You said she was stumbling," Allie started, zeroing in on the inconsistency. "Would you say she was drunk?"

"I'd say so."

"Are you sure about that?"

"She was swaying all over the place outside a bar, so yeah, I'm pretty sure."

Allie's eyes narrowed. "That's funny, because you didn't mention anything about her drinking in the statement you gave to the police."

Scott must have been a good courtroom attorney, because he didn't even flinch. "I probably just forgot to mention it," he told her. If Allie hadn't been listening for it, she would've missed the subtle wobble in his voice. "I told you what you wanted to hear. Can I go now? I'm going to be late for something."

"Sure." Allie grinned, cool and slick, like she imagined sleazy lawyers did all the time. "Right after you tell me the real reason you didn't mention she was drinking to the police."

She took a step forward. Scott took a step back.

"That *is* the real reason," he snapped, coat shoulders bunching toward his ears.

"Come on, Scott. If you lie to me, I'm going to start thinking you had something to do with what happened to Avery." Allie shifted to block his path as he made to sidestep her, throwing out her arm to barricade him into the alley. "Do you have anything to do with Avery's disappearance?"

"What? No!"

"You didn't see her stumbling out of that bar and think to yourself..."

"Look, I didn't mention her being drunk because I didn't want to make things harder on her family, all right? I told the investigators everything else I knew."

"Now we're getting somewhere. Why did you think that would make things harder on her family?"

"You know what? Fuck you, lady," Scott spat. When Allie didn't react, he tossed his gloved hand skyward, gesturing jerkily toward the horizon. "What do you care about her family? You didn't even know her. You think this is fun for me, talking to you soulless creeps? You think I want a girl's grieving mother to know her only daughter got herself killed because she was driving drunk?"

How interesting, Allie thought, that he'd pointed so confidently to the north while talking about Avery's family. It could've been nothing, but it might've been something. A thrill stirred in the pit of her stomach, a diluted version of what she usually felt on the hunt.

"Tell me, Scott. What was the nature of your relationship with Avery Burke?"

"The nature of our relationship?" Scott's agitated gaze went steely in the gloom. "What exactly are you insinuating?"

"I'm not insinuating anything. I'm just asking what the relationship between you two was like. Professional? Friendly?" Allie cocked her head. "Sexual?"

"We worked together, and that's it," Scott snapped. He'd shrunk away a moment ago, but now he was stalking forward, his smart coat flapping behind him, to pitch an accusatory finger into her face. "I know what you're doing. I know what PIs are like. You're scrounging for phony leads you can use to convince a dead woman's mother to keep paying you."

Yeah, Allie had definitely struck some kind of nerve. "I'd only be able to do that if there's something you're hiding from me. Is there?" she goaded, gently slapping his hand away from her nose. He stared at her, the skin of his neck simmering red under his collar. "Are you hiding something that might interest Avery's mother?"

"I don't have to put up with this slander. I've got two kids and a wife waiting for me at home. I told you what you wanted to know, and now I'm done."

He made to step around her again, but she blocked his way more aggressively this time, stepping right up to him.

"You're done when I say you're done." Scott had to know that she was in charge. "I'll get the whole story out of you, one way or another."

His mouth twisting into a scowl, Scott lurched forward to shove Allie out of his way. Instinctually, like it was happening in slow motion, she rebalanced herself and swung her fist into his stomach.

Allie felt an instant pulse of relief as her fist collided with Scott's unprepared body. He collapsed under her knuckles, coughing as she dropped him straight to the ground. It was the first real release she'd had since Bennett interrupted her thrashing of Dex, and it was so sudden and so sweet, running didn't even come close.

"What the fuck was that?!" he ground out through the pain, writhing on the asphalt.

"It was a lesson you needed to be taught." She glared down at him. As Allie savored the feeling of her fist in flesh, her desire for violence quieted a little, and her mind went blissfully smooth. "Remember it the next time I ask you a question."

As the relief rushed in, something new came with it—something that didn't feel quite right.

Scott scrambled backward, looking up at Allie with wide, terrified eyes that caught the streetlight glow from the ends of the alley. Realization hit her like a set of brass knuckles. That odd little twinge was regret.

It took her off guard for a moment, because she definitely didn't regret putting Scott in his place— he'd deserved that. When she traced the feeling to its source, her heart sank.

She'd already failed her test.

Allie was ripped out of her regret by a prickling sensation on the back of her neck that told her she was being watched, and a sound like a shoe on the pavement behind her. Without thinking, she spun around, swinging her tingling fist.

Phoenix ducked to the side just in time to avoid getting a mouthful of Allie's fist. Her fingers brushed the tips of his auburn hair.

"Down, girl!" he yelped. Allie couldn't even open her mouth. She just stood there, blinking wildly, trying to make it make sense.

She whipped around just as fast when she heard Scott staggering up behind her.

"You better stay right where you are, Scott," Allie growled. He shrank as if expecting her to lunge.

"She's kidding." Phoenix waved his hand dismissively. "You're free to go," he added, nodding once. "And I hope my associate here didn't cause you too much trouble."

All Scott said to him as he passed by, giving Allie as wide a berth as he could, was, "She's a lawsuit waiting to happen."

Allie—certified lawsuit-waiting-to-happen—glared at her target's back as he walked quickly toward his car, throwing glances over his shoulder every few seconds, and disappeared.

Chapter 18

Allie rounded on Phoenix and demanded to know just what the hell kind of stunt he was trying to pull.

"What are you doing here?" she hissed, clenching her fists, using every ounce of her self-control to keep them pinned to her sides. "Have you been following me?"

"Of course I have." He laughed in a way Allie imagined he thought was disarming. "I'm your chaperone. You didn't think Daniel was just going to send you out on a sensitive investigation by yourself, did you?"

She shouldn't have been surprised.

If Daniel had ordered Frustrating Phoenix to spy on her from the shadows, then he didn't trust in her abilities after all. A small part of Allie—a part she quickly squashed—whispered that he was right not to. Her anger burned hotter inside her chest.

"This isn't my first rodeo, Phoenix. I don't need anyone to spy on me, okay? I can take care of myself."

"This isn't about you, sweetheart." A slanted, punchable smile quirked up the corner of Phoenix's mouth. "I'm here to protect the business. You almost killed a senator's son last week, or did you forget that? You can't be going rogue at the drop of a hat—you'll ruin it for everybody."

"So... does this mean I'm done?"

"No," Phoenix added before she could kick up a fuss. "I'm glad to inform you that you haven't completely bombed yet. You're on strike one, and that means you aren't allowed to fly solo anymore."

"I wasn't anyway, as it turns out."

"And from now on, it'll be clearer that I'm shadowing you. You can still complete the test and make the cut, but you're gonna do it with me openly looking over your shoulder until Daniel decides otherwise."

Great. Allie would almost rather fail than have to spend the rest of her test being babysat by Phoenix. Almost.

A mixture of anger, disappointment, and just a little hurt twisted in her gut. "Well, I wasn't gonna kill Scott, all right? I don't need you watching me," she insisted.

"Maybe not, but you did punch up one of our only leads."

"I was just going to—"

"Listen, if you want in—and trust me, if beating up bad dudes is your idea of a fun Friday night, you *definitely* want in—you're stuck with me until Daniel's satisfied you aren't a liability to his pet project."

Even she couldn't argue with that. Bennett was her commander now, and she'd defied orders.

The two of them stood in the twilit alley for a few moments. Slowly but surely, the sounds of pedestrians, traffic, and Allie's own breathing began to filter back in through the haze of her aggravation.

"You wanna punch me, don't you?" Phoenix said suddenly, inexplicably.

Allie rolled her eyes, if only to lament the unfortunate fact that he continued to exist. "You're making it hard not to."

"So go ahead." He spread his arms out wide, as though to entice her with a hug. "I know that look of yours—the bull nostrils, the crazy eyes. You need to get a few hits in, blow off some steam to clear your head. Right?"

There had been a time not so long ago when Allie might have offered the same thing to one of her feistier recruits on a bad day. She was the recruit now, and a prospective one at that.

"I'll manage," she snapped.

"Will you, though?" He paused, but his arms didn't drop, and his eyebrows gave a maddening waggle. "Just go ahead and let loose, sweetheart. Raise that cute little fist of yours and—"

Without wasting a moment, Allie took the invitation. She socked him right in the gut.

He folded like a card. "What the hell!" Phoenix wheezed, gasping down a breath.

"You said I should let loose," she reminded him.

"I wasn't ready yet!"

Allie decided she'd sooner die than let this arrogant, patronizing, sad excuse for a coach get in one more snarky remark at her expense.

"Are you ready now?" she dared, and punched him again, this time sending the bony ridges of her fist to his face. His head whipped around with a delightful expression of surprise.

"Now you're talking." Phoenix cupped his hand around his bloody forehead and wiped the stream running down his lip with his sleeve. The sight of it sent a shiver of glee through Allie. She hated to admit it, but Phoenix was right. She needed this, and she wanted more.

"Are you going to fight back or—" Allie pivoted as Phoenix lunged at her, expertly slapping away his blow.

He'd underestimated her, but he wasn't the first one to make that mistake, so she didn't hold it against him. She held being a sleazy, disgusting asshole against him, but she could understand why he was flabbergasted when his second strike sailed uselessly through empty air.

Allie blocked his third punch, using his momentum to throw him off balance, but he managed to skillfully deflect her incoming kick. She hadn't expected such a quick, fluid reaction based on his muddled form, and she only remembered he'd been a Ranger when his fist connected with the side of her head.

Ears ringing, Allie dodged the next punch, wrapped her arms around his torso, and brought the two of them to the ground. Their landing knocked a painful yelp out of him. It wasn't as loud as she'd hoped, but it was still music to her ears.

She wanted to hit him again—it felt so good to hit Phoenix—but he'd done her a favor, and it sounded like he'd had enough. With her demons slightly appeased, she pushed herself off him, stood up, and stepped back.

"And don't call me sweetheart ever again, Phoenix," she told him, pointing threateningly.

"Got it." He sucked down a shaky breath, then rolled to his hands and knees to cough. "*Fuck*, you hit hard!" he swore with a satisfying amount of admiration in his voice.

"So I've heard." Allie wanted to keep a straight face, but she smiled wickedly.

After catching his breath, Phoenix hauled himself up, drying his forehead on his arm and running a hand through his fine, ruddy hair. "I don't know about you, Grecco. But man, I need a drink," he groaned, obviously fighting the urge to bow over and prop both hands on his kneecaps. "In fact, I think you might owe me a beer."

"What's that, now?"

"How about we head in to Scott's favorite hangout and chat over a pint? You don't have to buy. In fact, I'll pick up yours."

Allie's brows sank along with her smile, suspicion roiling within. "I've got work to do, and even if I didn't, I'm not interested in a chat or a drink with you."

"Okay, let me rephrase. The chat isn't optional, but the beer is. For you, anyway," he added. "I'm definitely having one."

"What do we need to chat about?"

"Oh, come on," Phoenix whined, rolling his eyes. "It's not a date, Grecco, damn. It's a business meeting. You know, about the little exam you're taking right now? About the little screwup I just saw? And when else can you have a business meeting over a beer?"

At least if they went to the bar, they'd be in a public place, and Phoenix had just sampled what Allie had to offer people who ambushed her, intentionally or not. If Phoenix's chat was really about Soldiers for Hire, she wanted to hear what he had to say.

"Fine," she relented, still not convinced his intentions were purely professional. She let him lead her around the corner and into The Outlet.

· · · ● · ● · · ·

The industrial atmosphere of the bar irked Allie, from its brushed metal tabletops and exposed ceiling pipes to its old black chalkboard menus. It postured like a man who wanted to be perceived as tougher than he really was.

The patrons irked her too, babbling about pretentious craft beer in their strategically distressed leather jackets and new-soled boots. Phoenix dropped Allie off at a discreet corner table, then moseyed to the bar, claiming he needed something to make him forget the ache of her knuckles. Allie declined a drink. Growing up in Logan's house had pretty well turned her off alcohol.

It wasn't long before Phoenix plopped down into the seat across from her, holding a tall glass of dark and foamy beer. He took a long gulp then wiped the foam from his lip.

"That's better." He sighed and set it aside. "Before we get started, and since I happily offered myself up for a dank-alley-ass-beating, can I ask you a personal question?"

"No."

"Cool," he cut in, blowing right over her *no*. "What's the story behind the tat?"

Allie's spine snapped straight in the uncomfortable wooden chair, and a lump swelled in her throat like a fist. She felt three hard pulses of her heart.

"The snake or whatever it is," he added when she sat there, as leaden and stoic as a stone someone had just dropped. "Don't take this the wrong way, but I didn't figure you for the body art type."

"How the hell do you know about that?"

"I made a note of it while your ankle was hurtling toward my face at high velocity," Phoenix informed her, incidentally.

Allie lunged down to grab the loose hem of her jeans, discovering the left leg and been yanked from her boot during their scrap. He couldn't have seen more than a glimpse as they swapped blows, and yet thinking about his eyes on her shin—upon even a tiny, three-inch byroad of the long trail of ink and scar tissue she'd worn throughout her adult life—made Allie feel sick. She stuffed the denim roughly back into the boot.

"It's not a snake," she croaked, strangely breathless, wishing she'd ordered that beer.

"So you're not a puppy girl, not a kitten girl, and not a snake girl. What is it, then?"

Allie couldn't tell a fellow soldier she'd marked her body with a ribbon of barbed wire, its metal thorns interspersed with white chrysanthemums, and she certainly wouldn't give Phoenix the mental imagery of a tattoo winding all the way up to her thigh. "It's none of your fucking business. That's what it is."

Phoenix heaved another dramatic sigh, but dropped the subject. He clanked his glass on the table and didn't let her smoldering glare so much as slow him down. "All right, then. Business it is. Item one: you, my hot-headed little trainee, need to understand that we do things a little more subtly around here than you're used to."

"Different how?" she demanded, clearing her throat, trying to slow her hopping heart.

"Well, we don't charge in like a drunk fuckin' cowboy posse to question a witness, for starters. We run intel, we wait until we get orders and an opening, and then we *stealthily*"—he threw Allie a pointed look—"dole out the punishments."

Allie huffed, scowling at Phoenix over the lonely glass in his fist. "I don't sneak around. I find an asshole, I punch him in the face. End of story."

Phoenix snorted into his beer. "Yeah, because that worked out so well with the last one." He took another long pull. "Wait 'til you see the people on our lists. Dexie Boy was just the tip of the iceberg. This is the big leagues, sweetheart."

"You might want to rephrase the ending of that arrogant sentence." Allie narrowed her gaze.

"Sorry. I guess old habits die hard." He shrugged, smiling wolfishly. "What I meant to say is that we deal in truly evil sons-of-bitches who are too slippery, too rich, or too powerful to be punished by ordinary means."

"Doesn't matter how big they are or how much power they have," Allie said, folding her arms across her chest. "They fall down just like everyone else."

"That's true, but if you're a Soldier for Hire, first you've gotta wait for instructions from Daniel and the General." He rolled his eyes, crooking two fingers to encase *the General* in air quotes. "No exceptions."

"Who's that?" Allie asked. "The General."

"It's no one. Just Daniel's imaginary friend who hands down the orders. He insists he's real, but anybody with a brain cell knows it's just his way of avoiding the fallout when an operator takes issue with an assignment." He gave Allie two seconds to process before he scraped his chair closer to the table. "Hey, Grecco?"

"What?"

"Since you're so good at personal questions... can I ask what's the deal with your attitude at work?"

Like she was going to spill her guts to Frustrating Phoenix over a beer in a hipster bar. "There's no 'deal.' I don't like being a paper-pusher," she barked, "and I just want to get out of there as fast as possible every day. Maybe it has something to do with you burying me in a constant stream of invasive, bullshit questions. That ever cross your mind? Maybe it's *your* deal."

Phoenix waved a hand as if he were shooing away the flimsy, smoky tendrils of Allie's lie. "Come on, we both know that's not all of it. What's the real story?"

Allie almost told him to get lost, but the memory of how Judd had once pushed her to confide in him dammed the words in her mouth. She could see his hand slide up her calf, up her knee, up her thigh as he'd condescended her about how *scary* her first overseas op had been while she was lying in the medical tent. She could conjure up the blind rage she'd felt when he'd said:

"You froze the second you saw that kid and your mommy instincts kicked in or whatever. This is exactly why women shouldn't be allowed on the frontlines!"

She could still see her fist colliding with the side of his head, feel the spike of cold terror that flooded her when his wide hands wrapped around her throat.

"—just like Daniel, don't you?" Phoenix was saying. "I know you guys think the silent warrior act makes you look like a superhero, but it's not as cool as you think it is."

Allie took a deep breath, letting the murmuring and tipsy laughter around them sweep her mind clean. She willed her heart to stillness for the second time since walking into this embarrassing bar.

Frustrating Phoenix, she insisted to herself, was *not* Judd.

His dumb jokes and belittling nicknames regularly made her want to take a sledgehammer to his eat-shit grin. But he hadn't tried to take advantage of her, he hadn't mocked her vulnerability, he hadn't ratted her out, and he didn't hide his violent side underneath a mask. Still—vigilante or not—he was just as annoying as the Phoenix who sat next to her at work.

With a pang of horror, Allie realized she thought it was a little bit endearing.

"If Daniel's such a hero, then why'd he let Dex go?" she snapped, shoving the unwanted twinge of fondness deep down into the bowels of her psyche. Her fist whumped the tabletop, compelling Phoenix to protectively scoot his almost-empty glass closer. "He ought to be dead. He deserves to be dead."

"See? You and I are not so different after all, sweet... umm... Grecco," Phoenix corrected himself, beholding her sidelong. "That's exactly what I told him, but this is where that subtlety I keep telling you about kicks in. If Dex decides he didn't get the message, Daniel will find a discreet way to stop him for good."

Allie swallowed, tightening her fist on the table between them, but her soul felt like it was a thousand yards away.

She had to tell him. Maybe he already knew about the OTH, but at some point, he had to hear it from her. Her mentor had to know why she was so determined to see Dex Riklis go down, why she needed to draw blood so badly, and why she was so eager to punch out lawyers to solve her case.

"Punishing guys like Dex, it's—what I do." Her voice cracked. Each word felt like brittle glass in her mouth. "It's kind of personal to me. I've been... hurt by men like him before," she admitted with great difficulty.

Phoenix didn't interrupt this time, and he didn't whip out any more jokes. He spoke quietly, as if to apologize. "Hey, Grecco," he said.

Her tongue felt heavy. All she managed was a small "yeah?"

"For what it's worth, I would have killed him too," Phoenix murmured, and something about the way he said it—something about the cold spark behind his eyes when they met hers—told Allie he wasn't just talking about Dex.

She nodded. Phoenix let them sit in contemplative quiet for no more than a few seconds.

"So," he proposed, tapping his fingers around his sweating beer glass, and swung his voice back up as though nothing had passed between them. "What's your next step with the case, chief? You're in charge of this investigation."

Allie did her best to shake it off, dragging her focus back to the mission. She resented being reined in, but now that she'd flirted with failure two steps out of the starting gate, she kind of wished Bennett would just hand down precise orders.

"I get the feeling that Scott is hiding something," she began, remembering the fishy way he'd squirmed. "He got defensive when I asked about his relationship with Avery."

"Then he's still a lead, but we won't get anything more out of him tonight."

Allie pulled at her chin, thinking back to the police report she'd pored over all evening. Each photo stewed in her mind's eye as clearly as if it were sitting on the tabletop. Since talking to Scott, something felt off about him, but she couldn't quite put her finger on it...

She mentally summoned a photo of Avery's car, picture perfect, just as she'd seen it a few hours ago. The black four-door sedan was tilted at a brutal angle, its front end crunched into the red-painted railing of the bridge. She could see the bent edge of the windshield, the glass scattered all over the blacktop. The rear fender—

"Grecco? What are you doing?" Phoenix's voice snapped her out of the trance.

"Thinking," Allie replied tersely, opening her eyes. She wasn't about to let anyone start dissecting the weirdest parts of her head. Besides, Allie didn't know how to explain what she did, how she saw. There were no words for the sharpness with which she could reassemble entire scenes— images, sounds, sometimes even smells. "Something wasn't right about the police photos. The ones of Avery's car."

"Oh, I've got those with me." Phoenix pulled out his cell, slipping it across the table. "You could have just asked instead of meditating about it."

"I'm not meditating," she said, curtly, and nothing more.

Allie flicked through the photos. Zooming in on Avery's rear fender, she panned around until she found it—just a small dent, just where she remembered. And wedged deep inside: a scrape of barely perceptible green paint.

"Did anyone look into that?" She spun the phone around, pointing to the splash of color. "The report said she crashed head on."

"She did. What's your point?" Phoenix squinted down at her finger, still jammed into the mottled pixels. "What am I even looking at?"

"There's no green paint on that bridge," she blurted, tapping her nail against the screen, frustrated by his confusion and his childish face. "So either that ding was already there, or she hit something else before totaling it—or while she was totaling it."

Allie dug her own phone out of her pocket. She'd already bookmarked Avery's social media accounts, and rummaged through the photos for a recent shot of her car. There was only a single pertinent image. An elderly woman—perhaps Avery's mother—smiled as she pulled a piece of luggage from the black sedan's trunk. It had been uploaded on the eighteenth of October.

The fender was spotless.

Allie thrust out her phone for his perusal, holding it stiffly over the table. When Phoenix looked up again, his mouth had drifted open.

"Grecco," he squawked, and glanced quickly back down at his cell, touching the minute drop of green as if to ascertain he hadn't imagined it. "I don't know what kind of questionable substance you swallowed, snorted, or shot into your brain to notice that... but you just might have something here."

"I know. If we can figure out what happened, we might be able to find another witness, and they might help us figure out what happened to Avery that night," Allie gushed, adrenaline bubbling through her limbs, tingling her fingertips.

This was it. The hunt was on again.

"Hold your horses, Grecco. You gotta tell Daniel first. After you tell him about your little oopsie with Scott's solar plexus."

The thought dampened Allie's excitement like an old candle in front of an open window. "Do I have to go tonight? Can't it wait until morning? What if he cans me before I get a chance to crack this case?"

Phoenix was quiet for a long time—long enough that Allie wondered if she'd actually managed to offend him, though she wasn't sure if she was glad or vaguely remorseful. He drummed his fingers against the table, clearly turning something over in his mind.

"I'm gonna tell you something because I respect you. But you gotta promise me you won't tell Daniel I told you," he said seriously.

"You respect me?" Allie raised an eyebrow. "You bother me at work every day. If you respected me or my time, you'd leave me alone."

"That's just teasing." He flipped his hand dismissively to-and-fro again. "You make it too easy; I can't help it. But I can't let my cadet go into combat without critical intel."

Was he just saying that, or did Phoenix really think of her as his cadet? Her temper rumbled at the honorary demotion, but Allie couldn't tell with him, and it did nothing to untangle her newly

complicated   thoughts—or   that   nagging,
undeniable burst of affection, still apparently alive
somewhere down there where she'd stuffed it.
Even if she was a cadet, she didn't mind Phoenix
thinking of her as another soldier. Not a female
soldier—just a soldier.

"Out with it already." Allie didn't want to like
Phoenix. But here she was, liking him despite it
all.

"No way. Not until you promise. Daniel will
have my ass if he finds out."

"Drama queen much? I promise, okay? I won't
tell him. You want me to pinky swear too?"

Phoenix looked like he was actually considering
it.

"You know what?" He lifted his hand and stuck
out the littlest finger, giving it a wiggle. "Yeah.
Pinky swear me."

She scoffed and rolled her eyes, but—incredibly
—obliged him. Allie snatched his pinky with hers,
sealing her promise to an adult man that she
wouldn't tattle on him.

"All right," he said, leaning far over the table and
speaking in a hushed tone, like he thought Daniel
might kick his way out of one of those ceiling
pipes at any moment. "Scott Dallas is a known
asshat. Hell, he's been rung up for drunken bar
fights!"

"How is that related to..."

"Daniel expected he would bait you into getting
physical."

So he *had* been setting her up to fail, just not in the way she'd been thinking. "Son of a bitch," Allie said flatly.

"Daniel or Scott?" Phoenix joked.

"Daniel. Mr. Bennett. Both."

"Listen, Daniel's not a bad guy, but he doesn't screw around about the back end. It's really the only thing he cares about. He is two hundred percent dedicated to helping vets demilitarize— he's been through his own last-mission baggage, like someone else I know—but he's not gonna be your buddy about it. He's got some serious reservations about you, and he's going to put you through the wringer before he makes a final decision."

She should have been insulted. No, she should have been *pissed* about his secrecy—about his refusal to say it to her face—but suddenly, it was hard to sit still. Allie craned forward, locking on to the irregular detail. "What happened during his last mission?"

"Come on, Grecco," Phoenix groaned, covering a hint of something unjovial with a flash of a jovial smile before Allie could identify it. "You think I'm gonna spill my best friend's secrets over a pinky swear?"

"All right, fair." She sat back heavily. Allie's curiosity was piqued, but at least she'd discovered Phoenix had a shred of loyalty.

"Now, this thing with Scott Dallas?" He picked up a fist and clapped it playfully into his palm. "Not on you. Everybody fails their first task."

"So he just sets everybody up?"

"Yeah, he does. It's supposed to teach you humility." Phoenix leaned back, sniffing theatrically, trying on the role of disappointed schoolmaster. "What you do next is more important than fucking up once. If you can prove you know what to do with a second chance, you'll be on your way to making it in."

Work was one of the two things Allie was truly good at. She hated that she'd already failed a task, setup or not, and she especially hated letting her CO down. Knowing everyone screwed it up did make the regret gnawing in the pit of her stomach feel less tangible, though. She could still do this. If she marched in a straight, soldierly formation—if she didn't stick one more toe out of the line Bennett drew for her—she still had a shot of getting her life back.

"You're feeling a little better after our chat, right?" he wondered, watching her quizzically, all his severity crumbling away. "Less like you're gonna punch the next guy who talks to you?"

"Sure." If Allie was being honest with herself, yeah, she did feel better. It was kind of shocking how good it felt to open up to someone, even a little bit. Granted, there was so much more she could have said, but nobody was ready to hear that, and Allie was nowhere near ready to tell it.

"Good. You'd feel even better if you'd let me buy you a beer," he said smugly, and just like that

—even if she was, begrudgingly, liking her talk with Frustrating Phoenix—Allie wanted to punch his face in all over again. "Now that you're not steaming out the ears, you've got an appointment at Daniel's."

Draining the rest of his beer, he walked Allie out to the sidewalk, where he waved down a cab.

A yellow taxi pulled up, and before she really knew what was happening, Phoenix herded her into the back seat. He gave the driver the address and closed the door on her.

"Wait! What am I supposed to tell him?" She rolled down the window to flag him before he could walk away.

"The truth," Phoenix said, leaning down to meet her eye through the open window. "Daniel can sniff out lies like a fart in a chopper, so don't even try it. Trust me."

Allie frowned. "Nobody can smell a fart in a chopper."

"Yeah? Well, that should tell you how good Daniel's nose is."

"Or it just means your farts are weak."

Phoenix let out a sharp guffaw, loud and genuine. "Hey look, you do have a sense of humor!"

Before Allie could say anything more, her driver pulled away from the curb.

Chapter 19

Allie sank into the lumpy cab upholstery and watched the city lights wink by.

Had she really been joking with Phoenix? Had she just exchanged fart jokes with a coworker? What was going on with her?

Maybe she was running a fever or something.

Lost in her thoughts, Allie only noticed she'd arrived when the taxi pulled over. She peered through the window, ducking to take in the top of the very tall, very fancy-looking building.

"Are you sure this is the right place?" she asked the driver.

He shrugged. "It's the address your friend gave me."

Allie's eyes lingered on the sleek modern facade before she passed over a fistful of bills and exited the idling taxi. Out there on the sidewalk, the building looked even taller. The apartments in Rego Park weren't half this imposing or half this glassy.

Frustrating Phoenix *had* to be hazing her. With nothing else to do, Allie soldiered her chin, climbed the concrete steps, and walked in.

The building's interior did nothing to ease her paranoia about being the butt of her mentor's practical joke. It was an assault of opulence, of marble and polished-steel grandeur. The blatant display of wealth and all the reflective surfaces made Allie uneasy. Did Daniel Bennett seriously live here? How much money did one make in the vigilante business, and what would her salary look like if she joined it?

A soft *ahem* interrupted her gaping. She approached the immaculate, gently curved front desk, occupied by an austere woman in a crisp vest that reminded Allie of a blackjack dealer. She probably did not have any casino chips, though.

"May I help you, ma'am?" she asked as Allie stepped up.

Allie didn't like being called *ma'am* by a civilian. It made her feel like she should be asking to see a manager while three kids hung off her arm.

"I'm here to see Daniel Bennett?" She eyed the wall of locked mail slots behind the clerk, hoping to spot his name, but they were only labeled by unit number, and there were a lot of them. "Am I... uh... in the right place?"

The clerk didn't even consult her computer. "You are. Mr. Bennett does live here. Is he expecting you?"

Was he? Phoenix had made it sound like he expected every visitor he had, especially when she'd just borked her first mission. "He might be?"

"May I inform him of your arrival?"

Allie couldn't help thinking that down-to-earth, no-nonsense Daniel Bennett probably hated the formalities of this place. "You may," she granted. "My name is Allie Grecco."

"Thank you." Allie's ears clambered for a note of Bennett's voice as the clerk picked up her desk phone and dialed, but the call was over in a heartbeat. "He is indeed expecting you. Head down the hall and take any of the elevators to the top floor," she instructed, and Allie—lost in this big, glittery, empty place—was grateful to be told what to do. "You will find another elevator to your immediate left. You've already been approved, so walk right in and press the button. Mr. Bennett is waiting for you at his penthouse."

Daniel lived in the *penthouse* of this place?

Allie mumbled thanks and retreated across the wide lobby to the elevator bay, stepping into one of the ready cabins. She was about to punch the highest button when her reflection stopped her in her tracks. It wasn't mirror-perfect, but she could see the vague shape of her body and face in the elevator's metal paneling.

It's fine, she told herself, *you're fine. It's just a freaking mirror! Stop being a baby.*

Gritting her teeth, Allie jabbed *100* and looked at the floor. She stared at her feet as the elevator climbed. It was stupid, and it was childish, but it was unnerving knowing that just behind her, a blurry vision of herself was waiting for her stop too.

She was relieved to escape onto the top floor. The second elevator was thankfully much less reflective than the first, and Allie rode it all the way up to the penthouse, where she still couldn't believe Daniel Bennett allegedly lived.

The second elevator slid to a smooth stop, the doors pulled back, and Allie almost laughed out loud at the sprawling, unbelievably lavish apartment laid bare before her.

Stepping out onto a dark hardwood floor that must've taken a hefty bite out of a rainforest somewhere, Allie's eyes swept around the fanciest room she'd ever been in. The place was more window than wall. A spiral staircase led from the open-plan living area to a second-floor balcony, only possible because the ceilings were so high. There was a fireplace; there was a giant wall-mounted TV; there were granite countertops spacious enough to fit all the unwashed dishes a girl could make and still have room to nuke cup noodles. Not that Daniel had a single piece of silverware out of place, and not that Allie cared about granite countertops.

The entire apartment was showroom clean. If you peered past the sleek modern decor that looked like it must've come with the place, it didn't seem like a real person with interests or hobbies lived there.

Allie's eyes drifted to the living room. There— standing by the edge of a long leather sofa that was certainly worth more than every damned thing Allie had ever owned—was Daniel, her vigilante boss, in a gray t-shirt and jeans he probably bought at a thrift store.

If Allie was being honest, she had kind of expected it to be the wrong Daniel Bennett.

"Nice pad," she said, lingering near the elevator. "Is electricity included in your six-million-dollar rent or is that separate?"

"None of your business," Daniel countered, unamused. "And it's separate."

He beckoned her to the couch, and Allie reluctantly approached, feeling as out of place there as Daniel appeared to be at home. She eased herself carefully onto the creaky black leather while he moved around the coffee table, then settled into a matching armchair.

"So," he said, not sparing a single pleasantry, "tell me about Scott Dallas."

Allie sat up straighter. If Phoenix told her the truth, Daniel wanted evidence his operators were capable of learning from their mistakes, and she sure knew how to make those.

She repeated what Scott had said about Avery, then recounted how she'd pushed him on that— pushed him too far—and ended up knocking him down. Allie did not mention the rush of relief and satisfaction she'd derived from putting that asshole in his place, or that she'd thrown Phoenix to the ground and bloodied his perpetual grin soon after. She waited, silently, to see what Daniel would say.

"Was there a confusion?" he said, finally, and Allie shifted another inch forward.

"A confusion?"

"Yes. A confusion. Were my orders about avoiding physical interaction not clear?"

"I'm sorry, sir," she said, forcing herself to hold Daniel's even gaze. "I should have waited for an approval to engage, but I let my temper get the best of me."

"I appreciate you saying that, Grecco."

Daniel didn't continue right away. Something about his silence and difficult-to-read expression pressed her to offer more, hoping it might improve his assessment, but Allie couldn't think of anything else. Just the case—and the pictures of Avery's pulverized car.

"I noticed something important about the police report, sir."

"Go on."

"In the crash photos, there's an indentation and an unexplained scrape of green paint on Avery's rear fender. I checked her social media, and it must have happened within a two-day window before she disappeared. It's possible she had a smaller accident that very night."

"Which might mean there's another witness out there who could help us build our timeline,"

Daniel finished. He tapped his middle finger on the chair arm thrice. "I'll ask the General about accidents involving green cars within that window."

Slipping his phone from his pocket, he typed out a text. If Daniel really was making up his mysterious supervisor, as Phoenix suspected, he was awfully committed to the illusion.

"Now..." He set his phone on the wide arm of the chair and fixed his eyes on Allie. "Please tell me if you're actually sorry you punched Dallas or if that apology was nothing but lip service."

She almost twisted the truth. Allie didn't want to jeopardize her acceptance chances, but to hear Phoenix tell it, Daniel was a human lie detector; lying to his face would be worse than just admitting she wasn't all that remorseful. That didn't make the confession any easier.

"If I'm honest, I really am sorry that I disappointed you," she said carefully, "but I'm not sorry about bringing Scott to the ground."

Daniel's eyebrows went up, inviting her to go on.

"He was hiding something, he shoved me first, and he's an all-around aggressive jerk. I don't regret knocking him down a peg. He had it coming. You'll probably say it wasn't in the mission's best interest, and I know telling you all this isn't in mine. But you asked for the truth, and that's the truth."

He nodded once, curt but approving, and Allie relaxed into the butter-soft couch.

"I appreciate your honesty," he said. "Everybody makes mistakes, yet very few people own up to them. That being said, if you're serious about joining us, you're going to have to follow orders, even when you're dealing with all-around aggressive jerks."

Allie waited for him to go on, but he never got the chance. His phone vibrated against the chair arm, and whatever lecture Daniel had been about to give her about humility or obedience or whatever was forgotten.

"It's from the General," he told her once he'd finished reading. At least this "General" of his worked fast. "Does the name Kimberly de la Rosa mean anything to you?"

Allie shook her head. "No, sir."

Daniel rubbed his chin, more stubbly than usual by this time of night, as he consulted the message. "She's a trust fund kid with more than a few speeding violations. She was picked up for driving drunk on the twentieth."

"The day Avery disappeared."

"Right. Mommy and Daddy took care of it, though. She was released within a few hours."

"If she's a reckless trust fund kid, she's probably had plenty of DUIs," Allie pointed out. "What aren't you telling me?"

Daniel looked up from his phone, and a sparkle in his eye caught the light from the overheads.

"That night," he said, and—ever so quietly—the sparkle sharpened into a flame. "Kimberly wrecked her green sports car."

Chapter 20

Daniel's apartment may have been outrageous, but it didn't hold a candle to the de la Rosa residence.

Allie studied its three-story brick facade through Phoenix's passenger window, shielding her eyes from the bright morning. The upper-floor balconies were empty, the wrought-iron fence looked deadly sharp in the sunlight, and there were no signs of habitation on the perfect lawn.

"Where is this kid?" Phoenix wondered, glancing at his dashboard clock. "Doesn't she have school?"

"If she doesn't care about being pulled over for driving drunk at seventeen, she probably doesn't care about being on time for school."

Phoenix grumbled. "Little brat."

"I thought you'd admire a party animal," Allie said, eyes trained on the garage door, which was ridiculously painted to look like a barn. But a really fancy barn—the kind that housed show horses whose life insurance policies were worth more than Allie's salary. "Or at least have some kind of grudging respect for them."

"Not when they're this rich, I don't."

As if the word *rich* had summoned her, the garage door wheeled up, and a shiny red sports car prowled down the driveway. The teen behind the wheel wore sunglasses large enough to eclipse half her face.

"That's her," Allie said. Try as Kimberly might, there were no sunglasses big enough to mask the aura of an intoxicated seventeen-year-old. She was a dead ringer for the photo Daniel had sent, though this suburban palace was admittedly a nicer backdrop than the bleak wall of a police station.

Phoenix pulled into the street, following the noisy red car. They tailed her at a comfortable distance, hoping for some sign of careless driving —anything that might be used as compelling blackmail. To Allie's bemusement and Phoenix's chagrin, Kimberly was driving more like a grandma than a teenage alcoholic, crawling to a stop well before every sign.

"*Now* she decides she's a model citizen," Phoenix growled, banged his heavy hand on the wheel, and heaved an exasperated sigh. "This is useless. Let's just spook this kid. You ready to jump in?"

Allie nodded, keeping her eyes peeled for a one-entrance parking lot. The moment they found one, Phoenix sped up, forcing Kimberly's car into the turn lane, earning himself a chorus of honks and choice words from the drivers behind them. He swerved into the lot behind her. Allie didn't wait for him to put the car in park before she opened the door, standing up as Kimberly threw open her own.

"Oh my god, what is wrong with you?!" the teen shouted, pushing her sunglasses up into her wild red hair. Kimberly de la Rosa looked rough—not like she'd been drinking, but like she hadn't slept in a week. Poorly concealed dark circles made her youthful face look ashen.

"Ms. de la Rosa, we're private investigators, and we'd like to have a chat with you about your accident on October twentieth," Allie said, and slammed her door.

Kimberly's face seemed to drain of all color. Her fear was visible even from one car length away. "How do you know about that?"

"A little birdie told me," Allie offered unhelpfully. She walked around the front of Phoenix's still-idling car, toward Kimberly, who quickly yanked her door shut. "Can you confirm that you crashed a green car that night?"

"Yeah," Kimberly responded quietly—meekly, even. This was not the kind of kid Allie had been expecting. "I don't speed anymore, okay? I learned my lesson."

Allie's pulse quickened. Hunting down Avery couldn't be this easy, could it? "I'm going to need you to tell me what happened," she pressed on, placing one palm on the roof of the little apple-red car, hoping to dissuade Kimberly from stepping on the gas. "Did you hit anyone or anything?"

Her bottom lip quivered, and her dark eyes filled with tears.

"I didn't see her, okay?" she said, her voice wobbling as the tears began to rush down. "I swear I didn't. She came out of nowhere!" She turned her gaze from Allie to Phoenix and back to Allie, probably trying to figure out which of them would be more sympathetic. "I would have slowed down if I had seen her!"

Allie could feel her nostrils flare. She was close to something big; she could smell it. "Go on, Kimberly."

"That's it. What more do you want me to say? I hit her! I killed her! I hit Miss Kensington!"

Vehicular homicide sure hadn't been in the police report.

Allie felt blindsided. Her mouth dropped open.

"What's that, now?" Phoenix called from the open car window, startling Allie out of her surprise.

"She's dead! She's dead, and it was all my fucking fault," Kimberly cried, full-on sobbing now. She dropped her face into her palms and wept in the driver's seat. "I'm so sorry. I didn't see her run— run out—and I was going too fast, so I—I didn't stop in time. I swerved and hit a light pole." She sucked down a loud gulp of air. "But I had already... oh god..."

It was her second day on the job. Allie sucked in a lungful of air, held it, and begged herself to stay calm.

Kimberly doubled over, cradling her ribs, looking like she was going to throw up. Allie thought she might join her. No one had trained her for murder confessions—or for crying teenagers. Her pulse fluttered up her throat, banging at the back of her ears. Her fist balled up inside her jacket pocket.

"Did you see the body?" she demanded, tongue drying up between her clenched teeth. "Are you sure she was dead?"

Kimberly looked up, fruitlessly wiping away the tears that were still coming as Allie whirled around to meet Phoenix's gaze, hoping he had some mentorly counsel to share. He gave her a cringe and an exaggerated shrug, as if to say *you handle it*.

Kimberly de la Rosa was genuinely distraught, but this witness testimony had just jumbled itself into a shitstorm. "Ms. Kensington" hadn't appeared in a single report, from either the NYPD or Soldiers for Hire. Worse, without evidence, Allie couldn't be sure if she'd really hit a pedestrian or if she was using her teenage outburst as a cover to hide something else. And if she *had* killed someone—

"I'm a monster," Kimberly blubbered, feebly hugging herself. Her eyes squeezed shut. "I shouldn't be out here. Just walking around like nothing happened. I still remember how she looked. Her teeny face... her twisted little feeties. Her jingle bell all—"

"Hold on." Phoenix's grimace twitched. His long arm hung out of the window, and he drummed for attention on the side of his car. "Are we... talking about a cat?"

"Yeah. And I loved her. You've got to believe me! I would never hurt her intentionally. I never meant to take that beautiful creature's life!"

Allie felt like a cartoon piano somebody had just pushed off a skyscraper. Maybe out of Daniel's penthouse.

"So Miss Kensington," she gritted out, turning around slowly, white-hot anger racing through her veins, "is a fucking *cat*?"

"Please, ma'am. You're not gonna tell Ms. Zhao, are you?" Kimberly mopped a strand of soaked hair from her cheek. "I know she hired you to find out who hit her baby. She said she was going to get to the bottom of it, but please don't tell her it was me. Do you have any idea how many times I've catsitted for her? She can't know I'm the one who killed Miss Kensington. She can't!"

Allie stared for a moment, searching Kimberly's tear-stained face. She was serious. "I think there's a bit of a misunderstanding here. The cat's owner didn't hire us."

"Oh." Kimberly sniffed loudly, wiping her eye with her sleeve, careful to dab around her remarkably unsmudged makeup.

The lead was a bust, but it couldn't hurt to probe a little further. Maybe, by some stroke of luck, her car might still play a role in Avery's disappearance. If it didn't, Allie was out of ideas.

"Which is why I'm willing to keep your involvement in Miss Kensington's murder between us," she added. "Can you tell me anything else about that night? What area were you in when you crashed?"

"A mile or two that way," she said, pointing to the northwest. "There's a woman who lives over there—Victoria Bryant?" Allie didn't know the name. "She lives on my friend's street, and she's such a bitch. She calls the cops over *everything*. That's why I was speeding. My friend dared me to get her to call 9-1-1. It's like... it's just this stupid game we play," Kimberly admitted, then buried her face behind her fingers in shame.

"And what time was that?" Allie asked.

"Around seven."

Damn.

If Kimberly was telling the truth—and her tears didn't seem like an act—there was no way her car could've left that paint on Avery's bumper.

"I don't even drive that street anymore. In case... in case..." The tears were welling back up in Kimberly's red-rimmed eyes. "In case I come across Ms. Zhao. I can still hear poor Miss Kensington scream. I have nightmares about it."

Dead end. Allie had wanted this to be a worthwhile lead so badly, and all she'd found was a spoiled teenager, a dead cat, and neighborhood drama.

A sharp "damn it!" burst out of Allie as she walloped her palm against the hood of Kimberly's car.

Kimberly jumped at the noise. "What the hell! Are you insane?" she shrieked, tears drying up. "This is a brand-new sports car!"

"I don't give a rat's ass about your shiny new toy, Kimberly." Allie felt her demons stirring.

Phoenix's warning was close on her heels. "Watch it, Detective!" he called, reaching for his door handle, just in case Allie—or Kimberly— needed a save.

Left in the awkward silence after her outburst, Allie muttered, "Sorry about the cat," and about- faced to stalk back to Phoenix's car.

"Way to keep it together, Grecco," he drawled, unimpressed, watching Kimberly shakily turn her keys in the ignition as Allie dropped into his passenger seat.

She slammed the door behind her extra hard. "Shut up and drive."

Chapter 21

L eaning back in her office chair, Allie stared at the dull ceiling above her cubicle, lost in her head.

The investigation so far had been a crapshoot. Daniel's NYPD contacts had called to confirm Kimberly's story—which meant the green paint didn't match Avery's car—and that meant Allie was no closer to her target. Worse still: no other DUIs had been issued to drivers of green cars in the nights before the accident.

Just like that, Allie and Phoenix were back at square one.

Allie drummed her fingernails against the surface of her desk. She'd asked Phoenix to call repair shops around the city, just in case any dinged-up green cars had magically appeared on the twenty-first. It was taking an annoyingly long time, which stood to reason, considering it was Phoenix doing it. Maybe they weren't looking for a totaled car, Allie supposed, eyeballing a pea-sized imperfection in the ceiling plaster. Maybe just one that had been in a minor fender bender.

Allie probably should have been filling out next week's schedule. Although Daniel had reduced her logistics workload for the duration of the test, she found herself unable to focus on anything but Avery. Did the police even care? Had no one really noticed the dented fender? Or had they written it all off as a drunk driving accident, secretly celebrating the death of a civil rights lawyer who'd dogged them for years?

Logan's snarling red face flashed before her, and she shoved him out of her mind.

It was more than a test. This was principle, and it was personal. She was going to find whatever was left of Avery Burke—one way or another—and if someone *had* killed her, Allie would make sure she got her revenge.

A thump jolted her out of her head, revving her heart. It was, of course, Phoenix.

"Did you find anything?" she asked him.

"Nothing about the cars yet. I put a guy on it. But I've got something else." He patted the manila folder pinned under his arm. "Come with me."

He led her to one of the private meeting rooms. As he closed them in and pulled the blinds shut, Allie felt a familiar squeeze of suspicion in her lower gut, warning her to distrust his intentions. That didn't surprise her. What surprised her was how mild—how tiny—the squeeze now was. If she'd been just a little distracted, Allie might have missed it entirely.

"I took a closer look at the officers who investigated Avery's death." Phoenix dropped his folder onto the table, flipping it open. Then he spread the papers into two piles, each topped with a stapled photo of a uniformed man. "Bernie Miller and Kirk Bedford. They've been partners for a long time, and the two of them are pretty buddy-buddy."

Allie went right for the photos. Miller was a white male, middle-aged; he had thin blond hair and a broad nose that was peppered with old acne scars Bedford was a neatly shaven man no older than his late thirties; he had dark hair, dark skin, and dark deep-set eyes. Nothing stood out to Allie about either photo. They just looked like cops to her. She ran her eyes over the men's faces, committing them to memory.

"Anything fishy about the investigation?" she asked.

"I haven't dug in yet, but this guy"—Phoenix tapped Bedford's photo—"took a leave of absence after they declared Avery dead, and hasn't gone back to work since."

"And the other one?"

"Still on duty."

"That isn't necessarily suspicious, but I've been thinking about that green paint..." Allie tapped her chin. "I wonder if the cops missed anything else."

"I think we should pay Kirk Bedford a little visit and find out." Phoenix grinned. "Don't you?"

• • • ● • ● • • •

Phoenix parked his junker outside Bedford's place. It was an old house—the gray-blue paint was a little faded, and the concrete porch steps had some unpatched cracks—but otherwise it was as well kept as Bedford himself. The droopy, dying plants out front seemed to indicate a more recent neglect.

Paired with the low-slung November clouds, the whole scene was pretty gloomy.

They walked up to the house together, and Phoenix pressed the doorbell. A muted chime rang on the other side of the door.

"How should we do this?" Allie asked, suddenly wondering if she should've come up with a plan before they were standing on Bedford's porch. She'd already used up her Strike One. She couldn't let Daniel down again.

"However you want." Phoenix shrugged. "It's your show, Grecco. I'm just the muscle to get us in."

Allie arched a brow. "Do we have orders to use muscle to get in?"

"You've got your orders, and I have mine," he said, and before she could scold him for being evasive, the door creaked open.

Bedford peered out from the gap between the door and its frame. His cheeks were hollower than they had been in his picture, and he hadn't shaved in a few days. With sunken eyes and his brittle expression, he looked damned near ten years older than the image Allie stored in her head.

"Can I help you?"

"I think you can," Phoenix replied cheerily, shouldering the door all the way open and jostling Bedford out of the way.

"Hey!" he exclaimed as Phoenix and Allie pushed mulishly by him, barging into his den. "What the hell do you think you're doing?"

Bedford's house was dim; he'd left most of the lights off despite the overcast day. Dust had accumulated on the knickknack shelf beside the door, and the living room seemed like it hadn't been vacuumed in weeks. It had the same look as the porch—that of a once-loved home suddenly let go.

"We're PIs looking into Avery Burke's disappearance," Allie snapped. "We've got some questions for you about the investigation."

"I am a police officer," Bedford said testily, enunciating each word. Standing there in his own doorway, jostled aside by two boorish self-declared PIs, he seemed to regain some of his footing, and his fist tightened around the knob. "Get out of my house"—his voice leapt for a moment, and he dragged it back down to a conversational level—"before I have you arrested for trespassing!"

"Somehow I don't think you'll do that," Allie retorted, pinning him with her glare. "I have the funniest feeling you know more than you're willing to share about what happened to Avery Burke."

Something passed over Bedford's haggard face, but Allie couldn't quite tell if it was fear, regret, or something more complicated. "I led the investigation," he snapped back, but then he paused, and let out a tired sigh that hardly backed up his words. "I do know what happened to her. She crashed on the bridge with no seat belt on and went into the river."

"Are you sure about that? Some people don't think she's dead."

His expression fell from one of annoyance to one of pain. "Am I to understand that Lorraine hired you?"

"Yes," Allie lied. Out of the corner of her eye, she noticed that Phoenix didn't even flinch.

Bedford looked between them, then let out a last harried sigh.

"I'll speak to you for her sake," he said, "but that's it. No mother should have to endure this. If I tell you everything I know, will you get off my property?"

Allie crossed her arms. "If you tell us what we want to know, yeah."

Bedford gestured jerkily for the door. "Out on the steps, then. I didn't invite either of you in here."

They let Bedford herd them out of his living room and onto his porch, where the desiccated plants were waiting for them. He seemed to stand up a little straighter now that they were outside. Maybe the chill gave him some much-needed energy.

"Now," he began, looking unenthused but resigned, "what do you want to know?"

Allie had never been a big fan of mincing words, and she wasn't about to start now. "Tell us about the investigation. And don't spare the details."

Bedford rubbed his face with a lean hand, dragging an eyelid to the side and letting it snap back into place. "I understand why some people"— he did not specify whom, but his furrowed brow made it crystal clear—"find the particulars of this case a little suspicious. Believe me when I say I deeply respected Ms. Burke and her work, even if she didn't have many kind words to say about mine. But it was pretty obvious what happened. We couldn't find any evidence of foul play or the body. I was forced to close out the case due to lack of leads. I'm sorry," he groused, "if that's not sensational enough for you."

Allie frowned. "That was pretty vague. I said I needed details. What leads did you look into? What did Lorraine say to you about it?"

The corners of Bedford's mouth drooped into a frown to match hers. "I'm sure you know exactly what she had to say about it. She's convinced Avery never went into the river and is still out there somewhere." His shoulders slumped. "You're PIs, so I trust you know that missing Black women are less likely to be found than white women. Mrs. Burke called me many times. She wanted me to do better—as a Black officer—and find her daughter. I wish I could have." Kirk's eyes looked far away, and his already weak expression grew precariously thin. "Believe me when I tell you this isn't a case of a missing person. Just a missing body."

"Is that why you haven't gone back to work?" Allie pressed.

"Yes. I tried my best to do right by Lorraine and I couldn't. That wears on a man."

So that explained Bedford's ragged appearance and his crusty plants. "And the leads?" Allie asked him, knocking a cramp of sympathy aside. "What did you look into?"

Bedford didn't rush his answer, weighing something in his mind. "Wait here," he said, and disappeared back into his house, closing the front door behind him.

"You don't think he's gonna lock us out, do you?" Allie squinted at Phoenix, who merely shrugged.

Bedford left them loitering for only a few minutes before he stepped back out with a small leather-bound notepad in hand, closing the door quickly behind him. "There wasn't much to go on, but anything or anyone I investigated is in here." He passed the notepad over to Allie.

"Did you look into other drivers who were involved in accidents or taken in for DUIs that night?" Phoenix asked, but Allie only half-listened to the rest of their conversation as she flipped through the pad.

Bedford's notes were immaculate. Each name and number were written in a flawless hand, and even the comments that seemed to have been written in a hurry were legible. Allie raced through the pages, memorizing every stroke and margin mark she could.

Her fingers stumbled over a stapled business card. The note scribbled next to the name read *racist POS*, underlined twice. It was a name she'd heard before.

A name she'd heard earlier that day.

"Hey," Phoenix said, smacking her elbow with the back of his hand as he eyed his phone. "We gotta go. That list you were waiting for came in. We have five names."

He handed it to Allie, she handed the notepad back to Bedford, and without so much as a thank you, they left him to process his failure.

Allie ducked into the passenger's seat, her eyes already raking down the shortlist of car owners, catching on the very last one. She had brought a green car in for repairs on the twenty-first of October.

Her heart seized. There it was again—that name.

Allie didn't believe in coincidences, so she told Phoenix to drive straight to Victoria Bryant's house.

Chapter 22

Rap rap rap!

Allie pounded her knuckles on the white door, just under the wreath of fake fall leaves and faker acorns that encircled Victoria Bryant's house number, shiny burnished brass. They'd ended up back in the suburbs as the sun began to sink, puncturing the clouds with the first light and shadows they'd seen all day.

"Here we go." Phoenix exhaled, glancing at Allie out of the corner of his eye. "How are you feeling about this one?"

"Really good," she answered, the truth. She was finding it hard to stand still as they waited for someone to answer the door. Almost all the lights were on—somebody was surely home. "If it's another dead end, I'll lose it. We spent all day on this."

"Coming!" someone called from inside, and the door swung open. A petite, comely middle-aged woman peered eagerly out from beneath a bundle of platinum-blond hair.

"Are you from the homeowner's association?" she asked, and went on without waiting for either of them to answer. "I've put in at least three complaints about that woman's door! I'm glad to see someone's finally taking me seriously!"

"The neighbor's front door?" Allie and Phoenix shared an arched look.

Victoria scoffed, pointing impatiently. "Yes. Do your job and get her to repaint it! What are people going to think of the neighborhood if her door looks like that?"

Allie followed Victoria's finger to its target. The tidy flowerbed-lined house across its manicured lawn looked like perfection to her, including the door. There wasn't a dead leaf out of place.

"We're not from the homeowner's association," Allie said.

Victoria's expression darkened. "Then who are you?"

"We're investigating—"

"Where are your badges?" she demanded. "You don't look like police officers."

"We're not." Allie felt anger tightening her face, and reminded herself to keep cool. "We're private —"

"I know my rights," Victoria snapped, grabbing for the knob, making a show of shutting them out. "I don't have to talk to you. Get a warrant!"

"How's this for a warrant?" Phoenix asked, raising his foot and booting in the pristine white door.

Victoria shrilled as she leapt backward, and somewhere in the house, a tiny dog began yapping just as shrilly. Her wreath plunked onto the carpet, losing a few of its plastic acorns.

"Get out, *get out!*" she shrieked, scrambling toward the grand staircase as if someone might rush down and save her. "My husband will be home any minute! I'll call the police!"

"Are you sure they'll come?" Allie asked, casually kicking the door closed behind her. "I hear you like to cry wolf."

Phoenix locked the deadbolt emphatically, then tossed Allie a grin, lifting his eyebrows as if to ask *are you having fun yet*? And damn it. She was!

"Somebody told us you had a little fender bender with Avery Burke last month." While Phoenix blocked the doorway with his body, Allie took one step toward Victoria, who fell back against the staircase railing as if she'd been threatened with a knife. "Care to tell us what happened?"

"I didn't kill her!" Victoria squawked.

Allie stopped dead. *Not possible.* It was too easy.

"No one said that you did." Her eyes drifted to Phoenix as she said so, searching for a suggestion, but—for once—his eyes were vacant.

"Well, I didn't! I didn't kill her!" Victoria insisted again, steadying herself just before she tripped on the first stair. "We did get into a minor accident, and I did take my car in, but I had nothing to do with what happened to her."

Allie didn't give her an inch. "So we both know why I'm here, then?"

"Obviously! You're looking into that accident on the bridge."

"That's correct. Care to tell us where you come in?"

"I don't 'come in' anywhere! You said it yourself: we just had a fender bender," Victoria swore. "And it was that Burke woman's fault, not mine. She backed straight into my car!"

"Did you know her?"

"She lives around here." Victoria scowled. Then her expression defrosted the slightest bit as she amended, "She lived around here. She and I did not see eye to eye about HOA regulations."

"I don't care about your petty rivalry. I'm here to ask about Avery," Allie snapped, and took another step forward. Victoria's palms fluttered over her heart, and she let out a canned moan of dread, though the fear in her eyes was genuine. "So you saw her that night? The last night?"

"Yes. I saw her arguing with a man outside that bar. The, um—The Outlet, I think it's called."

"A man? What did he look like?"

"I don't *know*," she shouted, a burst of surprising force. Allie waited while Victoria scrambled to collect her thoughts. "He was just a man! I suppose he had hair... brown hair," she added, "combed to the side. He had on a very handsome coat, which I noticed, because his face was rough. I think he had some kind of nick right here." She pointed to the outside edge of her eyebrow.

That was Scott Dallas or Allie would eat her socks. Her pulse quickened. Now they were getting somewhere.

"And you say they argued?" she pressed, leaning in. "What were they arguing about?"

"I—I don't remember what they were saying," Victoria stuttered, shrinking, "but it seemed like a lovers' quarrel to me."

Allie thought back to Scott's *fuck you*. The insinuation he and Avery were more than coworkers had provoked him, but was this true? Had they really been involved, and—if Scott's wife and kids were even real—had he been cheating on his spouse?

"So they argued. And then what happened?" A bite-sized thrill tore through Allie. It finally felt like she was on the trail of something worth hunting down.

"The man stormed off, and Avery got in her car. And backed straight into mine."

"Why didn't you mention this to anyone?" Allie demanded.

"Well, when I ran up to get her insurance information, she seemed out of it. Distracted. She handed me a fistful of cash—right there on the sidewalk! Can you believe that? Like a gangster or something! Anyway, she handed me the money and said no one could know she was at a bar, and that she'd cover any damage to my car if I didn't say anything. It makes you wonder what she might have been up to on the side, doesn't it?"

Allie frowned sharply. "What did you think was going on there?"

Victoria's confidence seemed to wither under scrutiny. She backed off, her eyes darting between Allie and Phoenix, her jaw working silently. "Well, well, well," she stammered, clutching at the neckline of her polka-dot blouse. "Isn't it a bit suspicious that she had so much cash with her?"

"Do you know what your neighbor does for a living?" Allie's question was not particularly friendly, and Victoria all but squirmed.

"I'm not implying anything uncharitable. I just wondered..." Whatever Victoria "just wondered" got stuck in her throat.

"Come on, Victoria," Phoenix piped up, eyes gleaming. He must've been enjoying watching this suburban busybody writhe. "Tell us exactly why you think a bigshot attorney having cash is suspicious."

"Just that for a—a woman to have so many bills on hand—it could have been drugs, or..." She trailed off. Bedford's investigation may have been a bust, Allie thought, but at least his *racist POS* note hadn't been off the mark.

"Or...?" Phoenix was struggling to disguise his delight. He looked like an unsupervised kid in a candy aisle.

Victoria must have noticed, because her fearful expression hardened, and she angled her body toward Allie, making it clear Phoenix would not receive another answer. "However she got the money, she was acting weird."

Allie only had one more question. "Did Avery seem drunk to you?"

It was difficult to tell if Victoria's long pause was the result of leeriness or lying. "I don't know," she said finally, drawing herself up and firmly meeting Allie's gaze. "I couldn't tell. She was arguing with a guy in public outside a bar, and she was acting strangely. She might have been. I don't remember."

Allie shot Phoenix a meaningful look. A few drops of his glee had dried up.

"Is there anything else you're not telling me about that night?"

"Ummm..." Victoria seemed edgy. "No. I don't... I don't think so."

With a parting glare, Allie led Phoenix back out onto the front step.

Whether or not Avery had been intoxicated when she crashed, it was time to pay Scott Dallas another visit. But first, Allie wanted to check in with Daniel. Her test had gotten off to a rocky start, but now? Now she was loving this game they were playing, and if she wanted to keep her seat at the table, she needed to keep to the rules.

Chapter 23

D aniel stared at the night sky, waiting in his armchair for Grecco to arrive.

It seemed like it might rain, and a surge of November fog had made his tall windows look like frosted glass. Beyond them, New York City spread out all the way to the Atlantic, and the reflection of his gaslit fireplace was just another light among countless others. He shouldn't have much longer to wait.

Phoenix had texted that he'd dropped Grecco off at the front doors a few minutes ago. Daniel didn't really need her report—Phoenix was keeping him up to speed—but this was part of the test. He needed to know how she dealt with authority outside the office, and how she dealt with him. It was a vital part of every new operator's evaluation.

The elevator dinged, and Grecco stepped out, entering his apartment with a confident strut. Her expression—the bright eyes, the slight upward arc of her mouth—told him she was pleased.

"Have a seat." Daniel gestured to the couch, guessing Grecco wouldn't mind if they skipped the formalities.

She marched over and sat down purposefully, her posture as stiff and attentive as ever. "Sir. We followed up with some leads about green cars that had been taken in for repairs after the twentieth."

"We can get to that later," Daniel cut in when she took a breath. Grecco blinked. "First, I'd like to tell you a little more about the trial run. One of the skills we're evaluating is your ability to gather information on your own. If you're accepted, you'll often be working on cases the police can't or won't collect enough evidence about to solve."

"Like in Avery's case," Grecco offered.

"Exactly." Daniel nodded once. "Someone has to do right by the people who fall through the gaps of traditional law enforcement. That's us. I'm telling you this because I need you to understand it's not going to be Army Rangers Two Point Oh. My organization is a kind of hybrid. It's a different animal than military service, and if you had any experience in law enforcement, I'd tell you the same thing." Something flickered behind Grecco's eyes, but it vanished quickly.

"When you say it's different from the military," she echoed carefully, "what exactly do you mean?"

"In the military, soldiers follow orders to protect and secure the interests of their country. The front end of Soldiers for Hire operates similarly, only for the client. The back end serves underserved individuals at my discretion—and the General's."

"So there's no formal hierarchy or structure to it? It's just you, picking out scumbags to dismantle?" She almost seemed disappointed by the possibility of complete freedom, as did most new recruits, who longed for what they missed from their active service days.

"And the General," he reminded her, offering his most reassuring look. "There is structure, but not like you're used to. Don't get me wrong—you will still follow orders—but if an operator thinks there's a better way to get something done, I want to hear it."

"And you'll listen?" Grecco's eyebrows raised.

"The General and I have the final say, but our ultimate goal is to catch criminals. So yes. I would."

"I guess I'm a little thrown to hear you talk about the army like that, sir."

"The Rangers—the military as a whole, I guess," Daniel admitted, tenting his fingers, searching for a semiprofessional way to describe having his heart broken, "disappointed me."

Grecco's eyes darkened. That eerie flicker was back, igniting and dispersing quickly enough that she might not have realized her expression gave her away. "Me too."

"I'm not surprised you feel that way. How long did you serve?"

"Long enough that it was everything to me."

She shifted anxiously, and Daniel knew her discomfort wasn't the couch's doing. Grecco had been so defensive in the office, so ready to bolt up and storm out at the slightest intrusion into her personal life. Maybe finding common ground in their disappointment made her feel safer about opening up. That was good. It meant she was willing to make compromises—sometimes—and that she wasn't completely closed off to communication. Daniel could work with that. He gave her the time she needed to decide what to share.

"When they forced me out, it was like—it was like they made me—"

"Leave your home," Daniel finished for her.

"Yeah. Yeah, that's a good way to put it." She paused, drifting, and Daniel swore he could see her turning something over as she cocked her head. "Sir, you weren't...?"

"No, I chose to leave."

"Does it have anything to do with what happened on your last mission?"

It was as if the question had snatched him by the throat. He stared, speechless, swallowing like a fish with a hook in its mouth.

"That issue is not up for discussion," Daniel said sternly. So much for communication.

An awkward silence fell upon his home. Grecco's gaze snapped down to the tips of her boots, and the creak of couch leather was maddening in the quiet, accompanied only by the hiss of the gas fireplace. Had she been investigating him and Burke in tandem? How else could she know about that?

"I'm sorry," she said, terse but sincere, "if that was too personal, sir."

"It's fine." Grecco's furrowed brows revealed that she didn't believe him. He should have tempered his reaction. "I'm considering you in no small part due to your investigation skills. I suppose I shouldn't be surprised you know a thing or two about me. It's only fair, I guess, since I also know a thing or two about you."

"Oh?" Grecco raised an eyebrow, daring him to go on. The amber light of the fire reddened her hair, and the boldness of her expression—an expression that reminded Daniel of someone else in the most uncomfortable, unwanted way—persuaded him to continue.

"I know you started school at East Point at a very young age. I know you were adopted by Olivia and Logan Grecco. I know your dad is an ex-cop, and I'm guessing you were inspired to serve and protect because of him." A smile tugged on the corner of his mouth. "I never took you for a daddy's girl, though."

The joke didn't just fall flat—it plummeted and shattered on his floor. Grecco's firelit face twisted into a scowl, and Daniel immediately knew he'd misstepped in a big way.

"With all due respect, sir, fuck you," she snapped, leaving Daniel caught between wanting to laugh, feeling offended, and regretting that he'd squandered his headway with her on a lazy gibe. "You don't know a thing about me and you can shove your bullshit act where the sun don't shine!"

She lurched to her feet and stormed for the elevator. She crossed his apartment in large, furious strides, smoldering as she went. She stopped sharp, and—as if to slam the door on him —she punched her palm into the button.

Nothing happened.

Normally the private elevator was fast, but it must have been open on some other floor, because it didn't come to Grecco's rescue. She stood there, fuming, waiting.

And waiting.

Daniel stood from his chair. His amusement drained away as he watched Grecco's bristling back, her hunched shoulders. She really was suffering through the wait to escape him. He didn't want that—he wanted to provide her with an outlet for the abundance of anger and pain she clearly carried around. He wanted Soldiers for Hire to save her, just like starting it had once saved him. Yet he couldn't stop wondering if she might need something beyond what the back end could give her. If he let her in and she snapped—got hurt, got killed—then he would be responsible for the death of another woman. The guilt would come rushing back, drowning him, eating him up from the inside out, and he knew he couldn't survive it. Not again.

Maybe he should cut her loose and end it here.

The ding of the elevator forced his decision. Daniel pulled the hook from his throat and reminded himself how to be a commander.

"I want you to stop by Lorraine Burke's place before you talk with Dallas again," he found himself saying, and he supposed that meant she wasn't fired.

The doors slid open and Grecco stalked inside. She glared at him, holding the elevator with one hand, her other poised over the button panel. "That doesn't make any sense. Dallas is the obvious next step. Why on earth would I give Avery's mom false hope by going to talk to her?"

Daniel smiled. She could use a lesson or two in restraint, but he couldn't help liking her fire, even if it was a little more like wildfire than it was something to curl up by. "Those are your orders. You can take it or leave it."

For a few moments, Grecco just stood there, her mouth twisting into a grimace, looking like she wanted to say something less than polite.

"Yes, sir," she groused, and pulled her arm in as the doors closed.

Not a second later, Daniel heard a muffled scream from inside the elevator, followed by a battery of some very creative profanity that made him laugh out loud.

Chapter 24

The dim gray morning with its thick, low clouds made New York feel chill and damp. Undeterred by the gloom, Phoenix's clunky car puttered up to its destination, a modest brick building stitched to the sidewalk by a cobblestone path. The yard's small trees looked frail without their leaves.

"Looks like it's time for your first crying mom duty." Phoenix shut up the noisy engine with a turn of the key. "If you ask me, Grecco, this is the worst part of the job."

Allie only grunted in reply, keen to get this ordeal over with. She wasn't exactly a delicate conversationalist, but talking to a dead woman's mother isn't something you fuck up casually, especially if you're a wannabe vigilante in danger of bombing her first and only test. Last night's spat with Daniel had already put Allie in a rank mood.

"Are you still moping about getting your knuckles slapped?" Phoenix asked, reading her mind in the most annoying way possible. "Did he at least tell you more about the business? Give any new instructions?"

Allie hooked her fingers on the door handle and pinned him with a glare. "He said some..." She couldn't find a word. "Things," she decided, heat swirling at the back of her neck as she spat out the flimsy excuse. "I don't wanna talk about it."

"I was just asking. I'm supposed to be your mentor."

"Then you should know when to take a hint and back off."

"Or"—he didn't seem like he was going to let it go—"I should be up in your face until you tell me how things went."

Rolling her eyes, Allie threw open the car door and got out. She didn't want to think about how she'd stormed out of Daniel's stupidly posh apartment; she didn't want to remember the humiliation of waiting for the damned elevator two heartbeats after she'd cursed out her boss; and she definitely didn't want to discuss her failure with Phoenix, who had somehow successfully passed *his* test, if he'd even been given one.

The driver's side door clicked open just as Allie was turning to slam hers, and Phoenix's head popped up across the top of the car. "C'mon, Grecco, tell me what went down. I can probably translate from Danielese to English for you."

Allie paused, sparing Phoenix's passenger door from her wrath. He had a point. And though it took her by surprise—and though he was still a constant annoyance—it felt good to talk to Phoenix. Not *good* good, maybe, but venting her anger to someone else provided a strange relief. Allie had always assumed people would run to the hills after one glimpse of what she was really like, but Phoenix and Daniel seemed to stick around, no matter how ugly her stories were.

She shut the door more tamely than she'd planned. "I don't know if I need anything translated. It wasn't anything he said."

"Ah-ha, so it was something he did." Phoenix spread his elbows across the top of the silvery car and propped his chin in his hands. It was a disarmingly chummy gesture, and Allie felt her nose wrinkle. He looked like a schoolgirl at a sleepover. "Did he give you the Disappointed Dad Stare? You know, like this?" Phoenix's eyes narrowed and his mouth compressed into a thin frown—an accurate impression of Daniel's displeasure.

Despite everything, a little smile crept across Allie's face. "No," she said. "He didn't stare."

"So what was it? He tell you off about Kim de la Rosa?"

"No..." Allie stuffed her hands into her jacket pockets, fiddling with her notepad and pencil, itching to experiment with sharing her feelings. "Like I told you, it wasn't anything *he* said."

"What does that mean?" His face lit up. "Is it something *you* said?"

"Well..." She examined her boot laces. "I might have sort of told him to fuck off."

Phoenix's guffaw whipped her glare back up. Delight twinkled in his eyes and his head bobbed like some kind of gangly bird as he laughed. "You are my hero! You gotta tell me what he did to deserve this. I have to know!"

She did. Standing there outside Lorraine Burke's apartment building, using Phoenix's junker as a coffee table, Allie couldn't figure out which half of her emotions to reveal and which to squirrel away. So she told Phoenix everything—from the doomed attempt to ask about Daniel's last mission to the "daddy's girl" joke that had sent her storming out of her CO's presence without being dismissed. Phoenix didn't make a peep as she talked. He seemed content to wait there, arms still perched on the cold tinny roof of his car, taking it all in.

"I see..." Phoenix rubbed his chin in contemplation. "That still doesn't explain your sourpuss face."

"I just feel like no matter what I do, I mess everything up."

"Look, I can't tell you what last night was about, but I can say jokes like that are out of Daniel's character. Maybe it really was an honest mistake, or maybe it's all part of your test. But if he sent you on your way and didn't chew you out for insubordination, I think you can wiggle that stick out of your ass and unclench, Cadet Grecco."

A truck with a noisy muffler choked by them while Allie digested Phoenix's advice. Clawing her way back into this boys' club couldn't be so easy, could it? She had willfully flouted the chain of command and popped off like a fresh recruit. There should've been mandated apologies, pages of groveling, official censure. There was no way Daniel would forgive her so painlessly.

"Are you sure?" she pressed. "You don't think I ruined my chances?"

"Nah," Phoenix drawled. "Daniel's stoic, not subtle. If he was done with you, you'd know."

That was... encouraging, Allie supposed.

"How come that set you off, anyway?" Phoenix rapped out a lazy beat on the roof to show her how uninvested he was in the answer. "If you don't mind me asking."

Allie did mind, but she curbed the instinct to tell him, too, to fuck off. "I don't know. Maybe it's..."

"Go on."

"I'm really, *really* not a daddy's girl." She pulled her hands from her pockets to crook two fingers, squeezing air quotes around *daddy*, then pushed on, too anxious to give Phoenix the chance to react. "My relationship with that asshole isn't great. It's pretty shit, actually."

It felt like enough, and she hadn't meant to say anything else. But before she could bite her tongue or step on her own foot, Allie found herself halfway through a rundown of her piss-poor childhood. She told Phoenix about Logan's alcoholism, his verbal abuse, how he'd shipped her off to military school the second Olivia succumbed to cancer. She even admitted how long it had been since they last spoke.

"Does Daniel know about any of that?" Phoenix asked when she'd finished. He looked as comfortable as ever, but he'd straightened up as her story darkened, letting one arm slip from the roof and lifting his chin from his hands.

Allie, meanwhile, had slumped forward, propping her shoulder against the hard support of the door frame. She shrugged, feeling the cold seeping from the metal and into her coat. So much honesty had left her in a murky, alien fugue, like she'd just been sucker punched by a trainee and hadn't yet found her bearings. "I guess he didn't. I think it's safe to assume he has some idea now."

"That sucks." Phoenix shot her a sympathetic glance out of the corner of his eye. Only his fingertips were hanging on the roof now. "Sorry about the bad childhood."

"Yeah, well." It had felt vindicating to lay Logan out in the open. But now it was over, and Phoenix was giving her some kind of mortifying, caring look, and she felt stifled. Allie was about to suggest they head into Lorraine's when Phoenix spoke up.

"If it helps—and it probably doesn't—I get it," he offered. "I don't have the greatest relationship with my parents either. They cut me off after Daniel and I joined the army."

Allie's ears perked at the new detail. She'd been wondering about the origins of their bond for almost two years, and now here Phoenix was, spilling secrets as if they were friends. *Were* they friends? Allie's internal snarl of *no!* didn't sound convincing, and it was a little too much to think about, so she plowed on. "You and Daniel go way back, huh?"

"Since high school." Even further back than she'd expected. "I was a wild one at the time."

"Claiming to be a more docile version of yourself now?"

"You have no idea." He laughed, and the swell of discomfort drained away. "I was always on the lookout for reasons to get out of the house and away from my parents. Looking back, though, I now see that they were usually crappy reasons."

Allie couldn't quite figure out what to do with her posture now that she was listening instead of defending. *Casual* seemed to work for Phoenix, so she turned her body to face him and stuck both elbows on the roof, mirroring her mentor. "A wild child straightened out by the iron fist of a drill sergeant. Yeah," she agreed. "Sounds a little too familiar."

"I'm glad that's the story of my childhood, though, because it's how I met Daniel. Picture this, if you will: I was hanging with the no-goods at school, sitting in the alley behind the 7-Eleven, terrorizing innocent bystanders."

Allie gave him a judgmental squint. "Why am I not surprised?"

"Would it surprise you to hear that Daniel was one of those bystanders, and he wasn't taking any of my shit?"

She snorted. "Not at all."

"He knocked me on my ass. And the thing was, he didn't even hit me—just gave me that look and read me the riot act. He was the first person I ever respected. It changed everything for me. It even changed how I looked at my parents and how they saw me. It was like they appreciated me more if a kid like Daniel wanted to be friends with me. Like maybe I wasn't a total fuckup, after all."

"That... that sounds a bit..."

"Fucked up?" He grinned. "I mean, don't get me wrong—they were totally right. I didn't give a damn about the army back then. I only signed up because Daniel did. I think that pissed off my folks more than anything," he mused, and backed off the car to huff a warm breath into his fists. "Not the army. Not that I dropped out of school to enlist. Because they forced me to choose, and I chose Daniel."

An ancient, uncomfortable ache caused Allie to shift her balance.

"They never forgave me for that." He shook his head, and the odd smile dented deeper into his face, bemused and sorry at once. "Long story short: I made my choice and Daniel became my new family."

Hearing Phoenix talk about Daniel like this twisted Allie's insides with fear. She knew they were thick as thieves, but she hadn't come close to appreciating the extent of their brotherhood. Maybe cozying up to Phoenix was a bad idea, she thought. Maybe she should ease off the gas and back out of this budding whatever-it-was. Matthew and Judd had taught her that lesson, and she wasn't interested in inserting herself between two mutually obsessed military men ever again.

"I haven't really talked to my dad since." His bitter chuckle interrupted Allie's descent into her head. "My mom's called me, what... a grand total of twice. Once right before I shipped out on my first real mission and once after the last one nearly killed me."

The thread of her anxiety snapped like a rotted violin string. "Nearly *what* now?" she squawked.

"Umm... I might be slightly exaggerating. Let's just say that I had my ass stuck in the hospital with a back full of lead and a fistful of discharge papers."

"Whoa," fell out of Allie's mouth before she could think better of it. She'd never been injured in the line of duty. Not physically—by enemy forces, that is—and the thought of being so vulnerable and dependent on someone else tangled up her guts.

Suddenly *whoa* felt like such a stupid thing to say. It hung inadequately in the air between them, like a stench that wouldn't fade.

"Cat got your tongue?" Phoenix asked, not without some amusement.

Allie struggled to rustle up a response that wasn't callous or dismissive. Her silence probably felt callous and dismissive.

"I don't really know what to say, Phoenix. That sucks," she blurted when nothing else seemed right. She wanted to end their chat, close up these soft scabs, but didn't know how to exit kindly. She only knew how to stomp off or snap *go away*. "Sorry about the hospital stay. And your parents. And the discharge."

Phoenix's bark of laughter was abrupt, but at least it sounded honest. He wasn't offended by much. "Get your own lines, Grecco. Do you want to know what happened?"

Allie shrugged, sticking her hands back into her pockets, their most comfortable home.

"Let's just say that Daniel owes me. I wasn't even assigned to my last mission. He was, and I volunteered."

"Can you even do that?" Allie thought back to all the rejections she'd received whenever she asked to be deployed overseas. Maybe Phoenix had earned his nepotism.

"It wasn't uncommon for us," he said. Allie's breath was getting heavier. "You may have noticed we work well together, especially as part of a larger team. Our CO knew better than to split us up."

Damn him, now she wanted to hear more! "If you were such a dream team, something must have gone seriously sideways to take you out of action," Allie needled, slipping in a backhanded compliment to sweeten the pot. "Are you going to tell me or not?"

"I'm getting there, Grecco, damn! It's a little stupid, so don't make fun of me, okay?" He didn't wait for a response, but at least he didn't make her pinky swear. "I won't bore you with the classified details," he began. "We came under unexpected fire in a bad situation. Daniel was ahead of the squad, planting an explosive, his whole ass hanging out. He jumped up, raced for cover, and suddenly —*whammo!* Dropped to the floor like a sack of Yukon Golds."

"Was he hit?"

"Nope, though he scared the shit out of me; I thought he was KIA. Fucker really set up a bomb, turned around, and twisted his ankle!" Phoenix laughed again, but it sounded phlegmy this time, like sawdust had stirred in his lungs. "Like a little old grandma."

Allie tried to imagine it—tried to imagine the chaos, the smell of gunfire, a younger Daniel's breath slamming in his lungs as he hit the ground under a spray of bullets. Bad falls happened even to the best of the best. But Allie had always assumed that lackluster version of "best" was reserved for people like her—not people like Daniel, who seemed hardwired against the mere suggestion of taking a wrong step.

"Was he spotted?"

"Well, he started crawling away like a worm, so sure. He was spotted." Phoenix sucked in his middle, tensing his jaw, as if he needed to brace himself before reliving his injury. "If I had any sense, I'd have just snatched up the carpet or something. Dragged him to us. Didn't occur to me at the time."

Allie frowned. "Oh, you didn't..."

"Oh, but I did. I hustled to that sorry-ass little worm and threw myself over him."

This was even harder to imagine. An uncharitable voice inside her snickered that Phoenix was lying, that there was no way this annoying loser had ever been capable of so much self-sacrifice. But Allie smothered that voice as a quieter, clearer one insisted his eyes were honest, and his story was true.

"Phoenix," she wheezed, succumbing to an inexplicable need to catch her breath. Her palms had wandered out of her pockets to clutch her lapels, and their extra weight dug her collar into the back of her neck. "You saved his life. Why would you think that's stupid?"

"Unfortunate thing is, Grecco, I happen to be made of meat. It took a lot longer for those damned bombs to go off than I anticipated... We both got riddled. At least my meat's not as squishy as Daniel's, because the bullets missed his important organs."

"Thank god!"

"Yeah, God's the best, right? So I guess I'm supposed to thank Satan for not being that lucky, huh?" He went on to share how he was badly injured, lost his place in the unit, and—after spending a lot of time in the hospital—was let go from the army with an addiction to pain killers that haunted him for years.

His decision to jump into the line of fire had saved Daniel's life, but it had also separated him from his one and only friend, and cast him out from the only true home he'd ever known.

"You could have died, Phoenix. You know that, right?" A shiver ripped through Allie. Standing out there beside his car, listening to the story of how he'd ruined his life for someone else, she didn't particularly care if it was a reaction to the truth or to the cold. "You understand you basically sacrificed yourself?"

"When you put it like that, you make me seem like a hero or something."

"Are you?"

"Hell no! I'm not," he hurried to say, and all but launched himself away from the car.

Allie looked up. The sky had steeped a darker gray, more like charcoal than fog, and it was threatening to drizzle. A gust of wind rattled the naked birch trees. As Phoenix turned toward the apartment complex, Allie fought against her imagination, desperate not to visualize weeping red holes in the back of his coat.

"Fat-chewing time's over, Grecco. I'm freezing my nuts off. Let's get up there," he said, already stalking his big strides onto the sidewalk and toward the stairs.

As they headed up the path to Lorraine Burke, Allie got the sense Phoenix liked the title *hero* more than he'd ever admit.

Chapter 25

I t was darker inside the unassuming building than outside. The front door was unlocked and there was no entry code, so they easily made their way up the stairwell to Lorraine Burke's second-floor apartment.

"Be careful with this one," Phoenix warned as they stepped up to 204. "Daniel doesn't mind if you rough up assholes, but he's got a problem with upsetting victims or their families."

Allie scoffed. The more she learned about Daniel, the tenser she felt, but Phoenix's insinuation that she'd harass a grieving mother overpowered her nerves. "I'm not gonna punch Avery's mom, if that's what you're worried about."

"You're still looking a little moody." Phoenix assessed her face. "I can do this one, if you want to take a back seat."

Holding eye contact, she reached past him to knock on the door with more confidence than she felt. But before her knuckles could connect, it swung open.

Lorraine Burke was a head shorter than Allie, dressed in a conservative calf-length skirt and a knitted sweater. Laugh lines nested around her nose, and well-defined crow's-feet suggested she was used to smiling. She wasn't now, though. She looked tired enough to fall into a grave.

"Can I help you?" she asked, her gaze passing between Allie and Phoenix.

Allie looked to Phoenix for guidance, but he just tipped his head incrementally toward Lorraine as if to say *well, go ahead*. It was Allie's show—even the talking parts.

She cleared her throat. "Are you Lorraine Burke?" Their host nodded. "We're investigators looking into your daughter's case. We have some questions, if that's okay."

Lorraine's eyes brightened, and she stepped back to open the door, gesturing for them to enter. "It's more than okay. Come in, come in!"

Allie hadn't expected the mother of a woman who'd been missing for almost three weeks to feel so talkative, but she stepped into the cozy apartment, Phoenix right behind her.

"Shoes off, please," Lorraine requested, clicking the door shut. "You can hang your coats on the hook."

Allie and Phoenix kept their jackets on, but paused to unlace their shoes and leave them by the door. On socked feet, Allie followed Lorraine into the living room, toward the vibrant floral print couch. A painted metal sculpture of butterflies in flight adorned the living room wall, along with plenty of framed photos—most of them of Avery. Allie's eyes traced a lifelong story of her missing person: Avery pouting in water wings, Avery hovering over a messy stove, Avery tossing her graduation cap into the air, Avery smiling beside a crowd of family members. Lorraine Burke had transformed her entire house, it seemed, into a living monument of her only child.

"You know, I was looking into hiring someone myself," Lorraine said, directing her guests to sit side by side on the couch. The soft cushions threatened to suck Allie in, and she struggled to hold her hip bone away from Phoenix's with limited success. "Someone upstairs must have heard me and delivered the two of you to my door. How did you hear about my daughter's case?"

"It came across our boss's desk, and he assigned us to look into it." She scooted to the edge of the sofa. From her new position, Allie had a good view of the trees outside, still hanging on to a few dry, yellowed leaves.

"I can assume you work for the government?" Lorraine lowered herself into a matching chair across from them.

"No, we're… from a private agency," Allie mumbled. "We're not NYPD."

Lorraine's tired eyes darkened at the mention of the police. "Well, I figured that much. I haven't heard anything from them since they closed Ave's case. I've tried calling their office, but they just keep insisting there's nothing to be done about it!" Her voice, once gracious, shook. She sank back into her chair with a fatigued huff, pausing to calm herself. "It's about time somebody willing to make an honest effort took over."

"You don't think the police were thorough." Allie's question was not a question.

"Absolutely not. They barely searched her car! The only person who would talk to me was the officer in charge of the investigation. If my Avery were a blond cheerleader, they would have flipped a few more stones before writing it off as an accident, I'll tell you that much. Ave's out there somewhere," Lorraine swore, eyes watering, voice steadying itself on her daughter's name.

Allie wasn't sure what to say, so she nodded, allowing a respectful silence to engulf the room.

"Do you have a reason to believe she's still alive?" Phoenix had waited for Lorraine to finish dabbing her eyes before pressing on.

"I don't know what to tell you other than 'a mother knows.' Please, if there's anything I can do to help you with your search, I'll do it. I just have such a strong feeling that she's not gone."

Lorraine's plea tugged heartstrings Allie didn't know she still had. She tried to focus, tried to file through the list of case details locked inside her head, but she couldn't stop wondering what Olivia Grecco would have done if it had been *her* daughter's body thrown into the Hudson instead.

Would Mom have taken the police report at face value, or would she have kept hope alive? Logan, she was sure, would've believed whatever his buddies in the force told him. He probably would've been relieved.

She'd like to think that Mom wouldn't have given up on her so easily. But if she was honest with herself: Allie didn't know.

"Well, you don't have to convince us to look into it, Ms. Burke," Allie assured her. "We're trying to find out anything the police may have forgotten to ask. Was there anything you didn't mention to the investigators? Was Avery acting different before she…" Allie hesitated. Lorraine had used the present tense. "Disappeared?"

"Why would I keep that to myself?"

Allie chose her next words carefully. Lorraine Burke was probably suffering from a bad case of desperate thinking, but she was eager to talk to them—something that couldn't be said for most of the witnesses they'd interviewed. Allie wasn't about to destroy their chance to find Avery's remains by antagonizing the person who had been closest to her.

"Was she nervous about anything?" she asked as diplomatically as she could. "Did she seem scared?"

Lorraine shook her head. "No, no, nothing like that. She called me on the nineteenth—a Thursday —and everything seemed fine."

"Did Avery have any enemies? People who might want to hurt her?"

Lorraine gave another sharp, cynical chuff, pursing her lips. "You know what my daughter does for a living, I'm sure. Ave steps on *plenty* of toes. I have a hard time keeping up with her when she gets started with the lawyer lingo, and the stories she tells me about her clients... they're just terrible to listen to. I don't know how she does it all day," Lorraine whispered, half in disbelief and half in admiration, as if Avery might overhear them from the other room.

"Did one of her clients maybe hold a grudge?"

"Oh, I don't think so. She protects her clients like a bear with her cub. You should see the pile of Christmas cards Ave gets. Thank-yous, flowers, baby pictures..." Lorraine's soft smile eroded into a forbidding stare. "But I'm sure some of the folks she's gone up against don't feel so charitable. I don't know if any of them would go as far as to hurt her. The other lawyers at her office would know better than me."

Allie sat up straighter, ignoring the way Phoenix knocked his knee against hers. She didn't need his prompting to pick up on this chance. "Do you have any specific suggestions about who else we should talk to? People who would have known what was going on with her personal life? Friends, colleagues... a boyfriend, maybe?"

She studied Lorraine's face. If Avery and Scott Dallas really had a lover's spat outside The Outlet,

Avery's mother might have information she hadn't freely shared.

"I can give you contact information for some of her friends," Lorraine offered. "I'm sure they would be more than willing to talk to you. As for boyfriends..." Allie held her breath through Lorraine's thoughtful pause. "She started seeing someone recently, but I couldn't tell you his name. She won't say much about him."

Allie's pulse sped up, and she sat forward another few inches on the couch, escaping Phoenix's kneecap and the cushion's spongy embrace. "How much do you know about this mystery boyfriend?"

"Like I said, not much."

"Even if it seems insignificant, anything you can tell us will help."

Lorraine tapped a finger against her eyebrow and dwelled on it, not without a little displeasure. "Oh, the usual things a daughter tells her mother, I'm sure. She really likes him, she has a good feeling about this one, et cetera. But she isn't ready for me to meet him—or know a single thing about him, apparently." Allie got the feeling it was a discussion Avery had dodged more than once. "All I know is that he works in law."

Allie hurried to dig the notebook and stubby pencil out of her jacket. "And how long had they been seeing each other?" she asked as she scribbled down *secret boyfriend—Scott Dallas?*

Lorraine hummed thoughtfully. "A few months. Two at most."

"That's a long time to be dating a guy and not mention his name," Phoenix murmured, whistling lowly as Allie scratched out a few more notes.

"That's exactly what I said to Ave!" Lorraine threw an exasperated hand into the air. "This man must really be something, one way or another. She's never been so secretive about dating someone before. She doesn't usually shut me out of her life like that."

Allie got the feeling that special something about Avery's mystery guy might be *married with two kids*.

"We're very close, Ave and me," Lorraine went on. "I'm just—I'm so glad the two of you dropped in. Nobody but Officer Bedford seems to care what the NYPD is hiding."

Allie looked up from her notepad. "Are we talking about Kirk Bedford?"

"Yes, that's him. He's a kind soul, isn't he?"

"We spoke to him. He, um..." Allie wasn't sure how to deliver such a weighty secondhand apology. "He said to tell you he's sorry," she rasped, barely finishing before Phoenix's knee smacked hers a little less kindly than the last times.

Lorraine sighed, her shoulders dropping as if *sorry* had deflated her, even as poorly as Allie had said it. "The only person of color on that case and they shut him down," she lamented. The criticism was plain in her voice. "He worked so hard to find her, he had a mental breakdown, do you know that?"

Lorraine's image of Kirk Bedford didn't quite match up with the haggard man they'd spoken to yesterday. He'd seemed exhausted and remorseful, yeah. Maybe even a little testy after they'd invited themselves into his house. But he'd been perfectly able to chat about the case with them. If he really had been on the verge of breakdown, Allie hadn't seen the signs.

"I didn't know," she said.

"That poor man. He wanted to bring Ave home so badly. But the department made him close the case and take a leave of absence. I don't think they want him looking into it anymore."

Allie and Phoenix exchanged a quick look of suspicion. Bedford had indicated he'd requested the time off—he hadn't mentioned anything about the department forcing him away.

"May I ask who told you about that?"

"Officer Bedford did, of course. He was in contact with me for about a week after the case closed, but then he stopped answering my calls." Lorraine shook her head, full of disgust and pity all at once. "I called the precinct, but they wouldn't patch me through. I wish he had asked me to leave him be, but I think I understand."

Maybe he had just wanted Lorraine off his back, Allie supposed. Maybe he couldn't handle the stress of telling her Avery was never coming home.

One thing was certain: she needed more information about Kirk Bedford.

"It sounds like you two really made a connection," Allie added mildly.

The ghost of a smile turned up Lorraine's mouth. "I was a wreck those first few days. His encouragement meant the world to me. He told me that I should never lose hope, that it wasn't over until it was over. He said that if Avery had passed on, someone would have found some trace of her. Poor dear, he tried so hard. If I had another chance to speak with him, I'd tell him he did everything he could."

Maybe Lorraine was confused, clinging to any conceivable reason her daughter had never been recovered. But the way she spoke about the investigation, it sounded like she thought there was some kind of conspiracy going on.

"Are you saying someone wanted him to stop looking for your daughter?" Phoenix asked.

"I'm saying it all smells a little fishy, doesn't it?" Lorraine grimaced as if someone was holding a plate of that fishiness under her nose.

"What is?" Allie wondered out loud.

"That almost no one besides Officer Bedford investigated, that they still haven't found a trace of her... and the fact they told me Avery was last seen coming out of a bar! As if I'm supposed to believe that," she puffed, crossing her arms.

Allie still thought they were looking for a body, but...

"Was that something Avery wouldn't normally have done?" Her pencil waited at the ready, poised above her notepad. Avery's last sighting outside The Outlet was an established point in the case's timeline. But if they couldn't trust the police investigation—if they couldn't take the official report for granted—it would change everything.

The question seemed to take Lorraine off guard. "Ah, no. We're Latter-day Saints," she explained, blinking away her surprise. "We don't drink alcohol."

"I'm sorry. I'd heard that," Allie lied, fumbling to recover their lost rapport. "I didn't want to assume you both practiced the same way."

"No offense taken." Lorraine shot her a small smile as proof. "My daughter isn't always one for following rules, religious or otherwise. But we're in agreement about this one. Even if she was seen outside that bar, she wasn't in it. She wasn't drinking. Much less drinking and driving."

Lorraine Burke and Scott Dallas had given contradictory statements, and only one of them could be right. While it was possible Avery might've been laxer with rules than her mother knew, if Allie had to pick a liar, she'd put all her money on Scott. He'd hidden the fact he'd supposedly seen Avery drunk from the police; he'd hidden her Mormonism, if he'd even known about it; and Allie hadn't bought his "spare the family" line. Everything about him was too slick, too convenient.

And Allie still didn't like him for being a damned lawyer, or for wearing that prissy coat.

Allie asked Lorraine a few more questions to be polite, and then she and Phoenix took their leave, promising to let her know if they found anything, and to stop by again if they thought of anything else to ask.

Descending the stairwell at a trot, ignoring Phoenix's suggestion they race, Allie wondered if she should check in with Daniel. She was surely supposed to, but her desire for answers was starting to rival her desire for the release of violence. She didn't want to jeopardize her mission or her acceptance test, but she was itching to find out what role Scott Dallas had played in Avery's disappearance, if any.

This couldn't wait. She had to talk with Dallas again. Whether or not she was going to talk with her fists, though, remained to be seen.

Chapter 26

Allie's boot heels clomped loudly, unpleasantly, against the polished granite of the business building. She and Phoenix had ridden the elevator to Scott's law firm office, and she was scanning the doorplates for their suite.

"I'll give you as much time to get in as I can," Phoenix reminded her, "so whatever you gotta get out of Scott, do it fast."

Allie nodded, watching the suite numbers climb.

In the end, she had called Daniel to update him. It turned out to be the best move, since he'd not only given her permission to proceed, but said she could use as much force as she thought was necessary. At first, it had seemed like an exciting opportunity to vent some rage on a callous jerk, but on the car ride there—as she'd been brought closer and closer to the reality of knocking Scott down again—a knot had grown, cold and dense, in the pit of her stomach. Allie's last bout of violence had felt less than cathartic once she realized it might have sabotaged her test and disappointed the CO. It had felt like shit.

Could she determine the "necessary" amount of force? Allie had never needed to consider it before. But Daniel was willing to trust her, and she wasn't going to let him down again.

It had dawned upon her somewhere between floors three and four. Allie wanted to pass her test and earn Daniel's approval more than she wanted to punch Scott, and that in itself was an achievement.

"That's it," Phoenix said, pointing to a frosted glass door.

Allie forced herself to slow down. "So what is your distraction plan, exactly?"

He shrugged. "We'll see when we get in there. I'll just wing it."

"Phoenix—!"

"Hey, come on. Who's the expert vigilante here?" he asked, earning himself a pair of crossed arms and a highly doubtful look. "You focus on sneaking in and just let me do my thing, okay?"

"Fine," she snapped, whirling back toward the frosted glass. "But if you screw this up for me, I'll kick your ass."

That said, she pulled the door open.

The office lobby reeked of lawyers: dry cleaning, printer paper, and cologne bereft of any shred of charm. It was all warm wood and cream-colored walls, interrupted only by a few plush chairs and a shiny firm decal stuck up behind the front desk.

Allie knew Phoenix wasn't exaggerating his gifts of distraction, but she sincerely hoped he wasn't going to fly by the seat of his pants.

The man behind the desk greeted them pleasantly. "Good afternoon. Can I help you?"

Allie was about to try and BS her way into—what? Getting the secretary to leave? Getting permission to wander into the back of the law office? Luckily, Phoenix shouldered past her, effecting the cool and confident swagger of someone who knew exactly what he was there for.

"I'm Detective Murphy and this is my assistant." He nodded toward Allie. "The NYPD conducted an investigation into the death of one of your former employees a few weeks ago. Avery Burke. I have a few routine follow-up questions for you."

When he stepped up to the desk, Allie lagged behind him, her eyes on the hallway just to the left. As Phoenix bamboozled the receptionist with rapid-fire questions, Allie slipped right past them and into the depths of the office.

It was quiet in the bowels where the lawyers worked, door after door after door. She was starting to get worried they had the wrong building when she spied it: *Scott Dallas*. His name frowned at her in officious black typeset, tacked neatly over dark wood.

Slowly depressing the handle, she opened the heavy door on silent hinges. A perfect office waited on the other side—the wide desk, the client chairs, the diplomas on the wall—and there, right in the middle, was Scott Dallas. *Just like the sign said*, Allie thought with a smirk. He was standing behind his desk with his back to her, his nose buried in an open folder.

Allie stepped in with a malicious smile corkscrewed across her face.

"Hello again," she said, and shut the door.

Scott whirled around. "I thought I told you not to—"

He sucked in a sharp breath as he saw Allie, dropping the folder. Papers slouched across the somber gray carpet. "Son of a... how the hell did you get in here?" he demanded, leaving his papers where they'd fallen. "If you think I won't call the police—"

"I have a few more questions for you, Scott. You know... more of what we talked about last time we met. Do you remember what we talked about?" Allie asked, staring him down.

Scott fell silent, probably deciding whether to threaten her with the cops or a trumped-up lawsuit. She hoped he was remembering her fist in his stomach.

"I do," was all he said, "and I answered your questions already."

"Well, I think you lied to me. Because I heard Avery was Mormon. You know what that means, Scott? It means she didn't drink. Ever." Allie advanced on Scott's large wooden desk. He didn't back away, but he eyed her with an open suspicion that suggested he wanted to.

"Do you think she was the first daughter to hide things from her mother?" He scoffed, lip curling in contempt. "Why would she tell her devout family that she drank? Please. Maybe you ought to go back to school—take a few night classes—before you stroll into a law office with flimsy claims that even a high school journalist would've known to fact-check."

Allie's fury was stirring, its warmth rising under her skin. Her fingers clenched into a tight fist before she forced them to relax, uncurling them one by one. She wasn't going to let this escalate to blows. She was going to handle it in a way that Daniel would approve of—the way a real back-end operator would.

"That's very cute, Scott. The thing is..." She let him stew in the tension, dragging out her pause, searching his face for a clue she'd struck interrogational gold. "Someone saw your little argument outside the bar."

"Me? I didn't argue with—" Allie cut him off midsentence.

"I'm sorry. Did I say arguing? I meant you were seen fighting with your coworker that night."

"I wasn't."

"Are you saying you weren't fighting with Avery or that Avery was more than your coworker?"

"What?"

"Well, you see, Scott," Allie watched his nostrils flare, feeling with every second that she was zeroing in on her mark, her hunter's instincts baying to go in for the kill. "I was told your argument was more of a quarrel. A lover's quarrel."

A furious flush rose in his face, and a tendon appeared on his neck. "Whoever you talked to is full of shit."

"And I think *you're* full of shit!" Her temper threatened to boil over. "Lorraine told me Avery was seeing someone, and I think that person was you."

"That's it," Scott growled, stalking around his desk. "I'm not going to stand for this. You barge into my office, accusing me of cheating on my wife?" He grabbed for Allie's arm, managing to catch it before she could pull it away. "You're going to leave," he commanded, dragging her toward the door, "and if you ever harass me at work, or at home, or anywhere ever again, I'm going to litigate you and whatever agency you work for into oblivion!"

His fingers dug into her upper arm in a way that reminded her of another pair of hands, and Allie's training took over her reflexes. Seizing Scott's wrist, she yanked his hand off her, using his surprise to spin him around on a heel and shove him across his desk. He made a meaty thump as his body connected and she wrenched his arms behind his back.

"If you scream," Allie menaced in a whisper, mashing his cheek into the polished wood, "if you even sneeze, I'll gouge that eye right out of your head."

"You're insane!" he blurted, voice trembling as he held it at bay. The eye in question—the one below the scarred eyebrow—rolled up to look at her. "You're out of your damned mind!"

She tightened her grip around his wrists, crossing them tighter over the small of his back. "Tell me the truth, Scott. No bullshit this time."

"I don't have to tell you anything! I'll call security!"

She twisted his arm hard enough to elicit a hiss of pain. It was almost as satisfying as knowing she was about to squeeze the full story out of him, one way or another. "You can make this easy or hard, Scott," she told him, low and dangerous. "And if I'm honest, I'm hoping you'll go with the second option."

"What do you want from me?"

"I want the truth, and I'll ask you for it one more time. Did you have a thing going on with Avery?"

"I did, okay? Yes," he groaned softly against the desk. "We were having an affair. Is that what you wanted to hear?"

His admission hung in the close quarters of the office, and for a moment, Allie couldn't quite believe that he'd finally admitted it, that she'd finally cracked something about this case.

"How long?"

"Just over two months," he offered without hesitation.

"Mormon girls approve of infidelity? You sure Avery was aware of this two-month affair, or were your affections a little more one-sided, you sick fuck?"

"No! No," he stammered, squirming in her clutches like a lizard caught by a cat. "It was consensual. She wanted more. That was the problem—she didn't know about my wife. I told her..." Scott choked to hold in a yelp as Allie hauled him up just enough to slam him again. "I told her my parents wouldn't approve. Because"—he winced as Allie rubbed his cheekbone into the desk, chafing the thin skin—"because of her race. I told her that's why we had to keep it a secret. But I swear to god, I never forced her, never."

There was another silence as Allie considered her next move. She'd gotten what she'd wanted— cooperation. While her blood was running hot and she'd enjoyed retaliating against Scott's manhandling, she was unsure if slamming her person of interest into the desk had crossed Daniel's unspoken line.

In an uncharacteristic show of mercy, Allie stepped back, releasing Scott. Lurching upright, he scrambled to put the desk between them, his eyes wide and his perfect hair pushed up at a cartoonish angle. She pinned him in place with a stern glare.

"Start talking." Allie moved to block the door, ready to counter any sign of attack or escape before she was finished with him. "And remember, Scott: the truth."

Scott braced one palm on the desk, lifting the other in a placating gesture. His voice was clawing to regain its composure, but his whole frame was shaking inside its dapper suit. "I lied about her being drunk, okay? She wasn't drinking. She didn't drink."

"Go on."

"And we did argue that night," he said hurriedly, stuffing his crooked tie back into his jacket.

"What was the fight about?"

"It was about us. I ended things with her. I didn't want my wife to find out, and I lied to the police because I didn't want to be considered a suspect. How would that look? A man having an affair with his coworker calls it off the night she dies?" He shook his head. "I would've been toast, and I didn't do it, so yeah. Sure. I left a few things out."

"You interfered with a police investigation," Allie corrected him. "You weren't worried about being caught in your lie? Didn't you care about finding out what happened to her?"

Scott shrugged one shoulder. "It was just an accident. A sad accident, but an accident."

Allie's teeth were grinding away deep inside her jaw with every callous word of indifference. Scott barely seemed upset his lover was dead. Maybe it struck him as convenient. The thought enraged her. She wanted to give him hell, to break his face on his own furniture, but she made herself push forward. She was there for information that might lead to Avery, not to punish her shitty ex-boyfriend, even if he deserved it.

"Where'd she go after the fight?"

"To her car."

"And you? Where'd you go?"

"Back into the bar," Scott said. "I stayed until close, got piss drunk, fought with some guy, and spent the night sobering up in a cell. You can check the police records."

An alibi. Scott fucking Dallas had an uncrackable alibi.

She'd have to check to be sure, but not even this smarmy bastard would be so confident if it wasn't true. Which meant he had nothing to do with Avery's disappearance. The lies were crumbling, the mystery was unraveling, but Allie was no closer to Avery than she'd been at the start.

"I'm not proud of myself, but I had nothing to do with her death." Scott cleared his throat. "Are we done?" he asked gingerly.

And with that, another lead was scratched off her list.

Damn it. *Damn it!*

"Yeah," Allie grumbled, turning to the door. "For now."

She kicked the doorframe with the toe of her boot on the way out, leaving herself with nothing but a throbbing foot and a fresh dead end.

Chapter 27

Phoenix was the brains behind the change of scenery. He insisted shaking things up would help them think, although a hole-in-the-wall diner that looked like it hadn't been renovated in thirty years wouldn't have been Allie's first choice. Letting him take the lead had been a mistake. The diner's coffee was cheap, but it sucked. Even she made better coffee than this. At least it went well with Allie's mood. Swallowing another bitter, burnt-tasting mouthful, she set her mug onto the scratched-up counter with a loud clack.

Beside it sat the heap of police reports Daniel had dug up for the twentieth of October, which—to her dismay—confirmed Scott's story. He was an incomparable asshole, but an innocent man. His alibi checked out. He hadn't killed Avery Burke.

"Hey, look at this," Phoenix said, rapping a knuckle against the page he was examining. "I found Kimberly in here too. Guess we can cross our cat-squasher at large off the list, huh?"

Allie didn't feel like humoring him with her usual sneer. With Scott Dallas and Kimberly de la Rosa officially expunged from the suspects list, they were left with Victoria Bryant, whose odds of murdering her neighbors Allie ranked as pretty damned low. She really didn't want to talk to Victoria again. And she really, really, really didn't want to slink back to Daniel empty-handed.

What would he say if she returned with the conclusion that this case truly was an unfortunate accident? What did that mean for Allie's test? Would he disqualify her, or just give her a different assignment? She'd felt like she'd been set up to fail, and Phoenix's confession about Daniel's reservations echoed loudly in her mind. Sitting in that crappy little diner, Allie was forced to consider the possibility that Daniel had given her an unsolvable case on purpose.

She was weighing the pros and cons of flat out asking Phoenix if this whole thing was a bust when her eyes caught on a dispatch entry recorded just a few minutes past midnight.

"Hold on. Check this out," she said, slapping his arm with the back of her hand. "A patrol car responded to a call about a Black woman driving recklessly not far from The Outlet, possibly under the influence."

Phoenix glanced up from his printout. "You think that was Avery?"

"Could be," Allie conceded. They knew now that Scott had lied about Avery's intoxication, but if she'd been upset by a breakup, maybe someone else had mistaken her for drunk.

"What does it say?" he prodded, eager to push his own stack away. "Was she pulled over?"

"The call they got specifically mentions that the driver was a Black woman, and—oh." She tripped flat over the two names printed there, sitting blandly before her eyes. "You're never gonna guess who responded."

Phoenix hunkered on his elbows, tipping his head forward in disbelief. "No way."

"Yes way. Officers Bernie Miller and Kirk Bedford made the stop." Allie slid the report along the countertop. The names still danced before her eyes, emblazoned in her memory. A lump was rising in her throat too fast to be gulped back down. "They didn't report that the driver was under the influence. They didn't report much of anything, actually. Just that they had no grounds for an arrest and let the driver go on her way."

"That's weird, right?" Phoenix's eyes flicked rapidly across the page. She had a feeling he didn't need to ask. "Nobody mentioned anything about seeing Avery at the station that night. I mean, you'd think Scott would have recognized her."

"Very weird," Allie agreed. Her pulse was banging in her neck again. She reached for a sip of repulsive coffee to wash out the buzz of adrenaline. "If he admitted the affair, I don't see why he'd hide this. It would have clinched his story."

When he was finished reading, Phoenix raised his eyes to Allie's, hiking his brow. "Bedford sure didn't mention anything about this, either."

"He sure as hell didn't." That fact alone landed him a spot right at the top of Allie's list. "Shit," she spat, choking on another quaff of coffee, scrambling for a napkin to hold it in. Phoenix dangled the metal holder in front of her until she'd snatched one, barely managing to swallow. "If the reckless driver *was* Avery, then our timeline is screwed. Scott wasn't the last person to see her alive. Bedford and Miller were."

"*Was* it Avery, though?" Phoenix scooted the report back to Allie as she swiped another paper napkin to wipe her mouth. "If it was some other Black woman in a black car, then it makes sense that he didn't mention it."

"Seems like a pretty big coincidence." Allie tapped her index finger against her thigh. "Bedford *not* mentioning he pulled Avery over also kind of makes sense. Maybe it was her, and he lied because he feels responsible for her death."

Phoenix frowned. "What would Bedford have to feel guilty about? It's not like he sat on his ass and gleefully let a drunk driver hotrod into the Hudson. Scott lied about Avery being drunk and he never even mentioned it to the police, so there's no reason for Bedford to make a connection between Avery and this discharge call."

"The report doesn't even say if they checked this woman's blood alcohol levels. Maybe it was her and Bedford thought she was drunk. Or maybe he thought she wasn't and regrets pulling her over."

Phoenix's eyebrow cocked in interest. "Go on."

Allie twisted herself around on the uncomfortable stool to face him. "Imagine this. They pull Avery over. She's newly distraught. She's crying, they feel bad for her, they don't want to harass an attorney, they let her go without breathalyzing her. And then she crashed."

Phoenix made a sympathetic—albeit slightly dubious—grunt. "Maybe. It would explain why Bedford took the investigation so hard."

"And why he feels guilty about not finding answers for Lorraine," Allie went on, her mind wheeling faster than her mouth. "Maybe he does know the truth, and he feels like he could have prevented the accident. Maybe he feels like if he'd arrested Avery that night, he might have actually saved her life. Or at least prevented her death." The splurge of maybes collapsed into a too-long silence.

Phoenix glanced up thoughtfully, tapping his chin, considering the dingy ceiling as if its water stains held better answers. His distinct failure to leap up, wallop the counter and declare her a genius left Allie feeling deflated.

"You ever been arrested, Grecco?" he wondered, finally looking down to meet her deadpan stare.

"No."

"You should try it sometime. The part where they arrest you isn't fun, but whatever you were doing before that is." He smiled mischievously, earning her glower.

"We have to talk to Bedford again. Right now," she said, determined to get Phoenix back on track before he dragged her into his next nonsense. But something else occurred to Allie as her boot soles hit the tile. "Am I going to have to ask for permission again?"

Phoenix's sly smile told her all she needed to know. "What you do is up to you, Grecco."

As they hovered in the quiet of the mostly empty diner, Phoenix openly relishing a chance to be coy, Allie's frustration foamed up until she couldn't hold it in.

"Come on!" She thumped her fist against the counter, sending a tiny ripple across the surface of her coffee. "Why can't he trust me with anything? All these check-ins are getting in the way of the investigation! It's going to be too late to question Bedford today if I check in with Daniel first," she groaned.

"He wouldn't be much of a boss if he risked one guy's PTSD blowing an entire op." Phoenix soothed. "Or girl's," he added as an afterthought. "Everybody who comes through the back end has something going on with them."

"Including the man himself?"

"Oh, Daniel's no exception." Phoenix paused, scanning Allie's face for something. Whether or not he found it, she couldn't say, but he let out a strangely subdued sigh as he looked away. A hand ruffled through his auburn hair. "I know I joke a lot, but if you ever need to talk about heavy shit... I'm here. Better not try it with Daniel, though. He's not good with that stuff."

Allie and Daniel hadn't exactly had a heart-to-heart chat the last time she'd reported in—not by a long shot—but they'd brushed against topics that were sensitive to them both. Until she'd gone and stormed out, of course.

"Yeah, you said that before." Allie was ready to retire the topic, but Phoenix seemed like he had more to say.

"And I meant it. I've known the guy for two decades and I'm probably the only person he opens up to, and he won't even talk to me about his own heavy shit. It was like he just shut himself off after Naomi. Like a—"

"Who's Naomi?"

A startled silence crashed between them, disturbed only by the clack of cutlery against plates. Phoenix dropped the fist he'd been clenching in pantomime of Daniel's closed-off self. His lips tightened until his mouth looked like an old scar.

"Nope. Scratch that! You didn't hear that," he insisted. "I never said that. Who's Naomi? Never heard of her."

Allie was intrigued, to say the least. Everything about Daniel was so shrouded in mystery, any tidbits Phoenix let slip were all the more enticing. She plopped back onto her abandoned stool.

"Does this have something to do with this famous last mission?"

"Please, Grecco." Phoenix's eyes darted around the diner like he was afraid somebody there was going to tell on him. "I know I tease you, but this was a real fuckup. Don't mention that name to Daniel. He'd kill me if he thought I was gossiping about her."

Allie huffed, feeling less agitated and more annoyingly charmed by Phoenix's antics by the hour. She had more in common with her cubicle neighbor than she ever would have thought possible.

"Hmmm," Allie answered, and for a few moments, that was all.

Phoenix regarded her hesitantly, anxiously waiting for something more substantial. She sighed again, then extended her littlest finger, rolling her eyes. "You win. I'll pinky swear you. I won't tell Daniel."

"Good." He looked comically relieved as he joined their pinkies. "I'll hold you to that."

"Now that I'm sworn to silence, if you wanted to tell me what that was about, I couldn't say anything to Daniel about it if I wanted to," she probed.

Phoenix clucked his tongue in admonishment, leaning back on his stool. "No way, Grecco. That was a free slipup. It's not my story to tell. Besides, don't you have an actual case to solve? What did you decide about checking in with Daniel?" he asked, steering the conversation home.

Allie was on the trail, and her hunter's instincts told her to press her advantage while she had it. She tapped a finger against her thigh while she considered the options. "You don't think he'd stop us from talking to Bedford again, do you?"

Phoenix shrugged, scratching the bridge of his nose with one finger. "Probably not, but I could also see him saying no. We don't usually make a habit of needlessly pissing off cops."

Allie chewed her bottom lip. On the one hand, she didn't want to cement her status on Daniel's bad side. On the other, she was *sure* Bedford was hiding something, and if she had to wait until tomorrow to find out what it was, she'd lose her mind.

"Better to ask for forgiveness than permission," she said decisively, "especially if we get something good out of Bedford. And I've got a hunch we will."

"If Daniel asks, I disapproved." Phoenix gave her a rascally smile.

A smile of her own crawled up Allie's cheeks. She could get around to respecting Phoenix, she imagined, one day. As long as he kept his barbs in check and his mind on the straight and narrow and never called her sweetheart again. Maybe she would even learn to tolerate him.

Fuck it. She liked him.

It had been a long time since Allie had liked someone apart from Libby, and even longer since she'd allowed herself to feel fond of a man.

Allie didn't say any of that to Phoenix, though. She just smiled back, grabbed a messy armful of police reports, and told him, "I'm glad you see things my way, Phoenix."

"What can I say? I guess I'm nothing but a stooge in your show," he said airily, standing up from the stool and gesturing grandly toward the door.

Chapter 28

Standing under the light of Kirk Bedford's porch, Allie banged her fist against the gray-blue door. A light November rain was pattering down on the sidewalk, darkening the road and bouncing back wobbly reflections of nearby homes and streetlamps.

The shades were still drawn, but she could see a faint glow somewhere inside. After minutes of hammering and calling his name in the cold, wet silence, the door finally creaked open, and Bedford peeked out.

"You two again?" His dour face fell into a sigh. "What do you want this time?"

She fixed him with a stern look. "I think you can guess."

Glancing warily at Phoenix, who was looming over Allie's shoulder with his hands in his pockets, Bedford slipped outside and closed the door quietly behind him. He was wearing the same shirt from the day before, and he obviously hadn't shaved.

"I'm not in the mood for guessing, so just tell me what is it. Do you need my case notebook again?"

"We looked over dispatch records and found something very interesting." Allie's stare locked onto Bedford's face, looking for any signs that she'd hit a sore spot. "You and your partner responded to a call about a reckless driver on the twentieth. You pulled Avery Burke over, didn't you?"

Under the dim porch light, Bedford's eyes grew to almost twice their size, and Allie knew she had him on the hook.

"No, it wasn't her. We pulled over plenty of people that night," he stammered, voice tightening. The disjointed response and panicked expression left no doubt in Allie's mind.

"I think it was." She dove in for the kill, her whole body leaning forward, tensed for whatever might come next. "And that means you and Miller were the last people to see her alive, not Scott Dallas! Why'd you leave that out of the investigation?"

Bedford's jaw dropped, and Allie expected he'd tell them to get the hell off his property. But then his bottom lip trembled, he sucked in an unsteady breath, and the tears began to fall.

Allie and Phoenix stood there on the man's front porch, their clothes damp, waiting awkwardly while Bedford broke down. She'd been ready for him to react poorly to her accusation of a cover-up. She hadn't expected the waterworks. As he drew shaky breaths and wiped the tears still flowing from his eyes, Lorraine's words *mental breakdown* flitted through her mind. Seeing him weep in the dim porch light while the rain poured around them, she wondered if maybe it had been the truth.

"It *was* her," Bedford choked once he found it in himself to speak. "I did pull her over. Miller and I stopped her just after midnight."

That lined up perfectly with Victoria's fender bender story. The thought that she might finally be about to crack this thing set Allie's blood thrumming. "Keep talking."

"That damned report." He sniffed, clearing his throat, managing to get a hold of himself. "A white woman called about a Black woman driving carelessly and flashing cash around. Dispatch said she was worried about a drug deal, and I just believed it. I should've known better." He mopped at his eyes, sniffing again. "I'm no better than the racist piece of shit who called it in."

Racist piece of shit.

Allie had heard that phrase before. Closing her eyes, she let the evidence they'd gathered over the course of their investigation rush through the aqueducts and pipework of her brain. Bedford's notebook popped up, clear as day, just as she'd seen it the first time. Victoria's business card had been stapled above a neat blue scrawl. *Racist POS*.

"Can you confirm it was Victoria Bryant who reported Avery driving recklessly?"

Bedford seemed surprised to hear the name, but he didn't deny it. "Yeah, that was her."

Kimberly claimed Victoria called the cops over anything. Since they'd had some kind of petty neighborhood rivalry going on—or Victoria had thought so, anyway—maybe she'd taken a ripe opportunity to get back at Avery for whatever imagined crime she'd committed.

"Is that why you didn't mention seeing Avery that night?"

"Yes," Bedford admitted. "It was a mistake. Obviously, I didn't recognize her until it was too late. I racially profiled that poor woman, and it got her killed," he said mournfully. "I see that crap every day. I live it every day. If I had detained her for the way she was driving—or maybe even if I hadn't pulled her over at all—maybe she'd still be..." He choked again, turning his head to gaze mistily into his dying bed of plants. "Maybe none of this would have happened."

She'd unspooled another loop of the mystery, but this wasn't the definitive answer Allie had been looking for. Her enthusiasm wilted. She wasn't going to report a victory to Daniel—not tonight.

"How did she seem when you pulled her over?" Phoenix interjected in the quiet. Allie had almost forgotten he was there.

"Upset. She figured out what was happening pretty quickly, and she was—rightfully—angry. I got the feeling that something else was going on, though. She seemed erratic before either of us had said a word."

"And what happened after she got upset with you?" Allie asked.

"Nothing," Bedford insisted. "She wasn't driving under the influence and she consented to a search, so we let her go. I watched her drive off. She was alive and well—although royally pissed off—the last time I saw her. You can ask my partner. Bernie will tell you the same thing."

Allie didn't doubt it; truth or lie, cops were good about keeping their stories in perfect sync. She'd confirm it anyway, even if it amounted to nothing more than another tied-up loose end. Not that it would do Avery any good.

"This case hit me like a train." Bedford's shoulders dropped. "I didn't think anything of it until I went in the next day and heard that she'd been in an accident. And then I was put on the investigation, and a mother begged me to find her daughter. I couldn't take it. This doesn't mean anything to a pair of PIs, I'm sure, but I cannot express to you how horrible I feel."

He trailed off, his lip trembling. Whatever else might be said about Bedford, Lorraine Burke and her plight had really done a number on him.

"I take it that this is why you suddenly stopped talking to Lorraine?" Allie asked, quirking an eyebrow.

"I beg your pardon?"

"You kept in touch with her for a while after you took your leave of absence, right?"

Bedford nodded lethargically. "Oh, yes."

"And you ghosted her because...?"

"Because I felt bad about hiding what I did. In the end, what good does knowing that do anyone? It wasn't going to help find Avery," he said, steadying his voice with a long and heavy sigh. "It certainly wasn't going to help Lorraine."

"It doesn't help *you* any either," Allie replied tersely.

Bedford winced. "Please don't mention this. I'm under enough scrutiny as it is, and something like this getting out could end my career. I honestly don't even know if I want to go back."

"Are you thinking of leaving the force?"

"I've been playing with that thought, yeah. As much as I hate it, the case is closed, there's nothing more to be investigated. So you don't need to ruin my life more than this," he pled, "do you?"

"We'll see about that," Allie told him, turning to leave. "My only obligation is to reveal the truth."

They left Bedford standing there on his porch, watching them disappear into the thickening rain.

Chapter 29

Allie hadn't had a morning this bad in quite a while—and that was saying something, considering how often she woke up screaming.

Standing zombie-like at the copier, she tried not to let its rhythmic bzz-*ka-chunk*-bzz-*ka-chunk* seal her drooping eyelids. She'd let Libby talk her into going to a party last night. Allie told her that *some* students had to work in the morning, but it hadn't stopped Libby's merciless puppy-dog eyes, and so it hadn't stopped Allie from caving.

Even if it had meant wrestling into a dress again.

Allie suspected the discomfort and guilt of pretending to be someone she wasn't had kicked open the door to last night's bad dream. After spending the week hunting down clues behind a woman's death, she'd found it extraordinarily hard to slip back into the soft mask of femininity. If not for Libby, she wouldn't have bothered.

Phoenix was happy enough to be around her after seeing her violent side—hell, he even seemed to like her *more* now, a fact Allie still couldn't wrap her head around. But Libby was no goofy, gangly ex-Ranger who lived a double life as a secret vigilante and as the most annoying officemate alive. And if she lost Libby now, when her triple lives were spilling into each other left and right and it felt like she could barely keep her head above water, Allie didn't know what she'd do.

A chipper, lazy whistle drifted in from the hall, so off-beat and off-key that Allie couldn't identify the song. Phoenix sauntered in a moment later, finishing on a shrill note when he saw her.

"Mornin', Grecco," he greeted, haphazardly throwing open one of the supply cabinets.

Before she knew what she was doing, Allie found herself smiling. "Hey there."

It felt wrong as soon as she'd said it. Ugh—*hey there?* What was wrong with her? She was definitely losing her grip on her sanity, or reality, or something. *Hey there* was one step away from shooting the breeze about the weather at nine in the morning.

"Have you talked with Daniel yet? You know, about that *project* we're collaborating on?" Phoenix asked over his shoulder, placing way too much emphasis on *project* to fly under anyone's radar. Thankfully, they were alone, and more thankfully, everyone in the front end thought Phoenix was the office's pet idiot anyway.

"Not yet," she answered, eyeing the ticker on the copier's screen. "He said we need to regroup today, but he didn't give me a time."

Allie wasn't sure if Phoenix had told Daniel they'd talked to Bedford again, but she hoped their new information would be a worthy peace offering. She didn't think she could handle being given a taste of the back end and then denied it. This hunt was different from the others; it wasn't the immediate wash of relief she felt whenever she snapped a predator's neck. But the knowledge she might belong to a structure again had muffled the howling of her demons, and it almost made Allie wonder if—maybe—she could be okay.

If Daniel snatched that away from her, she wouldn't be.

The nightmares were ready to roar back in force at any moment. The crawling lake of blood, the woman's unblinking eyes, the hole punched through her forehead and the screaming baby.

She couldn't survive being cast out again. The pain of losing her first real family was too fresh.

Not that Frustrating Phoenix was family, obviously. Not today. Not any time soon.

"...so you probably won't have to wait much longer." He startled Allie out of her thoughts. She had missed the first half of his lecture. "Daniel likes to take care of important business first."

"Sure. Important business is always first."

"Exactly." He tossed a glance over his shoulder, still elbow-deep in the cabinet. "And this one's very important, if you catch my drift."

"Yes," she assured him dryly. "I catch your drift." She didn't.

Suddenly feeling a touch less charitable about Phoenix, Allie glanced out the window and down to the sidewalk. She spied the shape of Daniel's broad shoulders and the top of his sandy blond head speaking with Stan out front.

"*There* it is!" Phoenix exclaimed. He unearthed something from the recesses of the cabinet, turning triumphantly to show her a plain black stapler with a piece of tape labeled *Moore* stuck to the bottom. "Somebody keeps stealing it off my desk and burying it in random places."

"Wow," said Allie, who was—of course—that somebody. "Sounds really annoying."

The copier graciously spat out her final page.

"If I ever find out who's behind this..."

"Let it go, Phoenix. And stop blaming everyone else for your lack of organization skills," she scolded him, picking up her stack before Phoenix could figure out he was in the presence of the stapler thief. One last glance out the window revealed that Stan and Daniel were gone.

Allie headed back for her desk, Phoenix trailing not far behind. She'd just thumped her ream of papers down when she heard a second pair of footsteps.

Standing up straighter, Allie smothered the urge to salute as Daniel appeared in the entrance to her cubicle.

"Good morning, Grecco," he said evenly. If Phoenix had tattled to the boss, at least he didn't seem upset.

"Good morning, sir."

He nodded in the direction of his office. "Let's have that meeting now."

Allie tailed him through the maze of cubes, knowing Phoenix would tag along even though he hadn't been invited. They filed neatly into Daniel's impeccable office. He sat down in his chair, Allie took the seat across from him, and Phoenix closed the door, leaning beside it.

"I've got new intel about the night Avery disappeared, sir," Allie said, sitting up straight. "It's about the officer who—"

"I know all about Bedford and Miller," Daniel said with a dismissive wave of his hand.

Twisting around in her seat, Allie glowered at Phoenix. He gave her a shit-eating smile. Whether she liked him or not, he was Daniel's mole first, and Allie's coconspirator second.

"Oh, I'm sorry," Phoenix said. "Did I forget to mention I paid another visit to Victoria Bryant after we finished up at Bedford's?"

He seemed ready to gloss over the fact that he'd gone off and interviewed one of their witnesses without her, and Allie made a mental note to drop his stapler into the toilet next time.

"What happened to this being my show?" She snapped, her sharpness covering up the sting of betrayal.

He was supposed to be mentoring her, not doing her work without her. But that burn paled in comparison to the pathetic sensation of being backstabbed by someone she relied on. Again.

Even though Phoenix had always been upfront about reporting to Daniel, after the way they'd bonded and how he'd entrusted Allie with so much insider information, she'd kind of thought they were a unified team. It was like he and Daniel thought she couldn't handle her own case, and the humiliation of it gnawed at her.

"You know how it is, Grecco." Phoenix shrugged with a nonchalance that drove the needle prick of shame deeper. "Orders are orders."

"So this is *your* doing?" Allie turned to face down Daniel, but Phoenix was still blathering.

"Victoria coughed up some interesting details she just happened to leave out of our first interview." He paused to soak in the drama until Daniel corralled him with a *get-on-with-it* twirl of his wrist that was, Allie noticed, not without affection. "All right, all right," Phoenix relented. "So Victoria was the one who called in that report about Avery driving erratically, right?"

"As *I* discovered yesterday." Allie knew she sounded like a sore loser.

"Well, you'll be glad to know she confirmed it. She said Avery was acting so wacky after their little ding-up, she thought it was her civil duty to report her."

If she couldn't beat him on the case, Allie wasn't above embarrassing Phoenix for his linguistic mistake. "You probably meant to say civic duty," she corrected, sending him a gloating look.

"Nope," he recorrected, waggling his eyebrows, swooping into a warbly impression of Victoria. "And I quote: 'Reporting suspicious persons is my *civil duty* as a member of the Neighborhood Watch!'"

Allie snorted, trying not to gratify him with her laugh. Just another piece of evidence that proved Victoria was a laughable person, eliminated from suspicion of anything beyond her insufferable racism and obsession with her neighbors' lawncare.

"Did you learn anything new, or did you just visit her to chat?" The frown sprang to Allie's face as if it had never left. "Did you figure out why she didn't tell us she was the tipster when we questioned her the first time?"

"I sure did," Phoenix boasted, pushing off the wall and moseying to his favorite perch on the edge of Daniel's desk, reveling in Allie's captured attention.

Determined to thwart him, Allie glanced to Daniel instead. She found him with his elbows resting on the surface, his fingers steepled, his face impassive. Whatever was on his mind was a mystery, and that made her more than a little nervous.

"Apparently," Phoenix said, sing-songing his crux, "Bernie Miller told her to keep quiet about it."

"Bedford's partner?" Allie gripped the armrests, forgetting all about whatever Daniel was thinking. "Are you joking? That's not a joke, right?"

"It's not," Phoenix swore. "As it turns out, Miller told her he'd make sure she wouldn't be mentioned in the investigation—as long as she didn't tell anyone she'd called in Avery. And if she did tell, he threatened to expose her for the 'racist piece of shit' that she is."

"Well, then we have to talk to Miller," Allie breathed, lurching up from her chair, pleading Daniel to see reason with her eyes. "Look, I'm sorry I went off-mission, sir. I really am. And I'm sorry about the words we had the other night. But this needs to be done ASAP. I have to interview him today." A subtle smile crept up Daniel's face. That felt like a good sign.

"Yeah. I figured you'd want to question him." Daniel rose slowly, comfortably. "Come with me."

Throwing an unsure glance at Phoenix, Allie moved toward the door. But Daniel didn't follow. Instead, inexplicably, he moved to the back of his office. She watched as he fiddled with a portion of the wall beside his sparsely populated bookcase.

A door swung open, cut right out of the boring office paneling. An escape route, Allie supposed—a shortcut to the fire escape and the alley, just in case one of the powerful people Soldiers for Hire routinely pissed off got a hold of Daniel's address. But as she drifted after him, squeezing into a narrow hallway and not bothering to check for

Phoenix's encouragement, it quickly became clear they weren't headed toward an exit.

Allie stepped out into a tiny viewing room, the cramped walls doused in expressionless white paint, the far wall made up entirely of glass.

One-way glass.

It wasn't a weird studio or a secret way out. It was an interrogation room.

Stunned speechless, Allie peered through glass to the other side. There sat a man at an empty table, blindfolded and handcuffed to a metal folding chair. She recognized the thin blond hair and pockmarked nose of Officer Bernie Miller.

What might have been an exciting surprise instead stoked Allie's already simmering anger. This was supposed to be *her* test. They'd given her a seemingly impossible task, and she'd taken the case this far on her own. Now it looked like the guys were going to swoop in and just yank it out of her hands!

Allie's fingers curled tightly into her palm. How could she prove herself to Daniel—how could she become a soldier again—if he didn't trust her enough to wrap up her own investigation?

Chapter 30

D aniel flicked his thumb toward Bernie Miller. He was sitting stock-still—if not a little shakily—in the dim, empty chamber on the other side of the glass. The glass of the secret interrogation room that had been behind Daniel's wall all this time.

Allie had seen a lot of extreme twists across her years of service and her years of hunting, but she knew processing this one was going to take a while. Every time someone had sat in Daniel's office for a performance review or dropped off reports, this whole setup had been hiding behind the facade of a plain wall. How many times had someone been interrogated here while she'd written emails and stared at schedules? How could she miss a whole back-end operation taking place right under her nose?

The reality was rushing at her like a truckload of dynamite, and Allie suddenly felt a little less fiery.

"This is it, Grecco," Daniel said, drawing her eyes away from their suspect—their captive? How had Daniel even managed this? Had his connection with the mysterious General really gotten a police officer into his clutches? "Go ahead."

"I'm going to need much clearer instructions, sir. Much clearer."

"It don't get any clearer than this, soldier. This is it. You got us this far, and now you get to take us through the finish line. He's all yours. Whatever happens in this room is up to you."

Allie's anger and hurt stalled. "And you won't interfere?" she asked, peering into the dark side where Miller squirmed against his binds.

"Not even a little bit."

The prospect sent a heady dose of adrenaline through her, but it was overshadowed by anxiety. What if this was all part of the test, too, and there *were* invisible limits—limits that would shatter her chances if she crossed them. She was so close to finding the truth for Avery and earning a place there. She couldn't bear the thought of screwing it all up after she'd come so far.

"I mean it," he promised. "You were the one who did the investigating. You led us to Miller."

"I'd like to think I also helped," Phoenix added, stepping out of the tight hallway and into the viewing room to join them.

Daniel skillfully ignored him. "How you proceed now is all up to you, Grecco."

Maybe Allie could let go of some of her desire to do everything by herself. If she wanted to be a part of the back end, she'd have to work with a team. Maybe that was the lesson Daniel was trying to teach her.

Turning to watch Miller as he scooted up and down in his chair, Allie swallowed her reluctance. It was time to end this thing—her test and the case.

She approached the nondescript door to the interrogation chamber, forcing herself to reach the handle, leaving Phoenix and Daniel to observe. She stepped inside.

The instant Allie passed through the threshold, everything felt like a movie set. Miller's head whipped around at the sound of the door opening and closing. Like an actor, he was right on cue.

"Who's there?" he demanded, or begged, or complained. Her head was spinning, and she couldn't tell which.

"Somebody who's got some questions for you." Imitating the hardboiled, take-no-shit detectives she'd seen on TV—since it already felt like a movie anyway—Allie stalked up to the table and leaned across it to rip his blindfold off. Miller jerked away the moment her fingers brushed it.

"I'm a police officer!" he protested, but his voice was unsteady, and sweat rolled down his temples. "Whatever this is, you're gonna regret it!"

Allie couldn't smother her irritated *tsk*. "Calm down," she scolded, "I'm just taking your blindfold off."

She reached out to give it a last tug, letting the cloth fall to the floor.

If he'd been standing, Miller would've been about as tall as Allie. He had a boxer's shoulders and a blocky jaw, and his scarred nose sat between pale eyes. He was still in his uniform, his light hair only slightly mussed from the blindfold. Whoever had gotten him in there must have snatched him up straight from work.

Miller blinked under the fluorescent lights, taking a look around. He'd be very familiar with this setup, Allie mused—the single table, the pair of chairs, the suspicious mirror set into the wall. "What the hell is this?" he growled.

"This is the part where I find out what really happened to Avery Burke," she menaced, "and you're going to help me."

"I don't know who you are or what the hell you're talking about," he spat, "but there's been some kind of mistake."

"Well, at least we agree on that one." Allie smiled. "I also think it was a mistake to close her case when you know what really happened."

"I worked that case, but I didn't have anything to do with that decision!"

Allie chuckled darkly. "Oh, I think you did, and I can assure you that I know exactly what I'm talking about." His eyes darted to the glass, but in his already agitated state, it was hard to guess exactly why. "I know you've been with the NYPD for ten years. I know your partner is Kirk Bedford. I know you're married to Stacy, you're thirty-two, and you have a baby daughter, with another on the way."

"Leave my family out of whatever this is," Miller insisted, his voice rising, turning his face fully toward the glass. "Hey! What's going on in there? I want to talk to the chief!"

Allie's fingers darted out to grab his chin, forcing him to look back at her. Details from his file danced obediently through her mind. She'd leave no room for doubt that she was in charge, and Miller was going to do what she asked of him. "I know everything there is to know about you, Bernie."

"There are no skeletons in my closet, so you can just—"

"For example, I know you're a secret fan of Jane Austen," she said, delighting in the way his eyes bugged out of his head.

"I don't—that isn't—"

"I hear you like her books so much, you write your own little stories and post them online. Does an account by the name of—"

"Okay!" Miller shouted.

"—HartfieldGuy26—"

"All right!" Miller's eyes darted back toward the mirror, his face stained an intense, unflattering crimson. "I get it. You've done your research. You've made your point."

Allie smiled wickedly, showing him as many teeth as possible. She released his face, stepping back to lean against the edge of the table and look down on him. "I know a lot of things about you, Miller, and so I know you know what happened to Avery."

"Of course I do. She crashed her car and drowned."

"That's what's on the official report, but it isn't what really happened, is it?" Allie loomed over him, her shadow falling into his lap. "Tell me the truth."

"That *is* the truth!" Miller exploded. "We pulled her over, we searched her car for illegal substances. We didn't find anything, so we let her go. Whatever happened to her after, that didn't have anything to do with me!"

Allie's patience was wearing thin.

Scowling, she hooked her boot around the leg of Miller's chair, yanking it out from under him. His bark of surprise was immediately followed by the heavy thud of his body hitting the floor, cheekbone first. The metal chair clattered beside him.

Miller stayed down for a moment or two, goggle-eyed, dazed. He scrambled to get up before realizing he was still handcuffed to the upended chair. Allie's boot landed upon it, collapsing the legs with a terrifying snap.

"The police chief isn't here," she told him, leaning forward, keeping her voice deadly calm. "Your badge isn't going to get you out of this. No one is coming for you."

She let that sink in, listening to his quick, shallow breaths, loud in the confines of the small room.

"Who are you?" he panted.

"I'm someone you should cooperate with. And you will, right?" she pressed, lifting her boot from the chair to give him a gentle nudge in the ribs. He flinched on the concrete as if expecting her to change her mind and break them. "You're going to willingly answer my questions with the truth, or I'm going to make you. Understood?"

Miller swallowed, his eyes glassy and washed out under the glow of the overhead lights. He nodded.

"Good." Allie took her time strolling around the table, easing into the chair still waiting for her. "Sit up. I'll run out of patience fast if you're going to lie there like a slug."

Shrimping his body, Miller reluctantly lurched his shoulders off the floor, doing what she'd asked. The collapsed chair raked the tile as he wriggled into a sitting position. From the way he winced, Allie imagined he'd be sporting a couple juicy splotches on his face by tomorrow morning. He'd be much more compliant now—unless he wanted more than bruises.

"So," she started anew. "You and Bedford pulled Avery over. The two of you were the last ones to see her alive, and after everything I found out from your partner—and considering who Avery Burke was—I'm starting to think her disappearance might not have been an accident."

"You spoke with Kirk?" Miller's gulp caught in his throat. "I'll tell you anything you want. Just... know it was all an accident. Just know that."

"Let's start with why you told Victoria Bryant to keep quiet about the police report."

Miller looked outright sickly. "I didn't have a choice, okay? He forced my hand."

"Details," Allie requested sharply. "Who forced your hand?"

"Kirk!"

"Kirk Bedford?"

"He has dirt on me. He's been holding it over me for years. He threatened to let it drop if anybody found out what happened with Avery."

"What does he have on you?"

Miller's face plunged, and he swallowed again. If Allie looked closely, she could just make out the beginnings of a blister on his cheek. "Promise not to tell my wife."

"You're in my interrogation room," she snapped, crossing her arms, pinning him with a hard stare. "I don't have to promise you anything."

"All right, Jesus." Miller winced, shifting sheepishly on the floor. The metal chair scraped an inch toward him, and when Allie threatened to bolt up, he unbuttoned his lips in a rush. "I cheated on Stacy, back when we were first married. It was a onetime thing, but Kirk knew about it. Hell, he has a video of it."

"Lovely." She cringed in contempt.

"I'm not that person anymore! I'm not and he knows it! But he said he was gonna tell her if I told anybody about what I saw."

Allie's blood pressure soared, the hair on the back of her neck bristling. "What did you see?"

"So the call came in and we stopped her. I stayed in the car while Kirk went to get her registration information and everything. I didn't hear what he said, but she got out and started shouting at him. She kept saying crazy shit like how she was sick of men thinking they could just do whatever they wanted without consequences. Nonsense like that."

Allie gritted her teeth, thinking of scores of men who believed they were above consequences—Scott Dallas included.

"Did they know each other?"

"Lady, we all knew Burke. Especially Kirk. He's worked with her on internal shit... hell, he told me once he *admired* that cop-hating bitch. That's why this was all so weird to me."

"So they weren't friendly, then."

"To say the least. I remember she was calling him all these names like fraud, sellout, traitor. Yeah, a traitor to his race. That's what she said. She was yelling that she was gonna go to the media and make an example out of him—the Black cop who profiles Black women."

"And that's when Bedford attacked her?"

"What? No!" Miller's gaze snapped up from his lap and landed on Allie so fast, she almost took him at his word. "She was the one who got physical!"

"Avery?"

"She shoved him. Kirk was trying to talk her down, and I guess he got too close too fast. Burke just *lost* it. I jumped out to help him subdue her, but before I got there, she slipped on the curb and slammed her head into the hood of her car."

Miller grimaced at the memory. Maybe in sympathy pain. Or maybe in the disbelief of hindsight, knowing he'd just described the moment that jump-started this long and serpentine story—one that ended with him handcuffed to a folding chair.

"She was bleeding," he added, gravely. "Her eyes were wide open, but she wasn't moving at all."

A crisp image of blood pooling in the cracks of a tiled floor flashed into Allie's mind. But this wasn't the woman from her nightmare or the mother Judd had shot. It was Avery, unmoving and unseeing. Allie blinked hard, clearing the grisly scene from her head.

"Kirk was freaking out. I'd never seen him like that. He said we had to get her to a hospital and lie our asses off, file a report that she'd assaulted him with a weapon, or plant drugs on her before she woke up—if she woke up."

"Didn't you just say it was an accident? You saw her slip and fall, so..."

"It really was! That's why I don't know why Kirk went nuts. I was trying to calm him down so I could call the whole batshit situation in, but he said he knew what to do. He said he was gonna drop me back off at the station and take care of it himself."

Allie looked down at the table. Blood that had once pulsed hotly went eerily, frighteningly cool in her veins. She saw how white her knuckles were before she felt how tightly she was squeezing it. "And then what?" She loosened her fingers.

"And then that's what we did. He dropped me off, drove away with her in the back seat, and I never saw her again."

"You just let him go?" Allie snarled. "Are you a fucking cop or not? It didn't cross your mind that your partner might be planning to commit murder? You never considered that maybe a veteran of the force could stage a car crash, drag a woman off to the woods, and—?"

"No. No, no. No fucking way!" Miller recoiled on the floor—fear, disgust, denial.

With the pieces snapping together and the sinking stones in her stomach, Allie was having a hard time making herself care how he felt.

"Kirk wouldn't kill anybody. I don't think that. And if you knew Kirk, you wouldn't either. Maybe..." He blinked, jaw flapping, desperate for any other explanation. "Maybe she died on the way and then he just—I don't know—got rid of the body."

"You never asked him what he did with her?"

Miller shook his head, a frail gesture that hid his eyes from her. "I was too afraid he'd send that video. Besides... Kirk's an idiot," he barked, "but he's my friend."

"So what? You just went on with your life while Lorraine Burke was tearing up the city in search of her child?"

"Hell no!" Miller blurted, looking up too quickly for his own good again. He glared at Allie before thinking better of it and dropped his eyes back to the tile. "You think I haven't been thinking about this every minute of every day? I have a kid too. I didn't know what to do."

"So you decided to do nothing."

"What could I do? Kirk took over the search and it was all downhill from there."

"And you still don't think he killed her?"

He sighed, stricken with grief that seemed genuine, but Allie didn't have a shred of sympathy left. "None of you people understand what this life is like. Can you picture how it feels to have the news—the entire country—screaming to keelhaul your ass over a mistake?" The grief sharpened, contorting into something uglier, angrier, more defiant. He raised his chin to meet her eye, but she didn't care to look at Bernie Miller anymore. "It was a shitty, shitty accident," he pledged. "It was a shitty, shitty move. But that's all it was. He didn't kill that girl."

Allie lifted her hand to her chin before she hurt herself by clenching the table too hard. She believed Miller. He was too raw, remorseful, and afraid for anything but the truth.

"Have you seen him since he took his leave?"

"No. Guy's coming unglued," Miller mumbled. "But he did start to sound better lately. He even told me he'll be back soon."

Allie's hand dropped, the seed of something sinister tickling at the base of her spine. "And why would that be?"

"I don't know. I talked to him yesterday and he said he was ready to put all of this in the rearview mirror."

Bedford had been roughhewn on her first visit and a blubbering wreck the second. What had changed between then and now that convinced him to go back? Allie mused that all the things they'd taken for granted about this case had been less stable than it seemed. Maybe—against all the odds—the biggest fact Allie had taken as a given should be reconsidered too.

She had only a second to feel the stirring of hope in her chest before her blood congealed.

"The last time you saw Avery," she said slowly, feeling that old buzz of dread begin to well up inside her head, "are you *sure* she was alive?"

"I am," Miller swore. "I took her pulse right before Kirk dumped her in the back."

Allie's breath stalled in her lungs, a rush of realization rooting her to the spot.

There was a chance Avery might not have died.

There was a chance to bring her home.

Allie slammed her fist onto the table, making Miller jump pitifully on the floor.

"If he was afraid of her turning him in, and she never died in the car, and the accident was a fake—what would he have done with her?" she demanded. "Where the fuck would he have her?"

Miller curled into a halfhearted fetal position, as if it would protect him from Allie's furor. He froze there, the look in his eyes guttering from one of conviction, to doubt, to fear.

"If she never died in the car, then..." He stopped midsentence, and—right there on the ground—started to shake. "No, no, no, no. He didn't kill her. There's no way he killed her. She must've died and he threw her in the river or something."

Allie's head felt like it was filled with cotton.

The thing that had changed for Bedford was Allie and Phoenix, poking around and getting closer to the truth each time they'd knocked on his door.

Allie threw a useless, knee-jerk glance toward the one-way glass.

Jabbering on their interrogation room floor, Bernie Miller couldn't tell them whether Avery Burke was alive or dead. There was only one person who could, and they'd given him ample warning they were on the trail to the truth.

To Avery. One way or the other.

Chapter 31

B *am bam!*
    The pounding of Daniel's fist on Kirk Bedford's door was jarringly out of place under the noon sun, startling the sparrows in the power lines.

Allie, keeping a close eye on Miller between them, could hardly bear the suspense. She eyed the street, the desiccated shrubs, the way the knocker trembled every time Daniel slammed his knuckles beneath it. A familiar feeling fluttered in her stomach. It wasn't an exact re-creation of her first and only mission with the Rangers—it was the middle of the day instead of the middle of the night, the air was filled with a damp November chill instead of the dry heat of the desert, their captive was alert, and Allie could only hope this home invasion wouldn't end with another murdered woman.

They'd left Phoenix to hold down the home fort while they rushed out, dragging their witness behind them. Somewhere during the frantic drive,

Miller had found his conscience—or his resolve. He'd come to the door without a struggle.

When nothing happened, Daniel called Bedford's name, insistent and sharp. Allie felt like she was waiting on the tips of her toes, but even in their rush to find Avery, he was keeping his head, remaining the disciplined leader she'd always known him to be.

"Do you think we should bust it down?" Just as Allie asked, she heard footsteps from inside, and the door swung open.

Bedford was already talking, probably demanding to know what the racket was about, when his eyes landed on Miller—who was still standing beside Allie, bruises blossoming around his flat expression. Taking stock of his partner's obvious beating, he forgot what he was about to say. All Bedford managed was an incredulous, "What?"

Before he could get anything else out, Allie charged in, just as Phoenix had done before. Daniel propelled Miller forward, bringing up the rear. Bedford, seized by the talons of shock, staggered weakly out of the way as they pushed him backward and jostled into his house.

"It's over, asshole," Allie barked, roughly inserting herself between her target and the exit, just in case he decided to pull a runner. "It's time to tell us what you did with Avery."

"Nothing!" Bedford blurted. "I already told you. We let her go, and…" His eyes flickered to his partner, searching wildly for an explanation, but Miller—under Daniel's control—merely looked down at his feet.

"Cut the shit," Allie snipped. Daniel bolted the door with an ominous click. "Your buddy squealed. He told us everything."

"You've got him under duress!" Bedford cried, bumping into an armchair as he backpedaled feebly into his den, sweat already pimpled across his forehead. "Of course he told you whatever!"

Miller stepped forward, a look of pain and determination settling across his battered face. "Come on, man, we can't do this anymore. It was an accident. I was there and I'll testify to that," he promised. "But Lorraine Burke deserves to know."

Bedford stared through him, mouth agape. He had run out of room to retreat, cornered by his own wallpaper, and seemed to be summoning every fiber of police decorum he had just to keep from about-facing and breaking for a window.

"Exactly. It was an accident," Bedford yammered. "She had an accident and was thrown into the river. You know that. And *you* know I know—"

Miller took a deep breath—to shore his courage, Allie supposed. "If you tell Stacy, then fine. Go ahead. But this is over."

"You hear that?" Allie wasn't half so delicate or patient with a man desperately clinging to his crumbling life. "Game's over, Bedford. What did you do with Avery's body?"

His back was flat against the wall now, body tight and shivering with stress. He scrubbed a hand over his face, squeezing his eyes shut behind it. "It *was* an accident," he warbled. "You have to believe me."

"What the fuck did you do with her?" she boomed, advancing on him.

Allie froze as a big, splintery crack split Bedford's calm in two, and the shell finally collapsed away from the truth inside. He shouted at her to *wait, stop*. His outburst rang through the house, a final, complete breakdown of his lies.

"I wasn't going to let the department hang me out to dry!" he shrieked, voice raw and quivering. He thrust a finger toward Miller, his whole arm trembling. "If this had gotten out, you know they would have."

The hunter was closing in. Allie could smell the blood, taste it, see it. She wouldn't—couldn't—ease off now. "Tell me what you did with her body."

Bedford shook his head rapidly, as if to dislodge an image he couldn't get out. Allie knew the gesture well.

"I sent Bernie away. I—I cleaned up the blood. I brought her someplace safe. I tried to explain what happened when she woke up, but she wasn't having any of it." He took in another shaky breath.

"So she was still alive at the time." Allie's heart was quaking as violently as Bedford's body now, rising inside her, threatening to chafe against the roof of her mouth.

"Oh, she was very much alive. She just kept yelling and saying she was going to get me for this. That she wasn't going to let me get away with it. I wanted to let her go. I wish I had never taken her, but I just... I couldn't. I couldn't let her do that."

"So you...?"

"I faked the accident. I requested to lead the investigation so I could cover it up. But then Lorraine begged me to find her daughter..." The tears began to roll down Bedford's cheeks again, fast and thick, and Allie's burgeoning hope withered away.

Disgust replaced her hunger, bubbling up like tar. He was the one who'd strung that poor mother along, fueling her hope when he knew there was no hope left.

"I need to know what you did with her body," Allie growled. "Where is she right now?"

He seemed to freeze all of a sudden, and the energy in the room grew denser. Allie didn't understand how, but in the next moment, time slowed, and each second was like a zoetrope spinning out its story. It was as if she saw what would happen before it really happened. Bedford's shoulder turned, jerking from the den wall; Miller leapt back in surprise, followed by Daniel's arm, instinctively snatching his shirt; she lunged; Bedford was dashing for the hallway, probably for a back door.

Allie leapt for him with the single-minded focus of a wildcat. She wasn't going to let him get away.

Not when she was so close to the truth about Avery.

He'd taken no more than five steps into the hallway when Allie collided with him, sending the two of them crashing forward. She came down on top of him, slamming him facedown into the floor before he had time to cushion his fall with his arms. Bedford let out a wounded cry, turning his head to reveal a stream of bright blood pouring from his nose and over his top lip.

Allie pinned him to the ground as Daniel and Miller hustled after them. She couldn't hear their voices, wouldn't split her hunter's focus, didn't care about anything else right now. Blood seeped into the beige carpet as she pushed Bedford to the floor.

"You said you took her someplace safe. Where did you take her?" she shouted, pulse pounding in her ears, muffling the roar of her voice. "Was she even dead before you—"

Bedford couldn't answer. It was like muscle memory, like a ghost that had followed her throughout her life grabbed her by a handful of marionette strings. Allie had wrapped her hands around his neck without realizing what she was doing. Her nails dug into the bobbing Adam's apple, piercing the skin. Red crashed into her vision from every side, and her arms were locked, and Bedford gurgled, and she couldn't seem to stop—men were yelling at her—the whole house felt like it titled on its axles—she could smell

Judd's sweat, hear the tent mesh flapping in the wind—

Allie stopped. Bedford gasped. Daniel's hands landed on her shoulders, but she'd already let go. The world had snapped back into place the instant she heard it.

A second drumming, quieter than the beat of her heart. One that wasn't coming from her.

Allie shook Daniel's fingers off, still poised over Bedford. She craned toward the carpet, straining to hear, lowering her ear to the floor as he choked and sputtered and wept between her knees.

"Everybody shut up for a second!" she snapped.

Allie heard it again: a muted banging from somewhere deeper in the house. *Under* the house.

"Keep him down!" Allie ordered, too sharp with adrenaline to worry about the chain of command or blowing her test or the man writhing on the floor. She shot through the hall, tearing for the basement—and a muffled cry for help.

Chapter 32

Fixation and obsession are powerful motivators of human behavior.

At the front of the classroom, the professor leaned casually against her table, surveying her students. From her usual desk at the back, Allie propped her chin into her cupped palm, waiting to learn something she didn't already know. Beside her, Libby stifled a yawn.

"Attachment disorders are complicated diagnoses, most often rooted in some kind of childhood trauma or abandonment. But don't believe what you see on nighttime TV—they don't, in fact, always lead to murdered ex-ex-ex-boyfriends," the professor sassed, earning a few unenthused laughs from the usual crowd of suck-ups. Allie and Libby shared a sidelong roll of their eyes.

The next presentation slide was a bulleted list labeled SIGNS OF UNHEALTHY FIXATION:

• Controlling/possessive behavior

- Obsessive thoughts
- Jealousy of interactions with others
- Low self-esteem

"Obsession doesn't necessarily have to be romantically motivated—though it certainly can be," the professor droned on over the scratching of pens. "Someone fixated on another person will often experience extreme jealousy, which leads to controlling behavior. These feelings are motivated by a low sense of self-esteem, a fear of being replaced."

"We see this in the case of Sara Paesley," she went on, clicking to the next slide, where a pretty young woman beamed at the camera, linked arm in arm with a friend. "What we have here is an apparently normal graduate student—good grades, a healthy social life—who was arrested for murdering her roommate's family. She later told psychologists that she committed these murders to protect her roommate—that her victims were a source of heartache, and that she felt she was the only person 'safe' enough to spend time with the object of her obsession."

The professor tapped her laptop shut, closing the presentation. "Now," she began, loudly cracking her fingers. "Who can tell me what kind of events in someone's life might drive them to commit serial murder in this style?"

Libby was scratching away in her notebook with a green pen, diligently coloring in a doodle of a seagull. Allie could take a guess as to what might drive someone so attached to another person to kill, but she didn't bother raising her hand.

Fiddling her pencil between her fingers, Allie's mind drifted back to yesterday afternoon, letting the sounds of the classroom be replaced with the sound of her boots thundering down Bedford's basement stairs.

· · · · ● · ● · · ·

Each step flew under her feet, her soles pounding the old planks as quickly and loudly as her heart as she raced toward the source of the cry.

Allie was running so fast, she crashed into the heavy door at the bottom of the stairwell, slamming her forearms into the wood. "Stand clear!" she shouted to the voice on the other side. "I'll get you out!"

Allie threw back the deadbolt with shaky fingers. She had barely turned the knob before someone on the other side tore it open.

And there she was: the face from the photograph Allie had been carrying in her mind all this time, held there between her thoughts as gently as a raw egg. It was no longer smiling. It was drawn, disbelieving, streaked with filth. Alive.

"Avery," Allie breathed. In that moment, she had forgotten they'd never met.

Avery's wide-eyed expression lasted for all of a second before her knees suddenly wobbled, threatening to give out. She winced away from the faint daylight that crept in through Bedford's windows, bouncing down the stairwell walls, now penetrating the pitch black of the room she'd been held in. Allie reached out to catch her, expecting she might trip or faint or scream—who knew what—but Avery didn't do any of those things. She just grabbed Allie's forearm for balance, blocked her face with the crook of her elbow, then stumbled forward out of the dark.

"Thank God," Avery sighed. As her socked foot touched the first stair, she exhaled heavily and closed her eyes against the light. "Oh, thank God."

· · · ● · ● · · ·

A smile quirked up Allie's mouth as the professor dismissed them with a reminder about the weekly reading assignment.

She had been living this triple life for what felt like forever, but *operator* was the least tiring disguise she'd worn in a long time. It was a new sensation, feeling this satisfied and well-rested without having bruised her knuckles or speared a pervert's throat. Delivering Avery Burke alive against the odds had washed the hunger for carnage out of her mouth that had been building for weeks. She only hoped Daniel saw the outcome of her test the same way.

Last night, Allie had slept like a baby, unbothered by dreams or nightmares of any kind.

The screech of chair legs and the murmuring of departing students drew Allie back to the real world, topped off with the familiar zip of Libby's backpack.

"So! Between the two of us," Libby asked, turning to her with a cheesy grin, "who do you think is the obsessed serial killer roommate?"

"Honestly?" Allie tucked away her own books, hurrying to catch up. "I think it's you."

Libby faked a dramatic gasp. "Nuh-uh! The only things you can cook are eggs and toast. You need me, and I think you might be willing to kill to keep me around."

"Okay," she conceded, "but you like my coffee an unnatural amount. The other day you said you'd 'literally kill a man' if I didn't make you some before Chemistry."

"That's not obsessed roommate serial murder," Libby pointed out, her grin widening, driving dimples deeper into her cheeks. "That's just regular murder. Try again."

They hefted their backpacks and snapped up their jackets. Allie made a show of pretending hers was a struggle to lift one-handed as they made for the door.

"I don't know," she teased, chewing thoughtfully on her lip, squeezing past a trio of slow-walking guys to match Libby's pace in the hallway. "I think you're neglecting the psychological profiles. Your other friends may come and go, but I'm the one constant. Wouldn't you kill to stop someone from taking me away from you, Libby?"

"That isn't as big of a burn on me as you think it is." Libby puffed a theatrical sigh at the ceiling. "Allie, I love you, but you're antisocial. You wouldn't go out at all if it wasn't for me! You're clearly the obsessed roommate murderer, babe, and"—she winked—"I'll just have to live with it."

Allie was barely listening by the time she got to *obsessed roommate murderer*. Libby had said I love you.

How long had it been since anyone said they loved Allie? Romantic, platonic, familial—any kind of love. She knew Libby was teasing, but that simple phrase of affection said so casually was enough to close up her throat with emotion.

She was lucky Libby didn't notice as they headed for the main stairs, shoulder to shoulder, the heels of their dainty flats clicking on the polished floor. Other students scurried this way and that—leaving class, going to class. No one spared Allie a second glance, especially when she was dressed in unassuming pastels, and especially when Libby was with her.

Who else did she have? Mom was gone, leaving nothing behind but a bank account of rent money and a sour feeling in Allie's gut. Logan would never step back into her life. And Soldiers for Hire was still, at its core, a job.

Libby was right. They really only had each other to depend on.

"Well, the good news is you'll never have to worry about somebody taking me away from you, so you won't have to kill anybody," Libby resolved, breaking the silence between them with her usual cheer. "You'll always have me!" she added, slinging an arm around Allie's shoulders and pulling her into a side hug as they walked.

It was getting easier and easier to let her do things like this. Not comfortable, not yet, but it was just a few steps away from feeling nice.

Until Libby leaned in, nestling her lips right up next to Allie's ear, and whispered, "At least until I kill you in your sleep."

She'd started to laugh before she'd even finished her threat.

Allie pulled away, rewarding Libby with a light and artificial giggle. "Maybe we're both the obsessed roommate."

"Maybe," Libby agreed, still smiling to herself.

They made it to the stairwell, going down two flights to the ground floor. Libby forged ahead, hugging close to the wall to avoid the students climbing up.

As they reached the bottom, Allie's heart skipped a beat. She couldn't say why, but all of a sudden, she got the powerful, hair-raising feeling that she was being watched. With one foot on the second to last step, Allie twisted around to look over her shoulder—up the staircase, and out the window toward the campus green. She saw nothing threatening. No one was watching her. But the spike of adrenaline was still coursing like ice water through her veins.

"Allie?" Libby's voice snapped her back around. She was standing there, gripping the strap of her backpack, red curls falling forward as she tipped her head in concern. "Are you... is everything okay?"

"Yeah," Allie lied, taking as deep a breath as she could manage. "Yeah, I'm fine."

As she forced herself to follow Libby to the front doors, the feeling of danger faded.

What the hell was that? she thought, letting the cool November air rein in her breathing. It must have been the lecture. She hadn't realized it during class, but the obsessive behavior the professor described—the murderously jealous roommate—reminded her of Judd. She'd always thought he had been deeply infatuated with Matthew, but at the time, she hadn't recognized his devotion to her then-boyfriend as such a wild red flag. If she had known, would it have saved her from Judd's wrath? Would she have stopped his attack on her before it started?

Would he still be alive today?

Would she still be a Ranger?

As they walked to the bus stop, Libby chattering happily away beside her, Allie shivered.

This was different. She and Libby were different. Allie was sure—very sure—so sure, in fact, she couldn't kick the unsettling image of Libby's hand around her neck for the rest of the morning.

Chapter 33

Allie jumped in her desk chair, shaken out of her thoughts by the pale face and accusing eyes staring back from her dark computer screen.

She jiggled the mouse to wake the monitor. Relief swept through her body as the reflection vanished, and a half-written email reappeared. Daydreaming on the job? Great. She'd be competing with Phoenix for the title of Office Idiot any day now.

Allie stood up with a frustrated sigh, wandering toward the copier room. It was hard to sit still when she knew she'd either be accepted or rejected from the back end today.

It was killing her, flip-flopping between feeling good about her chances and feeling like she'd screwed it all up. The case was closed, and—what's more—she'd found Avery alive, but Allie didn't know Daniel well enough to guess his decision. The strikes against her were just as certain as the plusses. She'd taken the bait and roughed up Scott Dallas, just as she'd been set up to do; she hadn't followed orders to the letter; she'd exploded at her CO over personal matters. Maybe Daniel wasn't satisfied with the way she'd handled Kimberly, or Victoria, or Bedford.

She wouldn't know until he told her. She hadn't seen Daniel yet, and at the rate things were going, she wasn't going to get any work done until she knew.

Allie loitered by the copy machine, digging for files to duplicate, until she couldn't justify it any longer. She closed the cabinet. She turned around.

Someone was right behind her.

Allie instinctively threw her hands up, defending herself with open palms instead of raised fists. When the surprise passed, she recognized it was Phoenix.

"Whoa! You're lucky I wasn't holding coffee," he said, lowering his own hands. "What's shakin', Grecco? Long time no see."

She barely heard his greeting. "Have you seen Daniel?"

"Oh, hey. It's great to see you too," he complained. Then he swooped into falsetto, turning his head as if to respond to himself. "'Good morning, Phoenix! It's so nice to catch up after we left you behind yesterday.'"

Allie frowned. "That's not what I sound like. And what do you mean, 'left you behind'? Nobody left you behind."

"Like hell you didn't! I worked on that case just as hard as you, and then Daniel swoops in at the final hour to save the girl, and I'm stuck here babysitting paper-pushers," Phoenix pouted.

He was teasing. He was always teasing. But for a moment, standing there together in the empty copier room, Allie thought she detected something nasty and deep-seated buried under the crabbiness. For the second time that morning, the hairs on the back of her neck stood on end.

Whatever this new sore spot between Phoenix and Daniel was, she wanted nothing to do with it— or the conflict it might spark.

"That was Daniel's call," she insisted, keeping her voice even. "Not mine."

"Yeah, well. Sometimes it's a little hard to tell," he mumbled, and the prickle creeping up Allie's spine spread into her scalp.

She nudged the conversation along so she could find an excuse to leave. "Where is he, anyway? I really need to talk to him."

A playful gleam returned to Phoenix's eye, and Allie's urge to get the hell out of there drained away. Man, the stress was really doing a number on her if she was feeling spooked by *Phoenix*. A pang of guilt and shame unsettled her stomach as she remembered feeling the same uncertainty with Libby earlier that day.

"Anxious to get your report card?" he asked, crossing his arms. "Daniel's coming in late today, so you'll have to wait a while longer. Stan invited him to talk business over breakfast with his wife or something."

"With his wife?" Allie was incredulous.

"They do that sometimes. It's kind of a family thing."

Allie's eyebrows hopped. It had never occurred to her that Daniel and Stan might be related. They didn't look anything alike, and she never would have guessed they were connected by something stronger than corporate fraternity. It sure explained how he could afford that opulent apartment, though.

"They must be pretty close," she supposed.

"Super close," Phoenix said, ducking through the threshold to retreat to their warren of cubicles. Allie fell into step beside him. "Not as close as yours truly, of course, but the Gibbinses are kind of Daniel's in-laws."

Allie choked out a loud, unkind laugh. "Is Daniel *married?*"

She couldn't imagine it. Daniel Bennett didn't care about anything except Soldiers for Hire. He wore boring jeans and had floppy hair and somehow managed to be nothing but a stern, logic-oriented, utterly neutral professional, even when he invited you to his ridiculous penthouse at the tippy top of his private elevator. He'd never struck her as the husband type.

Phoenix gave her a significant, sidelong look. "He almost was."

They passed another employee heading in the direction of the breakroom, and Phoenix's eyes peeled away from her as he raised his hand in greeting. Allie thought back to their conversation in the diner, when Phoenix had let the name Naomi slip and had sworn Allie to silence.

"Are the Gibbenses you-know-who's family?"

They stopped outside Allie's cubicle. Ensconced in the forest of blank, too-thin gray walls, Phoenix leaned toward her. "If you mean someone whose name starts with an 'N' and ends with a 'you-didn't-hear-it-from-me,' then yes," he muttered out of the side of his mouth.

"Well," she replied dryly, rolling her eyes, "I kind of figured."

Allie was about to press Phoenix for more details when he promptly made her forget all her half-formed questions.

"Want me to tell you another secret?" he taunted, waggling his eyebrows, sliding one step away from her, escaping her cubicle.

Allie narrowed her eyes. "That depends," she countered carefully. "Is it a secret I want to hear?"

"Oh, trust me, you do. But first, tell me... are you a good actor, Grecco? Are you going to be able to act surprised when you talk to Daniel?"

The breath caught in her chest and turned to static. It crackled there, loud enough to drown out the sound of her gasp. "Do you know if I got in?"

Phoenix's smug smile answered. "I do know that, yes."

All prospects of playing it cool hurtled out the window. "Tell me!" burst out of her. A chiding look from Phoenix reminded her they were still in the office, and Allie forced her voice into a whisper still far too loud, too excited, too—yes—friendly. "I'm dying here," she hissed. "Just put me out of my misery!"

Phoenix's smug smile grew into something even more infuriating. "I wish I had a diploma to give you, Grecco," he said, and Allie was ready to explode. She was starting to worry he might never say it outright.

Then he did. Without any more teasing or jokes or impish imitations, Phoenix told her. He said: "You're in."

Those two words hit Allie like a truck. A smile split her face, and she couldn't bring herself to dampen it. Her next breath snagged high in the back of her throat, and she needed a moment to collect her energy before she could ask him anything else.

"You're not shitting me?" Her whisper was harsh, even through her smile. "This isn't a joke? You're serious?"

Phoenix scoffed. "Do you really think I'd dangle that in front of you if I wasn't serious? Even I'm not *that* mean."

The joy that cascaded through her was palpable. She felt like she might need to sit down, and yet she had enough energy for her morning run and then some. Allie laughed. She couldn't hold it in— and she was so thrilled and relieved, she didn't want to. Phoenix laughed too, reaching his arms out for her and leaning in, though Allie flinched back.

The joy slipped off a shelf inside her and smashed on the floor.

Phoenix pulled back too, awkwardly lowering his arms. "Uh, sorry. I'm a hugger. I should have figured you wouldn't be into that." His regret melted into a jokey half smile. "Maybe a celebratory handshake is more your thing?"

Allie had barely let anyone touch her after Judd's attack, especially not men. It wasn't like she thought Phoenix's intentions were malicious, but accepting his touch put her in a position of vulnerability she wasn't yet willing to show to anyone except for Libby. Still, she needed to do *something* to show Phoenix that she appreciated his excitement on her behalf. Something to show she appreciated everything he'd done to help her.

Allie seized his hand in hers, shaking it so vigorously, his shoulder bounced.

"Ow—hey!" Phoenix's laugh was tinged with a yelp. "Yes, great, congratulations—you're *crushing* my fingers!"

Allie released her viselike grip after one final squeeze. He shook it out like he'd been bitten. But Allie's smile hadn't gone anywhere, and despite the pain, Phoenix's was still stretched across his face.

Yeah. It was time to face the music: Frustrating Phoenix was definitely going to be her friend.

"Jesus, I think you might shake hands harder than you punch!" he whined, giving his knuckles a final shake. "Now. I gave you the good news early, so I think you owe me a play-by-play of everything I missed at Bedford's."

Recounting Avery's rescue was the least she could do to thank him for easing her anxiety, but that wasn't the whole story. She wanted to tell Phoenix. She was excited to share it with him.

"Yeah, I can do that." Allie paused, peeking around at the tops of the other cubicles. "Maybe not here, though."

He waved his hand dismissively. "Just be quiet about it."

Allie told him, quietly, about how Bedford had broken down and admitted to everything, and how she'd only heard Avery's cries for help after she'd flattened him. Phoenix commended her on a job well done, and while his praise wasn't unwelcome, it wasn't quite enough to satisfy her. She needed to know Daniel approved.

She needed to know, without a shadow of a doubt, she was in.

She needed to hear it from the boss himself.

Chapter 34

There was plenty to look at in Stan's spacious office—polished knickknacks, an abundance of law books, wooden furniture as dark as espresso beans—but Daniel only had eyes for Naomi.

She was smiling at him, mild and knowing. It was the smile that told him she knew what he was thinking, even if he tried his hardest to hide it. Her hair hung loose over her shoulders, its warm copper tones burnished with a touch of gold where the sun hit just right. She was happy, young, and beautiful—the way she'd be forever.

Daniel's heart squeezed inside his chest as the doorknob dragged his attention away from Naomi's photograph. He gently set the frame back in its place of honor on her father's desk.

It was for the best. If he looked too long, he'd be distracted and melancholy all day.

"You beat us here!" Stan observed, holding the door for Abigail. Daniel was usually the first to arrive. Stan was the most defensive driver he'd ever seen, and he wasn't exactly a speeder himself.

Naomi gotten her looks from her mother and her fire from her father. The two of them were a sight together, after all these years. Stan was tall and broad, and his well-trimmed beard and prominent nose gave him the distinguished look of an old-school sea captain. Abigail was small and birdlike, with the same red hair Naomi had inherited.

"Hello, Daniel," Abigail said, her eyes warm and affectionate. Daniel moved around Stan's desk to accept her hug. She held onto him for a beat longer than he expected, even though he'd been hugged by Abigail a thousand times before. It was a mother's hug, the kind that managed to be immensely comforting and just a little awkward at the same time. She released him after giving his shoulder a few solid pats.

With a familiarity that felt somehow strange, even to him, Daniel settled into one of the plush client chairs. Abigail scooted the other closer to him, looking more petite than usual in the large furniture, and Stan eased in behind his desk.

"So! What's new with you?" she asked kindly, folding her fingers over her lap. "Have you read any good books lately? Have you *finally* tried that wonderful Thai place?"

"Not yet," Daniel admitted with an apologetic wince. "I keep forgetting. This week, I promise."

He didn't answer her other questions. There was never anything new with him, and he didn't read much these days, but Daniel didn't like showing

Stan and Abigail how little he had going on outside of work. He would frown and she would worry, and they'd go home after breakfast and murmur between each other in hushed tones, wondering if their (almost) son-in-law was slipping back into depression. Daniel had meant to dream up a fun and exciting fib beforehand, just to set their minds at ease, but he couldn't think of anything and talking about his latest binge-watch of *Queen's Bridge* was absolutely out of the question.

He looked to Stan, hoping to change the subject. "I hear you finally wrapped up that case that's been giving you so much trouble."

"Yes!" Stan was always happy to talk about his work. "A high-profile marathon, but we finally got our acquittal. It was a close thing, though. Half this place was working on that case at some point... you should have seen the aides scrambling. But the important thing is that we kept an innocent man out of prison. That's what we like to see at the end of the day."

Daniel hadn't been keeping up with the news, so Stan filled him in on some of the public details, describing each turn with the grandeur and embellishment of a fisherman recalling his biggest catch.

Abigail, though, could be counted upon. The moment her husband wrapped up his story, she clucked her tongue for Daniel's attention, and went in for the loving kill. "That reminds me. How did that new logistics manager turn out?"

The question startled him. He took a moment to reorient himself, glancing between Abigail's patient face and the clock on the wall.

"She's not really new anymore," he demurred. "It's been well over a year. But she's been a good fit. Diligent, very focused on her work." His brow furrowed. "Why do you ask?"

Her eyes slid over to Stan, and a secretive smile took root, growing quickly across her peach-painted lips. "Oh, I was just wondering, is all."

"Well, it's old news. No need to talk about her now."

Stan returned Abigail's smile. "I think *you're* the one talking about her now, son."

"Only because you brought it up." Daniel turned his frown on Stan; he wouldn't dare be caught frowning at Abigail. "Have you been gossiping about me?" he demanded, grinning flimsily, trying to insist it was a joke.

"Of course not! I can't help it if talk gets around the dinner table, though."

"What else have you been up to?" Abigail pressed, taking pity on him. This was the gene that had skipped her daughter. Naomi had been more likely to grill you like a murder suspect than disguise her interrogations as polite conversation. It was one of the things he'd loved most about her.

"Not much. I've been busy with work."

Abigail tutted, still managing to look gentle. Even her disapproval was motivated by care and maternity. "You're always busy with work. When are you going to take some time for yourself?"

"I do," Daniel protested, trying to squash the feeling that he was a teen defending himself from his parents' accusations of slacking off. He was an adult, and he was not going to be scolded for taking his work too seriously. "I have"—he struggled to come up with an example of something that wasn't a guilty pleasure show —"evenings and the weekends," he finished halfheartedly.

By the unchanged look on Abigail's face, it wasn't a convincing alibi.

"Everyone has evenings and the weekends. I just worry that you're going to burn yourself out one of these days. That's why I make Stan take our yearly vacation." She pulled her husband into their debate with a single look.

"It's true," Stan agreed. "It may as well be a doctor-ordered vacation."

"I went out with Phoenix for a beer last week," Daniel remembered, feeling vindicated by the truth. Abigail didn't seem nearly as impressed. "We even stayed up past midnight."

"You need a hobby, Daniel," she insisted. "You started Soldiers for Hire to help veterans relearn how to live fulfilling lives. And you've done such wonderful work for so many troubled soldiers..."

Daniel was really in for it now—Abigail loved compliment sandwiches. Of course, the problem with compliment sandwiches was the rotten meat in between.

"But...?" He guided her along.

"But it seems like the only soldier who hasn't graduated your program is you. You're doing so much good. Just remember to spare a little of that compassion for yourself, dear."

And there it was. Abigail wasn't wrong—Daniel had stagnated in his disengagement from the military, but not in the way his operators did. He didn't need the Rangers. He needed Naomi.

He'd been planning to marry her when he'd come home from what had turned out to be his final mission. But the love of his life had been taken away from him, so he had married Soldiers for Hire instead. He didn't expect Abigail to understand. How could she? The love of her life was kicked back in a cozy chair just across the room.

"Work is important to me," he explained carefully. "It fulfills me, and I like doing it. I swear I'm not overworking myself."

Abigail didn't buy it, but it didn't increase her displeasure. She just looked sympathetic and a little regretful, like maybe she thought she was failing to get through to him. The idea of causing her one more shred of grief made Daniel feel guilty.

He should try to be more charitable about Abigail's interrogations. She still had Stan—but she had lost Naomi too.

"I suppose I could use a hobby," he conceded. "I'll figure one out over Thai."

That made her smile, and it warmed Daniel to see a twinge of real happiness reach her eyes.

He'd seen both Abigail and Stan through the worst time in all three of their lives. It was a miracle to him that they'd learned to laugh again. But sometimes he felt like he was the only one not yet in on the joke.

"Good," she said. "Just don't spend so much time on work that you don't have time to socialize. You should get out around people more, dear. Invite some colleagues over for supper. Take an art class. Go on a few dates! I'm completely serious," she swore when he made a wickedly sour face. "I don't mean to bully you, dear. It's just that you're our boy, Daniel. We want to see you enjoying your life. And don't think I forgot," Abigail threatened, "that you promised me grandkids."

Stan laughed, big and jovial.

Daniel wasn't. He felt speechless.

It was just a joke. He knew that—and he knew he was supposed to laugh, too, bittersweet and filial. But the thought made his heart ache. It had been just shy of six years. If Naomi were still alive, they probably would have started their own family by now. He'd have a wife, a kid, maybe more than one. Daniel couldn't wrap his head around how different life might be if he had just stayed home.

He'd left on that mission to get out of her way as she finished planning the wedding. She'd made him promise on everything he held dear that he'd come home safe to her. He had been under the radar, out of communication with anyone but his superiors for weeks. When he'd packed his bag and stepped onto the plane, he'd never imagined fast-talking, firebrand Naomi would ever need protecting.

And so he'd returned, heart light with intentions of marriage, to find out his beloved had been abducted and murdered.

No one had even told him she'd gone missing. His superiors had decided that it was better for the mission if he didn't know.

"You've gone quiet there, son," Stan said, catching Daniel's attention. "Do you have anyone in mind to complete that mission?"

Daniel's laugh, when it came, was bitter cold. "You know I don't."

"Oh, Daniel," Abigail sighed, her eyes softening. "You don't have to hold out for us. Or for her."

"I know," he replied quietly. "That's not the problem."

"The problem," Stan groused, saving them all with a heavy slap of his blunt humor, "is that you don't know any redheads—aside from that Phoenix."

Daniel couldn't stop his chuckle. Stan had never let go of the joke that he had a type.

"That's right," Abigail remembered, snickering. "You had that saying in the army. How did it go?"

"'If you want trouble, find yourself a redhead,'" Daniel quoted, his eyes lingering on the back of the picture frame, his heart longing for the woman he'd lost.

Chapter 35

It was a miracle Allie hadn't worn a track in her floor with all this pacing.

Holed up in her room since she'd come home from work, she'd been too keyed up to eat dinner. Libby was out with friends, so at least she didn't have to think up an excuse for herself. Now the sun had set, she hadn't seen Daniel at work, and she still hadn't heard from him. Not knowing was driving her up the wall.

Phoenix reassured her that Daniel sometimes went dark after visiting with the Gibbinses, and it was only a matter of time before he called her in to tell her the good news. But he hadn't explained *why* Daniel was still hanging around with his ex's parents, and without knowing the details to explain his radio silence, Allie could barely keep her brain inside her skull.

She completed another lap around her bed, glancing toward her phone on top of the dresser. Allie moved to snatch it up, just in case she'd missed something, for the six thousandth time.

The moment she reached out, it lit up.

The ringtone rattled so loudly against the cheap wood, Allie jumped. She snatched it like a biting snake.

It was Daniel. The text said only:

Daniel: "I think it's time you and I had a conversation."

Allie let out the long breath she'd been holding all evening.

Allie: "I agree. Am I in or out?"

Daniel: "Come over to my apartment and we'll discuss it here." His reply did nothing to soothe her nerves.

Seriously? He left her in the dark all day, ignored Phoenix's inquiries, and now she had to take a taxi all the way over there? He was wasting their time with this pomp and circumstance!

Allie's blood froze as it occurred to her that he might be acting so evasive because he'd changed his mind. She fired off before she could reconsider her tone.

Allie: "It's a simple yes or no question."

Daniel: "That isn't how this works."

He was giving her no clues about his mood. She hoped it was fair and businesslike. It had to be. He always was.

Her fingers were suddenly cold, so she paused when another message came in.

Daniel: "We'll discuss it in person when you get here."

Allie: "Can't you just tell me?"

She hesitated for a long moment before adding one last thing.

Allie: "Please."

Allie hated to be so vulnerable in front of him, even over text, but torturous hours of waiting had worn her down. Funny that her need for a chain of command was driving her to argue with her boss.

Daniel: "You have your instructions."

She knew better than to keep pushing. It felt like the final word.

Since Libby was out, Allie didn't bother changing her clothes in the service room. She switched out her dress for a t-shirt and jeans, grabbed her coat, stuffed both feet into her boots, and headed out the door.

Caught between excitement and anxiety, Allie didn't recognize who was walking up the hall until a voice called out.

"Hey, you!"

Allie's head snapped up. Libby was trotting toward her, red curls pulled up into a ponytail and bouncing behind her head.

"Ooh, are you headed out?" Her eyes dropped straight to the combat boots as she pranced the last few steps between them. "Oh my god, you're wearing jeans! I've literally *never* seen you in jeans. I didn't even know you owned jeans. You look so different!" she gushed, lifting one of Allie's suddenly limp arms as if to get a better look at her outfit. "Confident. Casual."

If Allie had been asked a month ago—a week ago —to identify the most important part of her disguises, she would have said the clothes. She had worked so hard to keep up the soft colors, flowing skirts, and floral print around Libby. Now, faced with these bewildered *oohs* and *aahs*, she was surprised to find she didn't mind being seen out of her mask. This outfit was closer to herself—her real self—and somehow, it was a lot less scary than she'd thought it would be.

It was a strange feeling. It almost felt natural.

"Um, yeah," Allie said when she realized that Libby was waiting for an answer. "Gotta run to the office for something."

Libby's gaze flicked down to the baggy legs of Allie's jeans again, and she chuckled to herself. "I'm sorry for staring. I've just never seen you go out like this."

"I thought I'd try something different. I just couldn't be bothered dressing up, you know?"

Libby smiled brightly, and Allie breathed an internal sigh of relief. There was no hint of facetiousness or insincerity to that smile. There never was with Libby. "Of course, babe! I know that feeling all too well. Sometimes you just want to be comfy." She nodded toward her boots. "And it's a cute look on you, too. Very badass."

Allie thanked her timidly, unsure how to accept the compliment. "I'd better get going," she said, dealing Libby a halfhearted goodbye hug to satisfy her before sidling toward the stairs. "Coworker's waiting for me to pick something up."

Allie was only a handful of steps away when Libby's voice stopped her in her tracks again.

"Hey, babe?" Allie turned back to find that megawatt grin had grown a little sly. "Whoever he is, he seems like he's really good for you."

He? It took Allie a moment to realize that Libby thought she had some secret boyfriend.

"Oh, no. No, no," she denied, snorting out a laugh. "There's no guy."

And there never would be. No guy would ever make her feel accepted or seen again—not totally. The only place she had ever been truly welcome was the army. If she was feeling any less volatile or more comfortable in her own skin, it was because she had a taste of that life again.

It was because of Soldiers for Hire.

Allie tossed one last wave to Libby, promising to be home before it got too late, and headed out to the sidewalk.

The taxi ride to Daniel's place was excruciating. It was impossible to sit still, and just as impossible to keep her mind from volleying between the euphoria of finally hearing an official *yes*—and nightmare scenario of being fired, spurned, and kicked to the curb.

Allie barely waited for the cab to park before shoving open the door. She hurried past the fancy front desk with its somber clerk, up the uncomfortably reflective public elevator, and into the dark and empty hall. She had just pressed the button to call the private lift to Daniel's penthouse when her phone vibrated against her leg.

Digging it out of her pocket, she wondered if Daniel was getting impatient, or if Libby was prodding her for details about her nonexistent boyfriend. She found something else entirely.

Unknown: "I have your father held captive. If you ever want to see him alive again, come to Washington Square Park and sit on the benches closest to West 4th St. immediately. Once there, respond for further instructions."

Allie stared at the text, dumbstruck. This had to be some kind of joke.

No, her instincts corrected, and—lowering the phone—she swallowed her shock, and narrowed her eyes. This *had* to be part of her test.

It was Daniel. It must have been. Allie could think of no other explanation. Her CO was worried about the "daddy's girl" outburst, and he wanted final proof she was ready to put familial attachments behind her. He wanted to know Allie Grecco could serve a greater good with the unswerving loyalty of a Ranger.

And if it wasn't a test? Allie wasn't sure.

To say that she and Logan were not on friendly terms was the understatement of the century. She'd wished death on him more than once, and long after her raging teen years. But now that Allie was confronted with the tangible thought of his demise, a muffled voice inside—a child's voice, one that barely even sounded like her anymore—was wailing to stop it. Bedford and Miller hadn't hated Avery, but the guilt of their decisions had eaten away at both of them. Would she feel guilty if anything really did happen to Logan?

Even if she did hate him. And she most definitely did.

Allie stood there, marinating in her choice, a short elevator ride away from the only thing she'd wanted this badly in a long, long time.

Logan had never given up anything for her sake. Did she want to risk giving up her chance at a new life for his?

She was startled out of her thoughts by the ding of the elevator. The doors slid open to wait for her, silently asking her to make a decision.

What was she going to do?

The End

· · · ● ●·● ● · ··

All of the Allie Grecco Series books can be found on Amazon.

A Note From The Author

Now that you've made it through the hard times with Allie, I can safely say that this is only the beginning of her journey.

Before you move on, I wanted to share a little about me, the fast-typing lunatic who brought Allie to life.

I'm happily married to my non-fiction hero and I'm also an overprotective mom, though my kids are still too young to know what their mommy's doing all these hours in her studio.

When I write, it's as if the world comes to a complete halt. With each new book, I feel I can breathe just a little bit easier... which is where you come in. :)

I need you to help by submitting your honest review of my books. I've been writing about characters like Allie and Daniel for as long as I can remember, but I've always been too scared to show them. Putting my words out into the world took a lot of hope and courage. Now that I've finally gathered the strength to take this big step, I have to admit that I draw my power from your reviews. I'm addicted to your thoughts, and sometimes I spend hours reading comments over and over again.

So I'd like to ask you to help me keep my courage. Please take a few minutes and submit a review of my book on Amazon. Your reading experiences are the wind beneath my writing wings, and as long as you're with me, I'll be able to publish more books—and I'll be fast-typing with a smile!

Looking forward to hearing your thoughts on Amazon.

Katy

Acknowledgments

I've dedicated this book to everyone that's straggling to find their smile, so I'd like to end it by thanking the person who puts a smile on my face dan in and day out, my dear and wonderful husband. I'll never grow tired of telling you that you're the love of my life.

Thank you for bringing our two perfect souls into this world and thank you for being the solid rock that you are. I love you.

About Author

Katy Pierce is a born and raised New Yorker. Most of the time, she is a passionate, outspoken, cynical woman, but all that fades away when she comes home to her husband and two kids at the end of a long day, where she willingly turns into a cliché, soaking in every second of motherhood life has to offer.

For Katy, creative block is considered a hoax, since from the second she wakes up, new ideas keep coming to her, characters she never met before are driving her crazy and in a perfect world, she'd be writing books 24/7.

She enjoys the simple things like making her husband proud, making her children laugh, and making her readers gasp for air as they flip through the pages of her fictional creations. She's addicted to social media, has a terrible fear of spiders, and would rather speak her mind and be hated for it than keep quiet and fake being "normal". Come to think of it, she hates the word "normal".

When Katy writes, it's as if the whole world comes to a complete halt. In her mind, the stories, the emotions, and life-threatening situations are real. She can see it all and she simply writes what she sees.

With every new book of hers that gets published, Katy feels she can breathe just a little bit deeper than before, which is why she vows to keep at it for as long as humanly possible.

Follow Katy On Social Media:

Facebook Page:
Facebook.com/AuthorKatyPierce

Facebook Close Friends Group:
Facebook.com/Groups/KatyPierceCloseFriends

Official Website:
AuthorKatyPierce.com

Amazon Author Page:
Amazon.com/Author/KatyPierce

Made in the USA
Monee, IL
05 April 2022

94192154R00177